Other books by Gar Anthony Haywood:

Not Long for This World
Fear of the Dark

GAR ANTHONY HAYWOOD

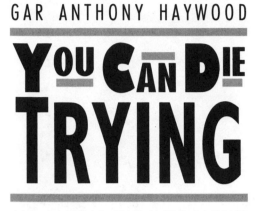

YOU CAN DIE TRYING

AN AARON GUNNER NOVEL

A·THOMAS·DUNNE·BOOK

ST. MARTIN'S PRESS
NEW YORK

Design by Basha Zapatka

Library of Congress Cataloging-in-Publication Data

Haywood, Gar Anthony.
    You can die trying / Gar Anthony Haywood.
        p.   cm.
    "A Thomas Dunne book."
    ISBN 0-312-09425-6
    I. Title.
    PS3558.A885Y68   1993
    813'.54—dc20   93-22467
                                                  CIP

First Edition: July 1993

10 9 8 7 6 5 4 3 2 1

For My Sister,
SHANNON MARIE
The Best Friend
a Big Brother Ever Had

ACKNOWLEDGMENTS

The author wishes to thank the following accomplices for their generous contributions to this book:

The Brothers Petievich, Gerry and John;

Lt. Fred Nixon, Los Angeles Police Department;

Mike Mooney, Hollywood Park;

Natasha Anderson, Central Juvenile Hall;

Det. Dennis Payne, Los Angeles Police Department;

Jerry Kennealy;

Karol Heppe, Police Watch;

Lt. John Durkin, Los Angeles Police Department.

ROLOGUE

Detectives from the Los Angeles Police Department, Hollywood Division, found out later that the loser who had inspired Jack McGovern to blow a four-inch hole in the back of his own head was a twenty-eight-year-old ex-con named Perry Timmons, though Timmons had been careful not to drop his name over the phone.

It happened that Timmons had a rap sheet as long as a small telephone directory, but he was no murderer; he had only one weapons-related arrest to his credit, and that was for attempting to resell an unregistered handgun someone had given him in trade for a little homegrown grass over four years ago. What Timmons was was a thief, bold and brazen but utterly harmless, and only someone with an overactive imagination would have failed to recognize the fact. Knowing the cops as well as he did, however, the black man had nevertheless taken the precaution of calling 911 within an hour of McGovern's death because he didn't want any misunderstanding: He hadn't *touched* the motherfucker.

They weren't going to believe him for a minute, he knew—no matter how innocuous his record made him seem—but he wanted his account of the way in which McGovern had died on the record all the same, early, so that no one could say later that he was just making it up as he went along. He would tell them now, as he would no doubt have to tell them later, that he hadn't killed *anybody* over one lousy little four-inch-screen TV.

Least of all an old demon of an ex-cop whose face he had remembered from the newspapers.

After asking his name a half-dozen times, as if he didn't know what fuck you meant, the desk sergeant on the other end of the line asked Timmons to repeat himself, not surprising the black man in the least.

"Shit," Timmons said impatiently, "you heard what I said. Man put the gun in his own mouth and pulled the trigger. I wasn't nowhere near 'im, I swear to God."

"What man is this? Where?"

Timmons took a deep breath, gathering his rapidly diminishing resolve, and said, "Old dude watchin' the loadin' dock at the store. The guard."

"Can you give me a name and a location of the store you're referring to, sir?"

"Look, officer—don't fuck with me, all right? The shit went down an hour ago, you know what goddamn store I'm talkin' about! You motherfuckers gotta be crawlin' all over the place by now!"

"This is a big city, sir. We're crawling all over a lot of places tonight," the cop said evenly, ever the consummate professional.

Timmons sighed, feeling more and more stupid for what he was doing by the minute. "I'm talkin' 'bout the Circuit City store, all right? You followin' me now? One over on Sunset, up by Temple. I ain't gotta tell you that's in Hollywood, do I? I told the fuckin' operator I wanted Hollywood."

Timmons could hear the desk sergeant lay the phone down to toss some hurried instructions over his shoulder, and he knew right then he'd fucked up, going out of his way to offer the police an alibi for a crime they hadn't even been aware of until this moment. Within minutes, he knew, a black-and-white would arrive on the scene at Sunset and Temple and the cops would start drawing their own conclusions about what had happened there an hour ago. Conclusions he had to dispel right here and now if he didn't want to end up either a ninety-nine-year-old cripple back in Chino or a twenty-eight-year-old stiff in the county morgue, which was where all the cop-killers he had ever known had eventually wound up.

"Why don't you tell me what happened, sir?" the policeman asked, getting back on the line only a split second before Timmons could act on the urge he was fighting to hang up and make a run for it.

"I told you. I didn't kill the man," Timmons said flatly. "I took a goddamn hundred-dollar TV, man, that's all."

"You were burglarizing the store?"

"That's right."

"Go on."

"Go on what? The motherfucker put his gun in his mouth and blew his head off! How many times I gotta say that?"

"He killed himself."

"That's right. He killed himself."

"Why would he do something like that?"

It was the same question Timmons had been asking himself, over and over again, since it had happened. He let his eyes glaze over with the memory and said, "I don't know why he did it. Cat must'a been crazy. I come out the back door and there he is, standing there waitin' for me. His piece was pointed right at my head, and . . . I didn't even know the goddamn store had a guard, he must'a been out the car, sleepin' or somethin'. . . ."

"Go on."

"He didn't say nothin'. I kept waitin' for him to say somethin', like freeze motherfucker, or kiss your black ass good-bye, nigger. You know, somethin' like that. But he never did. He never said shit. He just . . . stood there lookin' at me. He got this funny look on his face and . . . it happened so fast, man! . . . he put the gun in his mouth and pulled the trigger, bam! Blew the back of his fuckin' head off! Goddamndest thing I ever seen!"

Timmons was suddenly shaking like a scared kitten, and it wasn't because he was standing out in the open night air of Inglewood using a kiosklike pay phone that did nothing to shield him from the elements. He was seeing the old guard's head come apart again, the blood and bone jettisoning off in a wide, erratic spray behind him, and the vision ran a chill down the length of Timmons's spine as sharp as a surgeon's scalpel and just as hard-metal cold.

That was when he hung up the phone.

He wasn't going to tell them the rest, no way. He had said too fucking much already. They were going to find out soon enough who the crazy old bastard had been—what he had been—and Timmons understood that that was when the shit was really going to hit the fan. They'd come for him in earnest, then, once they'd seen the old guy's face and recognized it, just as Timmons had.

Nothing could bring the heat down on a black man's head faster than a dead cop, former or otherwise, and Timmons knew it.

He walked three blocks before he actually started running, because he knew once he did, he wasn't going to be able to stop.

When they finally picked Timmons up two days later, as he had known damn good and well they would, sooner or later, he was amazed by the LAPD's relative courtesy toward him. It was not at all what he had been expecting. From the pair of blank-faced uniforms who had stumbled upon him in MacArthur Park down in the Wilshire district, thinking they were just rousting another homeless bum trying to catch a little shut-eye on a public bench, to the plainclothes detectives working Hollywood homicide who interviewed him at the station later that same day, the cops had treated him with uncommon respect, and he didn't know what to make of it. They raised their voices from time to time to make a point, as all cops did, but they never came on with any of the rough stuff he had braced himself to suffer, short of an earnest shove here and an emphatic push there. Even their questions were halfway polite.

It took Timmons a while to catch on, but in time he came to realize what, exactly, was going on.

They believed him.

They had believed him almost from the very beginning. His account of the Circuit City security guard's death was bizarre, to say the least, but nothing about the physical evidence at the scene seemed to contradict it. And when the dead guard turned out to be Jack McGovern, it all made a perverse kind of sense. Because the last time the forty-seven-year-old ex-cop had drawn a gun on someone of Timmons's ethnic persuasion, it had cost him nothing less than everything he had.

4

Once the cops realized this, Timmons was basically in the clear. By the time a thumbprint on the Hollywood Circuit City's loading dock door had identified the man they were looking for as Timmons, they had pretty much made up their minds that the story he had told over the phone the night of McGovern's death had been a fairly accurate one. His instrumental role in the ex-cop's suicide didn't win him any friends on the department, and he was going to have to do a little time, at least, for the Circuit City burglary, but no one was going to mistake him for a murderer. He was a thief, that was all he had ever been and all he was ever likely to be, and he was fortunate in that the homicide detectives working the McGovern case were bright enough to understand that.

Just as they were bright enough to know that McGovern had been dead long before he had actually blown his own brains out, in any case. Someone had killed him, all right, but it hadn't been Perry Timmons. A man named Dennis Bowden had done McGovern in a good eight months before, and every cop pulling down an LAPD paycheck knew it. Bowden was a cop-killer, plain and simple, but it was highly unlikely that he would ever hear such an outrageous accusation made to his face.

For Chief Bowden was, after all, the biggest and baddest LAPD cop of them all.

I

He was working on the back door. He had little more than a crescent moon overhead to rely on for light, and the tools he was using had not yet made peace with his hands. He was making a lot of noise, picking and scratching on the tumblers of the lock, and he knew he was running out of time.

"Goddamnit," Aaron Gunner said irritably.

He shot a quick glance at his watch, but its face was just a mottled shadow in the darkness on the porch. The windows of the little duplex were still pitch black, but he feared they wouldn't be for long. A pair of dogs had broken into a heated debate a mere three yards away, and they were making enough racket to raise the dead. It was getting more and more difficult to concentrate.

A sharp clicking sound gave him reason to hope he had solved the lock's riddle, but the tumblers still refused to turn. He dropped the tool in his right hand clumsily—a wicked sliver of metal with a sickle-shaped tip—cursed again as he retrieved it, and was attempting to reinsert it into the lock when the door swung open before him and someone on the other side of the threshold pressed the barrel of a pistol into his right eye, nearly blinding him.

"Why don't you come on in and make yourself comfortable," the big man with the gun said, stepping gingerly out onto the porch.

He was grinning, infinitely proud of himself. He was a dark-skinned black man with a head full of yellow hair and a face as square as a cinder block. He was taller than Gunner, by at least three inches, and that put him somewhere in the neighborhood of six foot six or six foot seven. He looked like a bank vault walking. It was nearly midnight, but he didn't seem to know it; he was still fully clothed and his eyes were bright, not at all indicative of a man who had just been stirred from sleep by a prowler at his back door.

Gunner came up slowly from the crouch he'd been found in and held his hands out and away from his sides, dropping the tools he'd been using on the lock without having to be told to do so, but the big man wasn't impressed. He kept the nose of his revolver right where it was, up against the soft flesh of Gunner's right eyelid, apparently as unwilling to speak as he was to move.

"The gun's a nice touch," Gunner said.

"Yeah. I thought you might think so."

"There wouldn't actually be any bullets in it, I hope."

"Bullets? I don't know, partner. Let's see. . . ."

He cocked the hammer back on the gun and Gunner slapped it away from his face with his right hand, stepping quickly aside. The big man stumbled backward and broke out laughing, tickled by Gunner's reaction.

"You're not a funny man, Fetch," Gunner said, watching the big man fall all over himself at Gunner's expense. "Don't ever let anyone tell you that you are."

"Ain't no bullets in the fuckin' gun, man," Fetch Bennett said, holding the revolver forward for Gunner to inspect. "Check it out."

Gunner snatched the gun out of the big man's hand and said, "Kiss my ass," before walking past him into the house. He turned the lights on in his kitchen and immediately went to the refrigerator, setting Bennett's revolver on top of the box in order to withdraw a pair of cold beers. He sat down in a chair at the kitchen table and Bennett finally stepped inside the house to join him.

"You were too damn noisy," the big man said, twisting the cap from his bottle. He was still grinning.

"I couldn't see a fucking thing out there. I told you I needed a light."

"You're not always going to be able to use a light. Besides, you're going to need two hands free to do most of the locks you're going to find out there."

Gunner nodded his head in silence, his mouth full of beer.

The private investigator was paying Bennett thirty-five dollars a lesson to tutor him in the fine art of breaking and entering, and every time the big man opened his mouth, Gunner became more convinced that he had picked the perfect man for the job. Bennett's given name was Bill, but everyone on the street called him Fetch, because his was the sterling reputation of a good hunting dog. There wasn't anything you could send him off to get that he couldn't retrieve, once he had the scent. As near as anyone could tell, he had been out of the burglary business for years—his last stint in the joint had ended back in '85—but everyone who knew him had no doubt that he still had the touch, and would probably use it again if the right set of temptations ever came along.

"You notice I never turned on any lights? That's because most people won't. They're smart enough to know better. What you want to do is listen up when you're working on a door. Worry about what you're *hearing* inside a house, not what you're *seeing*. You wait around for somebody to turn on a light before deciding to take off, you're going to get caught with your pants down around your fucking ankles, just like you did tonight."

"You didn't give me enough time, Fetch," Gunner complained halfheartedly.

"For that sorry-ass lock you got on that back door? A minute and a half should've been plenty."

"Another twenty seconds and I would have had it," Gunner said.

Bennett shook his head, suddenly very serious. "You don't learn to do a lock quieter than that, you're not gonna get half the time I gave you. There's a lot of light sleepers out there, man, and one out of every ten's got a loaded twelve-gauge waiting in the closet, or under the bed." He used the index finger of his left hand to point to a spot on his right arm where a huge chunk of flesh appeared to have been removed from his biceps with an ice cream scooper. "Take it from me."

Gunner took another swallow of beer and nodded his head, slightly taken aback by the big man's mood swing.

"That the doorbell?" Bennett asked shortly, reacting to a muffled buzz emanating from the front of the house.

"Sounds like it, doesn't it?" Gunner looked at his watch. It was twelve-thirty in the morning. "Somebody must've got the wrong address."

"Maybe it's a lady friend," Bennett said. "Lookin' for a little late-night action." The thought made him grin again.

Gunner got up from the table, taking his beer with him, and said, "Maybe you've had too much to drink."

As the doorbell rang again, he entered the living room of his little duplex and squinted into the peephole on his front door, cursing himself for being disappointed when he found a man he didn't recognize standing on his front porch, appearing to stare right back at him. Bennett's comment about a lady friend had been made entirely in jest, but Gunner had allowed it to get his hopes up all the same. The fact that Claudia Lovejoy had been making herself scarce around his home lately didn't seem to matter. Some small, sadistically optimistic part of him had sold him on the idea that this midnight caller might be her, looking to renew their suddenly stagnant affair, and now he was slightly devastated to learn that an idea was all it was.

Stupid.

Gunner opened his front door abruptly and the middle-aged black man standing beyond it froze, caught in the yellow glow of Gunner's porch light as he was reaching for the doorbell one more time.

"Can I help you?" Gunner asked.

The man put his outstretched arm down and straightened up, trying to make a good first impression. He was a black Joe Average: medium height, medium build; conservatively dressed and groomed. The hair just above both ears was Christmas-card white, but that was about all anybody would be able to remember about him if he ever took to robbing banks. Gunner guessed he was an ex-navy man with a wife and four kids and a garage full of Chevys who did all of his shopping at Sears.

"I'm looking for the Aaron Gunner residence," the man on the porch said.

Gunner looked at him for a long moment before saying anything. "I'm Aaron Gunner."

"Mr. Gunner, we spoke on the phone this morning. We were supposed to meet in your office tomorrow afternoon, but I've decided that might not be such a good idea. Discussing what I have to discuss with you over there, I mean."

"Your name is Flowers?"

"Mitchell Flowers. Yes." He held out his hand for Gunner to shake, and his grip was something to be proud of. "I know it's late, but I'm afraid this was the earliest I could get over here. I had to pull some overtime out at the plant and I only got off about an hour ago. You mind if I come in?"

Gunner was ushering him inside when Fetch Bennett appeared from the kitchen, his sizable curiosity apparently aroused by his host's extended absence. Flowers appeared to be unnerved by the sight of him.

"You have company. Maybe we should do this some other time." He started to back toward the door.

"Hey, no, no, no," Bennett said, heading the smaller man off. "I was just leaving, brother, really."

"Fetch, this is Mitchell Flowers," Gunner said, trying to ease the three of them out of the sudden awkwardness of the moment. "Mr. Flowers is thinking about hiring me to do some work for him."

"Fetch Bennett. Pleased to meet you," Bennett said as he shook Flowers's hand, then opened the door to let himself out. "We still on for Thursday?" he asked Gunner.

"Same time, Thursday, yeah. Thanks for everything, Fetch."

"Any time, partner. Nice meeting you, Mr. Flowers."

Flowers dipped his head in reply and Bennett was gone.

"My piano teacher," Gunner explained after closing the door, deciding to answer the question before Flowers could think to ask it. He showed the other man to a seat in the living room and found one for himself, then pretended not to notice as Flowers's eyes wandered across the room, searching for a piano that wasn't there.

"Can I get you a beer, Mr. Flowers?" Gunner asked, putting the finishing touches on the one he had started earlier.

Flowers shook his head. "No. Thank you."

The doorbell rang again.

It was Bennett, the picture of embarrassment.

"Forgot my gun," the big man said sheepishly, trying to tone his cannon-shot voice down to a whisper.

Gunner laughed, told him to hold on a minute, then left for the kitchen. He could feel Flowers watching him as he returned to the door with the revolver at his side, not wanting to make the weapon any more conspicuous by trying to hide it.

Bennett took the gun and said thanks, then disappeared again.

Gunner rejoined Flowers in the living room and said, "When Fetch tells you how he wants a piece played, he only tells you *once*."

It was a lame joke, but it didn't deserve the cold shoulder Flowers gave it. He looked at Gunner like someone had just told him his shoelace was untied.

"There somebody watching my office I don't know about, Mr. Flowers?" Gunner asked him, writing off levity for the remainder of the night.

"Excuse me?"

"You said you didn't think our meeting there in the morning would be such a good idea. I'm wondering why you think so."

Flowers paused, choosing his words with care so as not to inflict any further injury upon his host. "Your office *is* a barbershop. Isn't that right, Mr. Gunner?"

Gunner didn't see the relevance of the question, but said, "That's right. Mickey's Trueblood barbershop. I lease a little space in the back. That a problem for you?"

"No, no. Please. Don't misunderstand." Flowers used both hands to wave off any unintended insult. "I'm sure it's a fine place to conduct business, in general, but . . ."

"But?"

"But it's a *barbershop*. A place where old men generally go to talk about everybody's business but their own. You understand what I'm saying?"

Gunner did, of course, though he had never given the matter much thought until now. There might be other places of business besides a barbershop where a man's secrets could take flight on the neighborhood gossip wires faster, but there weren't many. For all the disparaging things men had to say about the way personal confidences were scattered to the far winds by the ladies seated under the dryers at any corner beauty shop, a men's barbershop was usually just as bad, if not worse, and Mickey's was no exception. If the barber's bombastic crew of regular customers wouldn't be able to report what, specifically, Gunner and Flowers had to say to each other behind closed doors, it would at least be within their power to make Flowers's very presence in Gunner's office a matter of public record, and maybe that alone was the kind of indiscretion Flowers was looking to avoid.

"Okay," Gunner said, shrugging. "I guess you've got a point. If confidentiality's critical, we could be better off here. So . . ." He looked at Flowers expectantly.

The older man shifted about on the cushions of his chair uneasily, buying time, and then said, "I want you to set something right for me, Mr. Gunner. Something I did—or something I *didn't* do, actually—that I just can't live with anymore." He pulled in a deep breath and, without waiting for Gunner to urge him on, said, "One night last September, I saw a cop shoot a kid in an alley near my house. A bad cop, an evil one, a white man's been busting black heads in our neighborhood for years. You know the kind I mean. This cop, he caught a pair of kids trying to rob a liquor store over on Vernon and Third Avenue, chased one of 'em for six blocks down into this alley, then shot him dead. Just a twelve-year-old kid, named Lendell Washington. Maybe you remember hearing about it."

The name and the story did ring a faint bell with Gunner, but he chose not to say so, preferring for the moment to let Flowers's story run its natural course.

"Anyway, the cop tried to say he'd shot the kid in self-defense.

That's what they always say, right? He said the kid had fired on him first. Only, three people came forward at the scene to say he was lying. They said he was the only one who had fired a weapon. Now, you and I both know, Mr. Gunner, that three people—three *black* people, especially—aren't usually enough to get a cop slapped on the wrist for jaywalking, let alone murder. So everybody figured the cop was going to walk. Only, he didn't. Not after the police came right out and admitted that all the evidence proved the cop was lying."

"This cop you're talking about. His name was McDonald, or McGovern. . . . Something like that?" Gunner finally asked.

Flowers nodded. "McGovern. Jack McGovern. Then you do remember."

Gunner shrugged. "Vaguely. He was a real ball-buster, supposedly. The kind of foulmouthed, bigoted jackass that used to be all the rage in law enforcement twenty, twenty-five years ago."

"That was him. Shocked the hell out of a lot of people how they handled his case, didn't it? No excuses, no denials—just a quick board of rights hearing, then his immediate dismissal. A fast and dirty firing—something we don't see a lot of where the police down here are concerned.

"Of course, most people were able to read between the lines. Chief Bowden had been in charge of the LAPD for less than a year, and the riots were still fresh in everyone's mind. Crucifying McGovern was obviously just the chief's way of trying to show the black community there was a new sheriff in town, one we could all count on to be sensitive to the community's needs."

Flowers paused, seemingly having trouble getting to the point.

"You see something wrong with that?" Gunner asked him.

Flowers picked restlessly at the foam stuffing peeking out of a hole in the left armrest of his chair as he considered the question. "I shouldn't," he said in time. "I have a wife and three kids to worry about, Mr. Gunner. I should be as happy as anyone to see that madman off the street."

"But you're not."

"Not entirely, no."

"Because?"

"Because McGovern didn't murder Lendell Washington," Flowers said simply. "I told you I was there the night the kid was shot, remember? I saw the whole thing. And McGovern was telling the truth when he said the kid had fired on him first. I saw and heard him do it. It all happened exactly the way McGovern said it did."

"But you never went to the police to tell them as much."

"No. I never told anybody I was there that night." He smiled a halfhearted smile and shrugged, apparently not knowing what else to say.

"Any chance you're simply mistaken? Your eyes can play funny tricks with you at times like that."

"I know what I saw, Mr. Gunner. The Washington boy fired twice at McGovern before McGovern fired back. I'm sure of it."

"You said there were other witnesses," Gunner said.

Flowers nodded. "There were. A man and two women. They turned up near the alley that night, claiming they saw the kid get shot, and McGovern putting a gun in his hand afterward and firing it, but I don't think any of them really did. The streets were deserted when I walked past that alley, I didn't see anybody else around. I think those people just showed up afterward, saw a chance to make a cop look bad, and took it."

"But you didn't."

"No. I didn't."

"Because you didn't want to get involved."

"Because I *chose* not to get involved."

Seeing no way around it, Gunner braced himself to ask the obvious next question: "So why get involved now?"

Flowers just looked at him, stuck for a feasible answer.

"Your conscience is bothering you, is that it?"

"I guess you could say that."

"This is going to sound rather cold, Mr. Flowers, but don't you think you're a little late? McGovern got his walking papers from the department eight months ago."

"I understand that. I regret that I didn't come forward sooner, of course, but I guess I just didn't feel like I was responsible for what happened to him until now. You'd feel the same way if you were me, I'm sure."

"Well, that's certainly a possibility, Mr. Flowers, but it's not very likely. Judging from what little I can recall having heard about the man, what happened to McGovern was very likely inevitable, especially under the aegis of the LAPD's new regime. Even if he were only *half* the monster everyone says he was, the odds are good he would have made a career-ending mistake of one sort or another eventually, with or without your help."

"So?"

"So my advice to you is, go back to forgetting about it, because you couldn't get the man reinstated now, even if your sense of guilt were warranted. The department invested a lot of time and effort into dismissing him, as you pointed out, and I don't think they'd be particularly anxious to admit, eight months later, that it was all just a big mistake."

"Reinstated?"

"That's right. Reinstated. Isn't that what you were thinking? That you could maybe get him his job back if you came forward now?"

Flowers eyed him curiously, seeming to be at a loss for words. "You don't know, do you?"

"Know what?"

Flowers's incredulous gaze turned into a glare. "That McGovern is *dead*. He committed suicide three days ago."

He watched Gunner sit there like a dunce, having been made to feel like an uninformed idiot in the confines of his own home.

"The newspapers say he'd been working as a night watchman for the last few months, and was watching a stereo store out in Hollywood when he caught a man trying to rob the place early Friday morning. The man says McGovern caught him sneaking out the back door with his arms full of portable TVs, then just froze up. Turned his own gun on himself and blew his brains out, without ever having said so much as a word."

He waited to see how Gunner would react to that, but Gunner had nothing to say.

"It sounds crazy, but I can see him doing it," Flowers said.

"Because I've seen the thief's picture in the paper, and on TV, and he's a black man not much bigger or taller than the Washington boy was when he died. A *black man,* Mr. Gunner. Do you follow what I'm saying?"

Now Gunner remembered. He had caught a few words of a television news report announcing McGovern's death the day after it had happened, Friday, but not enough to identify McGovern as the pathologically violent cop the LAPD had so uncharacteristically raked over the coals back in early November. It would have been easy to miss this latest chapter of the ex-cop's story entirely, as McGovern had picked the start of the Fourth of July weekend to reenter the headlines, and in competition with the usual glut of holiday car wrecks, spectacular fireworks displays, and drug-related homicides, coverage of his suicide had received the short shrift such poor timing deserved.

"The police are certain it was suicide?" Gunner asked Flowers.

Again, Flowers nodded. "They say they are. They say it was the would-be thief himself who called them to the scene, and they admit there's no way he would have done something like that unless McGovern died just the way he says he did. Besides, they know what happened to McGovern eight months ago better than anybody. If I can picture him killing himself under those circumstances, I'm sure they can, too."

Gunner nodded his head, thinking along the same lines. Other than his general build, the thief probably bore no more real resemblance to Lendell Washington than Flowers did—but it had likely been Washington's face McGovern had thought he was seeing that night, all the same.

"I'm not going to try and tell you that I feel sorry for the man, Mr. Gunner. I think he got exactly what he deserved, when you get right down to it. Trouble is, he got it for all the wrong reasons, and I can't help but feel like I'm to blame for that."

Gunner shook his head and said, "Don't flatter yourself. What you said about Chief Bowden earlier was right on the mark. He's been looking for an opportunity to prove himself to the black community, and the Lendell Washington shooting was it. His boys would have probably treated you like someone reporting a UFO sighting had you approached them earlier in McGovern's defense."

"That's beside the point," Flowers said indignantly. "Whether or not I could have done McGovern any good isn't what matters to me. What is is that I didn't do what I knew was right, and only because I was ordered not to."

Gunner raised an eyebrow, not sure he had heard this last correctly. "Ordered?"

Flowers reached behind his right hip for his wallet, drew a folded sheet of white paper from its billfold section, and, opening the note meticulously, handed it over to Gunner.

"Read this," he said.

It had the distinctive look of a blackmail note. Somebody had clipped mismatching characters out of newspapers and magazines and pasted them haphazardly together to form a succinct and crude message:

DEAR UNCLE:
WHY DONT YOU SIDE WITH THE BROTHERS FOR ONCE. DONT NOBODY BUT US KNOWS YOU WAS THERE. LET THE FUCKING PIG BURN AND YOU WONT GET HURT.

"I found that in my mailbox two days after the Washington boy was shot. It came just like that: no envelope, no address, no postmark. I figured whoever it was must have just come by the house and dropped it in the box the night before."

"Any idea who it could have been?"

"No. I never told anybody I was there, remember?"

"So it had to be someone who saw you near the alley that night."

"Yes."

"And knew who you were."

"Yes."

"This the only note you received?"

"The only note, yes. But I got a phone call a day later, in the evening, early. This man asked me if I'd gotten his message. The message he'd left in my mailbox, he said."

"You didn't recognize the voice?"

"No. I'd never heard it before."

"Go on."

"Man was brief and to the point. He said he knew who I was, and what I was. He kept calling me 'Uncle.' Uncle this, and Uncle that." Flowers's eyes narrowed with anger as the memory came back to him. "He said he knew where my daughter Kisha went to school. Martin Luther King Elementary School; room nine. He told me what color clothes she had on that day and how many braids were in her hair." He was looking at Gunner, but seeing something beyond him that wasn't really there; a what-might-have-been nightmare that had come too close to reality for comfort. "Maybe I would have kept quiet about what I saw that night anyway, I don't know. Like I said, I was no friend of Jack McGovern's. But I'm a conservative man, Mr. Gunner. Too conservative for some people. If I told you I could never see myself helping a policeman in trouble, I'd be lying to you. I think cops have a thankless job, a difficult job, and most of them are all right. I don't think that opinion makes me a cop-lover, but to some people, it does. Apparently, this man is one of them."

He breathed a deep sigh, resolutely pushing on, and said, "If they had let me make up my own mind about going or not going to the police, I wouldn't have had to come here tonight. No matter what I'd decided to do, I would've been able to live with it, without any regrets. Only, I didn't get to make up my own mind. Somebody followed my little girl to school one day and made up my mind for me. And that's why I need your help."

Gunner waited for him to spell it out.

"I want you to undo the damage my cowardice has done, Mr. Gunner. I want you to find out what really happened in that alley the night Lendell Washington was killed, and I want you to tell the whole world about it."

Gunner still didn't say anything.

"The man who sent me that note obviously wanted McGovern to lose his badge over something he didn't do," Flowers went on, "and he used me to make that happen. He took advantage of my insecurities as a man and bought my silence—*cheap*. If I let him get away with that, now that it's cost a man his life, I'll be everything he accuses me of being—and worse."

He gave Gunner a good look at the determination he'd brought into the house with him, and Gunner found himself suitably impressed. Appraising the older man with more professional interest than he had shown him to this point, it occurred to Gunner that Flowers fit the profile of a man who might have had to deal with being thought of as an Uncle Tom all of his adult life, and he knew what that yoke was like to bear. Being made to feel answerable to the whole of one's own race was a burden few white men ever had to shoulder, yet it was a black man's birthright from day one. To wander off too far from the beaten path of conformity, daring to expand upon what some people insisted were the unalterable parameters of "blackness," was to purchase the guilt of treason, and for some that guilt could be so incessant as to be crippling. Gunner himself was no such victim, but he had felt the sting of the phenomenon more than once, enough to know its symptoms when he saw them, as he realized he was seeing them now.

Unfortunately, being able to commiserate with Flowers did not preclude Gunner from recognizing the absurdity of his request. One was always risking a broken neck playing cops with cops, no matter what you were trying to prove or who you were trying to vindicate, and only morons didn't know it.

Gunner was no moron.

"Mr. Flowers," he said, making his best effort to be delicate, "I'm afraid I can't help you. I doubt that anyone could, frankly."

"I don't understand," Flowers said.

"Look. I can appreciate your motives in all this, but there really isn't anything you can do. The book on Jack McGovern was closed a long time ago, and that's probably just how the cops want to keep it."

"So?"

"So that means the poor devil who takes your case isn't going to have their cooperation. In fact, he's likely to have them leaning on him every inch of the way. Hard."

"I've lived in Los Angeles all my life, Mr. Gunner. You don't have to tell me how hostile the police can be toward private citizens looking into police affairs."

"Then you must know that a man could get himself seriously hurt asking them the kinds of questions you want asked."

"I know that, yes. But I understood that was the nature of your work. Taking risks, I mean."

"Excuse me?"

"I was told you weren't easily intimidated. That you'd taken cases like this before, and done well."

"Told by whom?"

"I spoke to several different people. Ex-clients and the like. They all spoke very highly of you, Mr. Gunner."

"My publicists always have glowing things to say about me when someone else is buying the drinks, Mr. Flowers."

"Then you're not interested in helping me. Is that what you're saying?"

"This isn't a matter of my being interested or disinterested. It's a matter of my being *capable*." The investigator shrugged. "To be perfectly honest with you, my present client list wouldn't have three names on it if I added two. The timing of your offer, at least, couldn't be better for me."

"Then what's the problem?"

"The problem is, I can't guarantee you anything. Nobody could. Best effort is the most you can expect on a case like this, and you'd be insane not to understand that from the gate."

"All right."

Gunner paused, realizing with some dismay that he was sounding more and more like a man about to accept Flowers's case, rather than one trying to politely decline it. "Granted, it should help that the intent here is to try and *clear* a cop of misconduct, for a change, but that's only if I—that is, your investigator—can get anybody to believe for one minute that that's the case. And that won't be easy. Cops are a skeptical bunch by nature, anyway, but their antennae don't really go up until they hear the words 'I'm on your side' uttered by a perfect stranger."

Flowers just nodded, suddenly very agreeable. He was waiting for Gunner to get to the bottom line.

"What if I prove that the police are right, and you're wrong? Have you thought about that?"

"I've thought about it. Naturally. But since I'm not wrong, it doesn't worry me. I saw the kid fire on McGovern, Mr. Gunner. Twice. There's no doubt in my mind."

He was knocking down every wall Gunner was throwing up before him, determinedly refusing to withdraw his plea for help. Down to the last poisoned arrow in his quiver, Gunner went for broke and said, "All right. Let's assume I agree to be your man. You want me to play twenty questions with the LAPD, you're going to have to foot the bill for some upgraded health and dental insurance. You may as well understand that right now."

"How much will you need?"

"A fifteen-hundred–dollar retainer up front, then a-hundred-and-fifty dollars a day after that. Plus expenses. You have that kind of money?"

"Yes." Flowers never flinched, just nodded his head once more.

Gunner wanted to ask how Flowers could have come into that kind of wealth—he didn't exactly look like someone a banker would race down the street to meet, deposit slip in hand—but the investigator couldn't think of a way to phrase the question that any self-respecting adult wouldn't find insulting. So instead, he merely asked, "You're sure this thing means that much to you?"

Again, Flowers's head inched up and down affirmatively. "I've had eight months and all weekend to think about it," he said. "I'm not going to turn back now."

He was giving Gunner one final chance to bow out gracefully, his eyes issuing a silent promise that he would bear no grudges if the investigator did. For a split second, Gunner almost had the sense that he really had a choice in the matter—but of course, that was only a hopeless delusion. What he had told Flowers about the sorry state of his client list had been no overstatement; he needed the work, and badly.

And so common sense lost yet another duel with practicality. The wide berth he was always so careful to give the police in Los Angeles was about to be dispensed with, and all because he didn't know where his next meal was going to come from.

Chalk up another one for hunger, Gunner thought to himself. The great motivator.

"You're going to have to tell me everything, starting at the very beginning," he told Flowers, trying to sound optimistic. "But first, I'm going to need another beer."

He stood up and headed for the kitchen.

2

One good thing about Matthew Poole was, he wasn't a fancy eater. You could take him to any International House of Pancakes in town and he would feel more than sufficiently bribed. Gunner considered himself lucky that Poole, one of his few decent contacts within the LAPD, didn't have richer tastes; homicide detectives, in general, usually charged a private operator an arm and a leg just to relate the time of day.

"Nobody's gonna tell you shit, that's number one," Poole said, stuffing a sausage into his mouth with great relish. "Do you really need a number two?"

He and Gunner were part of a small, prenoon crowd patronizing the IHOP franchise on Manchester Avenue in Inglewood, only a short jog west of the Great Western Forum where the Lakers mourned the loss of Magic Johnson when they weren't doing it out on the road. As usual, Gunner had called the detective on short notice—less than ten hours after having agreed to take Mitchell Flowers on as a client—but Poole had driven halfway across the city from his Seventy-seventh Street station environs to meet with Gunner nevertheless. His love of a free meal was that reliable.

"I was kind of hoping it would help to be on the home team's side for a change," Gunner told Poole, stirring some stale cream into his coffee.

"Hope springs eternal, friend, but it won't save your ass in a pinch."

"If I put that on a plaque and hung it up somewhere, would you charge me for the privilege, Poole?"

"Look, Gunner—I'm not telling you anything you don't already know. Nobody down at Southwest's gonna talk to you. You're a private ticket, it's not gonna matter who you say you're working for." He went to work on his eggs without missing a beat and said, "Who'd you say your client was, again?"

"I didn't say. And it wasn't because I forgot to mention."

"You see? You fucking PI's are all alike. Take, take, take, that's all you know. You wanna ask a shitload of questions, but not have to answer any. Is that fair?"

"I'm not implying that you'd let it get around, Lieutenant, but if I were to tell you who my client is, it's possible I could regret it later. This is a person, after all, whom some might accuse of having stood idly by while a twenty-two-year veteran of the Los Angeles Police Department took the rap for something he didn't do."

"You say that as if that's not a perfectly accurate description of what your client himself claims to have done."

"Maybe it is, and maybe it isn't. I, for one, think that's a pretty harsh way of looking at it. In any case—and you'll notice that, unlike yourself, Poole, I make no reference to gender here—it's my professional opinion that it's in my client's best interests to remain anonymous for as long as possible. Even to you."

Poole shrugged with seemingly genuine indifference and reached for the salt. "Suit yourself."

Gunner watched him eat for a full minute before pushing on. "So are you going to tell me where to start, or what?"

Poole looked up as a stumpy black waitress in an overinflated blue uniform made use of the full pot on their table to top off their coffees, having noticed they had shown no inclination to do it themselves. Gunner couldn't tell whether Poole wanted to laugh or cry, but that was the way the cop's face always worked; it was a jowly caricature of a young Walter Matthau that never betrayed a thing. It moved—here, there, sometimes in a thousand places at once—but that was all it did. Even the man's smiles were hard to make out in certain light.

"What is it with you?" the detective asked as soon as the waitress was gone again. "You don't understand the Queen's English? Give the man—or the *lady*—their retainer back and find something else to do with your time. Because number one, you're brain dead if you believe that anybody familiar with McGovern's unique brand of police protection would pay you or anybody else a hundred-plus bills a day to clear him of the Washington kid's killing; I don't care what they say their reasons are. And number two, if you think what I'm doing now is turning a deaf ear to you, wait 'til you start talking to McGovern's pals down at Southwest. You're not gonna hear a damn thing over there but the sound of your own voice."

"I already took the case, Poole," Gunner said.

"Un-take it. You're your own boss, right?"

"And what about McGovern?"

"Do I have to actually say it? Fuck McGovern. He was a bad egg, and everybody knew it. Not having to split my pension with an asshole like that will be one of the highlights of my life."

"You two were that close, huh?"

"I never had the pleasure, actually, but I'd heard enough about the guy over the years to know I didn't miss anything. We're no brotherhood of saints, Gunner, but even we cops know a uniformed sociopath when we see one."

"Then you think his dismissal was warranted."

"Warranted? I don't know about warranted. All I know is, the department's case against him was ironclad, and I don't see how it automatically becomes null and void just because one ass-hole—of undetermined gender—steps forward damn near a year later to say that they saw something in a pitch-black alley three other people on the scene didn't. Give me a break.

"I mean, if the Washington kid had fired two rounds at McGovern the way your client says he did, they would've found a couple of slugs out in the street, where McGovern said he was standing at the time of all the shooting. Right? And the prints they found on the gun he turned in would've come from the Washington kid's left hand, because he was strictly left-handed. You with me so far?"

"So far."

"All right. Good. So guess where the two slugs they found that had been fired from the gun McGovern turned in were dug up?"

"In the alley."

"In the ground. That's right. And guess which of Washington's two hands made the prints on the gun?"

"His right."

"Right again. Two rounds fired into the ground, and fired with the kid's weak hand around the grips. Geez. I wonder what that means."

Gunner paused for a moment, a little surprised. "Hope you don't take this the wrong way, Poole, but you don't often hear a cop jump to another's defense the way you've just jumped to Jack McGovern's."

"Heresay is inadmissible, Gunner. You see anybody around here wearing a wire?" Poole spread some butter on his pancakes and then splattered a quart of boysenberry syrup on the front of his shirt wolfing them down. "What do you want me to do? Lie to you? Tell you not to worry, those guys are gonna just spill their guts, all you've gotta do is lay on the charm?"

"I want you to tell me who to talk to first. Never mind all the well-intentioned encouragement to quit before I've even gotten started."

"Okay. Okay. Square one for me would be McGovern's watch sergeant. If there's anybody over there who'd likely be anxious to see the book reopened on him, it's the man—or *woman,* as the case may be—he worked for. McGovern was under their command, right? I'd be willing to bet whoever it is took what happened to McGovern very personally."

"Fine. His watch sergeant first. And after that?"

Poole shrugged again. "After that, it's a toss-up. His last partner, of course. Some of the other officers in his squad. People like that. I don't have to tell you everything, do I?"

"What about Internal Affairs?"

Poole dropped his fork and actually stopped eating. "No. No. Forget Internal Affairs. Those guys are gonna get you nowhere fast, save yourself the heartache."

26

"You don't think they'd be willing to help?"

"Help? No. Help is not their thing. Breaking balls, that's their thing. You want your balls broken, Gunner?"

"Not if I can help it, no. But I sure as hell can't see how I'm supposed to find out how McGovern came to shoot Lendell Washington without reviewing the department's own investigation into the incident. Can you?"

"I told you. This case is a dead end. Nobody's gonna talk to you, and least of all the boys in Internal Affairs. With everybody else it'll just be a matter of choice; with them, it's gonna be departmental policy. Without a court order, they're not gonna show you so much as the cabinet they keep the files in, and without a detective's badge—a *real* detective's badge—they're not gonna say gesundheit when you sneeze. Are you getting the picture here?"

"What about off the record?"

"Off the record, on the record—they're not gonna give a shit what you call it."

"Even if the investigation in question has been closed for nearly a year?"

"It doesn't make any difference. Once a verdict has been reached, the files are sealed; they don't reopen them for anybody. Especially not for some black private license whose very mission in life is to prove that their investigation into an officer-involved shooting was a total fuck-up."

That was, Gunner had to admit, exactly how they would be likely to view him.

"Nobody said they fucked up anything," the investigator said, sweeping yellow egg yoke across his plate with a slice of blackened white toast. "It could be the conclusions they came to were essentially sound, based on the evidence they had to work with at the time."

"Which is another way of saying, maybe they overlooked something. Or worse, were misled."

"Is it?"

"I'm sure they'll appreciate the distinction, being accused of mere stupidity as opposed to utter incompetence. Shit!" He had picked up his coffee again and burned the hell out of his mouth, forgetting that their waitress had just been by to refill his cup.

"You okay?"

"Yeah, sure. I'm fine," Poole said, brushing coffee off his tie with a napkin already smeared with syrup. "Exasperated, but fine." He looked up to gaze at Gunner evenly. "You've got the thickest skull I've ever had the displeasure of trying to dent, Gunner. You know that?"

"When a cop follows through on a commitment, everybody calls it 'dedication.' When a private ticket does the same thing, they call it being 'hardheaded.' Why is that, Lieutenant?"

"Because we cops can afford to be 'dedicated,' you asshole. We've got something called 'backup.' Who the hell are you gonna call when the shit gets thick, the ACLU?"

"It's a job, Poole. That's all. If somebody had come along and offered me a couple grand to track down the missus, I'd be doing that instead. Believe me."

He picked up the check and grimaced. Poole was cheap enough to bribe, it was true, but that didn't stop Gunner from wishing he could get away with treating the detective to a breakfast at McDonald's, every once in a while.

"Any last words of advice, Lieutenant, before we call this meeting adjourned?"

"Yeah. I've got some advice." The abrupt change in Poole's tone earned Gunner's full attention again. He wasn't a jocular man, Poole, but his usual, astringent professional demeanor hadn't really shown itself until this moment. "Use your head. Watch your ass. Talk to these people like you've got some respect for them, and leave the snappy comebacks at home. Are you with me so far?"

"Yes."

"Nobody's gonna like you. Understand that up front. You're not a member of the social club, and you're gonna be rootin' around in club business, a definite no-no for anybody, no matter what they say their motives are. So they're gonna give you a hard time—if they bother to deal with you at all. *Just don't take it personally.* Try to see the situation from their perspective, and keep a cool head at all times. You swallow your pride and show them a little deference, you might just get somewhere with somebody. You never know."

Gunner nodded his head silently, wordlessly. He knew that what Poole was telling him to do was not far removed from kissing a little collective ass, but he also knew how much wisdom there was in the suggestion, and he wasn't going to say anything now to make Poole think otherwise.

"Anybody asks for references, would you mind if I dropped your name?" Gunner asked instead, having waited until the last possible moment to bring the subject up.

Poole's latest shrug was as lazy as the others, just like the muscles in his face. "If you think that'll do you any good. I've spoken for you before, I guess I could do it again. We Seventy-seventh Street characters don't carry much weight over at Southwest, but I'll give anybody who asks for it my opinion of you, if that's what you want."

"Maybe I should hear what your opinion of me is, first."

"Sure. I tell 'em, 'He's not half the dickhead most private licenses are, and he never makes me pay for breakfast.' "

"Whoa. Take it easy. You come on with a five-star rave like that, Poole, you're gonna lose all your credibility in this town."

"Hey, we're not exactly drinking buddies, Gunner, all right? We get along, that's all. You don't make my job any easier, but you've never made it much harder, either, and that's the most I can say for you. So don't go rushing out to buy that engagement ring just yet."

Gunner fell out laughing. Poole was being earnest. He was obviously having a tough time figuring out what could prove more damaging to a man of his position: a reputation for flashing in the park, or having a private investigator as a friend.

"I love you, too, Lieutenant," Gunner said.

Poole scratched his nose with the middle finger of his right hand conspicuously extended, then got up to follow Gunner out.

3

"Aaron, I don't think I want to see you again for a while," Claudia Lovejoy said, flat out.

"I've been getting that impression."

"I just think we've been moving too fast. I need some time alone. To decide if this is really what I want or not. Please."

"Would have been a nice gesture on your part to tell me as much over the phone, don't you think? I've been trying to call you for two weeks," Gunner said. "It shouldn't have been necessary for me to stake your place out like a goddamn process server just to hear you say good-bye."

"I'm sorry. I guess I just didn't want to be talked out of doing this anymore."

"May I come in, at least?"

She stayed where she was, blocking the front door to her Lynwood home like a diminutive sentry, and shook her head with authority, her mind made up. "No. That wouldn't be a good idea."

It was the third day in a week that he had come knocking at her door, but only the first time she had rewarded him with an answer. Now that he had officially started in on the Mitchell Flowers case, he had better things to do with his time, but after leaving Matthew Poole in the restaurant parking lot fifteen minutes ago, he had found himself drawn here like a moth to a flame, despising his inability to wait her out all the while.

It only made things worse that, as always, she was beautiful, maybe the most beautiful black woman he had ever been fortunate enough to know. Black hair combed straight back on her head, scattering light like a clear-water lake in the sun, and with eyes as green and piercing as backlit emeralds, she should have been the easiest woman in the world to say yes to, but Gunner wasn't going to go away just because she issued the command. He was in too deep to be that obliging.

They had been seeing each other now for almost a year, and up until two weeks ago, when she had suddenly stopped taking his phone calls, Gunner had thought they were leading up to something substantive, not just killing time. It had mattered little to him that killing time was all she had ever claimed she could offer him; she had some wild ideas about the nature of his work and the broad scope of temptations it made available to him, and he figured her reluctance to acknowledge the long-term possibilities of their relationship was a simple matter of mistrust and nothing more. She was a devout Christian and he was a pitifully dormant excuse for one, and it was true that that occasionally worked against them, but he considered this, too, a negligible thing upon which to base a breakup. To hear him tell it, in fact, her cautionary approach toward him was wholly unjustified— though he knew that was a lie.

Now he was paying the price for not accepting the fact earlier.

Claudia had been less than a month into widowhood when the two first met, just a fair-skinned, thirty-two-year-old beauty in black whose husband had been murdered in a drive-by shooting Gunner's gangbanging client at the time had been accused of committing, and from the start, Gunner had spent nearly as much time and energy wooing her as he had proving someone other than his client had killed her husband. Without granting her a moment to think about it, like an obnoxious insurance salesman too dense to realize he's shown up at a bad time, Gunner had wedged his foot in Claudia's door and invited himself into her life knowing full well he was taking advantage of a woman too disoriented to fend him off. Had he been a smarter man—or at least, one less romantically deprived—he might have understood that, sooner or later, Claudia was going to realize that he had moved in on her while her judgment had been seriously impaired, well before her descent from grief could reach its own natural conclusion, and that she would consequently lay down some nasty skidmarks applying the brakes to their affair. But Gunner had never come to any such understanding. He had been too consumed with the false optimism of a lonely man on the brink of successful monogamy for that.

"Aaron, please. Try to understand. This isn't your fault. You haven't done anything wrong. This is just something I feel I have to do."

He chuckled in spite of himself, seething.

"I should have never agreed to start seeing you in the first place. I must have been insane," she said, angered by his obvious intention to make what she was doing feel as cold and inhumane as possible.

"Forget it. I'm the jackass who wouldn't take no for an answer. If anybody's to blame for this, I am."

"I'm sorry."

"Yeah, you said that already. You've been sorry ever since you came to the door."

"I want some time to think. That's all. If you want to make your own assumptions about how I'll feel about you afterward, that's your business."

"What's that supposed to mean?"

"It means you're giving up too easily. You're acting like I've told you I don't love you, when that's not what I've been trying to say at all. What I am trying to say is that I think I *am* in love with you—and I'm not so sure I *want* to be. Maybe what we've had together up to now is real, I don't know. It *feels* real enough. But you caught me right after Darrel's death, before I ever had a chance to really come to grips with being alone, and I can't help but wonder why I'm as inclined to stay with you now as I am. Because being with you is right—or because it's *safe*?"

"It makes no difference to me either way," Gunner lied. Poorly.

"Maybe not today, no," Claudia said. "But I think in time, it would make a difference. To both of us."

Gunner didn't say anything. He knew she was right.

"All I'm doing is testing my instincts. That's all. I'm just trying to convince myself that what they're telling me about you, about us, can be trusted. And I've decided I don't want to go on sleeping in your bed until I know, one way or the other. I've done that too long already." She started to say she was sorry again, but her lips had barely parted when she caught herself. She let a little shrug pass for another apology instead.

They stood there on her front porch and passed a moment frozen in time silently, painfully. "And what am I supposed to do in the meantime?" Gunner finally asked her, making the question sound almost rhetorical. "Take three cold showers a day and wait for the phone to ring?"

Claudia shook her head. "You're free to do whatever you like. I can't very well make demands on your behavior when I can't promise you anything in return."

"No. You can't."

"But I'd like to think, if I were to call, at some time in the future . . ." She shrugged again, not really wanting to finish the thought. "It'd be nice to catch you at home."

"Uh-huh."

"And it wouldn't hurt if you were alone." She tried to smile.

Gunner thought about it, never letting his eyes leave her face, then nodded solemnly and said, "Sure." He leaned down to kiss her softly on the mouth, his left hand bracing her chin, and then pulled away before she could beat him to it. "Take all the time you need, Claudia. I'm not going anywhere."

He turned away and started down the walk toward his car, wondering if she was fool enough to believe he'd really meant that.

The next morning, whoever the cop was working the phones for the LAPD's Southwest Division made a liar out of Matthew Poole. He answered Gunner's questions like somebody trying to win twenty-five thousand dollars and a new Buick Le Sabre on a TV game show, and asked precious few questions of his own. Gunner just told him he was a private license working a case and the man opened up like he'd spoken the secret password. A uniform with three stripes on his sleeve by the name of Harry Kupchak was the officer Gunner was looking for, the congenial cop said, but Kupchak was out in the field and could not be reached by phone. Gunner left a brief message for Kupchak to call him at Mickey's, then recited the number and said thanks, actually sorry that there was no way to pass the remarkably friendly desk sergeant a fiver for his kindness.

Kupchak himself, as it turned out, was another story.

He never picked up the phone to call. Gunner wasted half the day watching Mickey Moore cut hair before he figured out that his phone wasn't going to ring. He tried to reach Kupchak again at the Southwest station a few minutes after four, and this time the patrolman was in.

He had a voice like marbles passing through a meat grinder, and his disposition was worse.

"Yeah?"

"This Harry Kupchak?"

"I came to the phone, didn't I? Who the hell is this?"

"My name is Aaron Gunner. I'm a private investigator. Local. Didn't you get my message?"

"Gee, I'm sorry. My secretary must've misplaced it. What the hell's a private ticket want with me?"

"I understand Jack McGovern was under your command before his dismissal from the force last November. Is that right?"

Kupchak let the silent phone line echo in Gunner's ear before answering. "Jack McGovern? Never heard of 'im."

"That's not what I've been told," Gunner said.

"Fuck what you've been told. Cut the bullshit, pal, all right? You're no private license, you're a goddamn reporter. Who're you trying to kid?"

He hung up.

Gunner sat there at his desk, holding the phone's receiver away from his face like something that had just bit him and spit in his eye for good measure.

Maybe Poole knew what he was talking about, after all.

* * *

Fifteen minutes later, Poole was on the phone.

"I don't think that did you a whole lot of good," he said, "you wanna know the truth."

"You talked to him?"

"Yeah. I talked to him. He wanted to know what kind of lubricant we use. K-Y or somethin' more exotic."

"Sticks and stones, Lieutenant."

"Yeah. Right."

"Question is, did he believe you? About me, I mean."

"I think so. Who knows? The guy doesn't know me from Adam, for all he knows I'm the media's resident pimp down here."

"If he's worried about that, he'll ask around about you. Sooner or later he'll figure out you're okay. Right?"

"Depending on who he talks to," Poole said pessimistically.

Gunner said thanks and good-bye before Poole could hear him crack up at that.

"All right. So you're a private ticket, so what?"

Kupchak's voice hadn't changed much in five hours. Maybe it was only the phone, Gunner thought, but he still sounded like a handsaw attacking the hull of a battleship. He also sounded like he was calling from a bar, and not merely because the ambiance of the place appealed to him. He'd obviously had a few drinks before calling.

"I was about to give up on you," Gunner said, and it was true. He had had the barbershop all to himself for three hours now, since Mickey had locked up just after six, and he was getting tired of walking around the little shop's dark confines like a ghost.

"Your pal Poole says you're out to prove that Maggie got fucked over by the department, that he killed that kid in self-defense, just like he always said."

"Maggie? You mean McGovern?"

"That's what we all called Jack. Maggie. Don't change the goddamn subject, Mr. Gunner. You want me to hang up again?"

"Poole told you right. Sort of. My client's hired me to take another look at the Washington kid's shooting, to see if maybe

35

McGovern was telling the truth about how it went down. That's not the same as being hired to prove McGovern got screwed by the department, but I guess it's fairly close."

"So who's your client?"

The investigator had prepared himself for the question while waiting for Kupchak to call. Without a moment's hesitation, he said, "A local citizen with a guilty conscience. Somebody who was there the night Washington died and saw the whole thing, but never came forward to issue a statement."

Kupchak fell silent. In the relative hush his grating voice left behind, Gunner could hear someone in the background curse a jukebox loudly, followed by the sounds of a chair tipping over and glass breaking. Gunner could almost smell the spilt beer flowing across the hardwood floor. "This client of yours wouldn't be an Afro-American like yourself, would he?" Kupchak asked at last.

"That make some kind of difference?"

"To me? No way. Just thought I'd ask, is all." Incredibly, Kupchak's laugh was harder to take than his speaking voice. "Okay, so maybe it don't matter what color your client happens to be. I've got an open mind. You say this person was there the night Maggie shot that kid, is that right?"

"Yes."

"And they told you it all happened just the way Maggie said, that the Washington kid had a gun?"

"Yes."

"They see the gun?"

"No. My client never got that close. But they saw Washington fire two shots at McGovern, from the back of the alley, before McGovern fired back."

"Two shots, or three shots? Maggie said there'd been three."

"No. That's not what 'Maggie' said. He said there'd only been two shots, and my client says likewise. Quit trying to trip me up, Kupchak, I'm giving it to you straight."

The patrolman let Gunner hear a few more brief snatches of the drunken horseplay going on around him, and then said, "I'd like to believe you, Gunner, but I don't. Not about what you're after, anyway. Sorry I can't help you."

He hung up again.

Gunner said some unkind things about the men and women in local law enforcement and then rushed home to a cold, unfriendly bed.

It was like flushing seven hours down the toilet.

That was how long he grappled with the expectation of sleep before he was ready to accept the fact that he was never going to get any. He was dog-tired physically, but his mind simply refused to shut down for the night; an army of scantily clad Claudia Lovejoys was at the controls, and they had all of his sensory inputs cranked over to the redline. By six o'clock Thursday morning, he was sick enough of staring at the back of his eyelids and the lifeless black profiles of his bedroom furniture to throw himself into an ice-cold shower and go back to work for Mitchell Flowers.

When he left the house a good fifteen minutes before seven, he knew exactly where he was going and what he was going to do, which for him was an all-too infrequent departure from the norm. He hadn't lain awake all night just to form a single idea, but he had a funny feeling this one could make all the lost hours pining over Claudia Lovejoy almost seem worthwhile.

Through a damp gray mist that was all Los Angeles could do to remind the native San Franciscans in its midst of the impenetrable black fog back home, Gunner led the pre-rush-hour charge along the northbound Harbor Freeway toward Hollywood, pushing the '65 Ford Cobra convertible he was driving like a man with two speeding tickets already to his credit this year intent on collecting his third. Every now and then, the black man grew weary of treating the loud, red Cobra like an urban wimp-mobile and dared to open it up. This was one of those times.

He had been making good time up to now, but heavy traffic finally made a legitimate bid to collapse upon him as he reached the rolling parking lot where the Harbor and Hollywood freeways unloaded on one another. Some deft maneuvering and a brief, all-out sprint, however, got him past the congealing interchange and safely onto the northbound Hollywood, where he again assumed the role of point man for the onrushing mass of nine-to-fivers behind him. In short order he was in Hollywood proper, and he didn't have to read the exit signs to know it. Here, in the dry and dusty shadow of the Hollywood Hills, there was nothing so innocuous as fog to blame for the poor visibility ahead. Only three hours after daybreak, smog had assumed its daily post in the heavens; it blotted out the sun and the true colors of the sky like a burnt orange veil of smoke, difficult to breathe and even harder to stomach.

Gunner turned on the radio and tried to remember what the wind had felt like on his face only ten miles back.

He eventually left the freeway at Highland and made his way to Fountain, where a florist shop called Arturo's was located. He parked the car out front, totally ignoring the parking meter standing there, and went inside. Five minutes later, he was moving south on La Brea again, a dozen long-stemmed, red roses in a fancy gold lamé gift box sitting on the passenger seat beside him. It was almost eight o'clock.

He had to cruise along the northbound side of Santa Monica Boulevard, heading west, then reverse his field to La Cienega to peruse the southbound side of the streets before he found exactly what he was looking for. Half the citizens of Los Angeles had yet to peel their first eye open, yet the Santa Monica Strip skin trade was already open for business, and in earnest; there was an eclectic crush of male hustlers striking suggestive poses all along the boulevard, some dressed as men, some dressed as women, some only barely dressed at all. Still, for all the willing and able bodies from which he had to choose, Gunner knew the one he wanted the moment he set eyes on the sweet young thing.

She was a giant. The three-inch spiked heels she was wearing had nothing to do with it. She could have walked out into the street and stood in a pothole four inches deep, and she still would have passed for someone six foot two. She was as black as India ink and her ensemble was designed to match: black fishnet stockings, black shoes and handbag, black leather skirt and bustier. She

38

filled out the last two with what appeared to be two parts flesh, one part foam padding, but her legs were the real thing.

She was lighting a thin gray cigarette with unassailable flair out in front of a XXX-rated movie theater when Gunner and the Cobra rolled to a stop at the curb. The car caught her attention immediately, but she didn't start toward it until she was fully satisfied that the look on Gunner's face was meant to be an invitation of some sort. Even then, she took her time coming over; the cigarette in her hand was half spent when she finally took her first step, grinning from ear to ear.

"Ummmm, ummmm, ummmm. That is the most beautiful car I have ever seen!"

She reached her free hand out to touch the paint, gingerly stroking the aluminum flesh of the door with five long-nailed fingers too squared off at the ends to be a woman's. Gunner noticed it right away. Her voice was a giveaway, too, but only marginally; the hard, masculine edge to it, almost totally obscured by a smooth, mellifluous layer of camouflage, was an oddity you had to be listening for to catch.

"Were you going to offer me a ride?" the giant asked, finally redirecting her gaze, and the overplayed lust that came with it, from the car to the man who was driving it.

"That was going to be part of the deal, yeah," Gunner said. "Are you free?"

The dense, coarse mass of fake black hair she was wearing swiveled on her head as she shook it from side to side. "Free, no. But reasonable. Very reasonable. What did you have in mind?"

"I thought we might discuss that on the way."

The wig spun about atop her head again. "You thought wrong, honey. If I look that stupid to you, maybe you need to go home and get your glasses. Peaches don't get in nobody's car 'til she knows where she's goin', and what she's gotta do when she gets there. That's how I make a 'deal.' " She flicked her cigarette into the street with some annoyance and, for the first time stopped grinning. "Now. Just what is it you want me to do for my . . . ?" She waited for Gunner to fill in the blank, like any streetwalker with a full day's experience on the job would have been careful to do.

"Twenty-five dollars," Gunner obliged.

"Shit. It almost sounded like you said twenty-five dollars. Ain't that ridiculous?"

"Okay. We'll make it thirty."

"Thirty. Thirty dollars. Now, what in the world could you be expectin' me to do for that kind of money?"

Gunner opened the box sitting on the seat beside him and showed Peaches the roses. The buds were deep red and in full bloom, the water they had been sprayed with only moments ago still shining brilliantly on their open petals.

"I want you to give a man some flowers," he said, smiling like a cat with a mouthful of the proverbial canary.

And thinking she could read his wicked little mind, Peaches smiled again, too.

4

Legend had it the kid's name was Pokey, and that Pokey had been a sixteen-year-old high school dropout who was trying to get jumped into a neighborhood Crip set known as the Down Nines. The idea was to do something bold and audacious to impress his friends with his courage, but all he did in the end was make a name for himself as the dumbest little shithead in the 'hood. What else could you say about a kid who had tried to rob the one taco stand in the city that had an LAPD station house sitting right next door?

The taco stand was a Taco Bell situated on the southwest corner of Martin Luther King and La Salle, and the station house, home to the Los Angeles Police Department's Southwest Division, occupied the southeast corner. Both faced Martin Luther King. Supposedly, this kid named Pokey had sauntered up Martin Luther King from the east and gone around back to the employees' entrance of the restaurant, where he knocked quietly on the door, standing off to the side and away from the peephole. He was planning to force his way inside, clean out the cash registers, and then race back out again before anyone even knew a robbery had taken place, but he may as well have just stepped up to the order window and demanded the cash from there, because several of the many uniformed patrolmen eating lunch under the pale and rusted patio umbrellas out front had seen him coming and recognized his intentions immediately. They let him knock on the door a second time and get the Saturday night special halfway out of his back pocket before a small group of them fell on him like a 747 and removed him to the station house across the way, the sarcastic applause of the officers who stayed behind ringing in his ears.

Gunner didn't frequent the taco stand often, but it seemed like every time he did, one cop or another was relating the story of Pokey's Folly to his or her partner, raucous laughter punctuating every line. Today, a pair of black patrolmen were sitting off to Gunner's left, damn near having a party at Pokey's expense, when a red-faced cop with silver gray hair and three stripes on his sleeve appeared over Gunner's shoulder to ask, with obvious irritation, "Your name Gunner?"

He was wearing a name tag, but Gunner didn't bother to look at it; Kupchak's voice was unmistakable, as easy on the ears as a garbage disposal feeding on a bag of pennies.

"I guess you think that was pretty funny. Sending your girl-friend over to the station with the flowers."

He wasn't smiling.

"Pleased to meet you, Sergeant," Gunner said, setting down a half-eaten taco.

"Fuck you, wise guy. I ought to kick your face in for humiliat-ing me like that."

"If I embarrassed you, Kupchak, I apologize. But begging you nicely didn't seem to be getting me anywhere, did it?"

Roughly three hours ago, following Gunner's instructions to the letter, Peaches the transvestite had left the investigator's long-stemmed roses with the desk sergeant across the street, along with orders that they be given to Kupchak as soon as he came in. She was supposed to act as if she hadn't seen "Harry Baby" for a long time, and was having a tough time getting by. Gunner had affixed the gift card to the outside of the box, out in the open where the desk sergeant was sure to read it, and in his most effeminate, anguished hand, written the following:

My Darling Harry,
Why are you avoiding me? You sound so cruel over the

phone. Please talk to me. For Maggie's sake. Lunch across the street at eleven? Please?
                        Love,
                        A.G.

Gunner didn't figure Kupchak would see the whimsy in it, but he didn't think the cop would be able to ignore it, either. Gunner's proxy, Peaches, had just made certain that Kupchak would be the most talked-about uniform in the whole Southwest Division for the next several days, and Kupchak wasn't likely to appreciate the honor. Once he spotted Gunner's hand in the joke, he was bound to come running. The only question was, would he come to talk, or just to kick some ass?

"I'm not talking to you, Gunner. Get it through your head."

His voice said his blood pressure was dropping, but his face still looked like an overly ripe tomato. The bushy white caterpillars over his eyes were all bunched up together and the veins in his flat, off-centered nose were aglow with blood. Gunner had the feeling that were he to stick a hatpin in either of Kupchak's cheeks, the cop's head would take off in a rush of hot air like a runaway model rocket.

"Tell me something, Kupchak," Gunner said. "You one of those guys with a hard-on for all private tickets, or is there something about me in particular that bothers you? McGovern used to be one of your boys. You talk about him like he was a friend. Seems to me you ought to be busting your ass to help me clear his name, rather than giving me all this shit."

"You've got no interest in clearing Maggie's name. You don't give a rat's ass about him, and you know it!"

"I don't remember ever saying I did. All I said was, I'm being paid to prove he shot the Washington kid in self-defense."

"Bullshit."

"What?"

"You heard me. I said, 'bullshit.' You're being paid by Harriet Washington to prove her case against the department. Who the fuck do you think you're kidding?"

So that was it. The family of Lendell Washington had brought suit against the LAPD, as all of the Western world had known they would the minute the news broke of Lendell's death, and Kupchak had assumed—perhaps understandably—that Gunner was on their payroll.

"I don't even know Harriet Washington," Gunner said evenly, trying to cool Kupchak off before he finally said something the black man could not take lying down.

"Then tell me who you're working for."

"I can't do that."

"Damn right you can't."

"Look. Believe what you want to believe. I've told you what I've been hired to do, and why I was hired to do it. You want to assume because I'm a soul brother, I must be lying to you, that's your privilege. And your hang-up."

He let Kupchak feel the weight of his gaze and refused to turn away.

"What makes you think I can help you?" Kupchak asked.

"You were McGovern's watch sergeant. You probably knew him as well, if not better, than anyone else. Who better to talk to about what happened to him?"

Kupchak didn't say anything. He was running Gunner's logic through the churning machinery of his own, and it was a tedious process. Finally, having reached what was obviously a difficult decision for him, he took a seat at Gunner's table, moving like a man taking the long walk down death row, and said, "Assuming this client of yours really exists. How do you know he's not just jerking you around?"

"Jerking me around?"

"Yeah, that's right. Jerking you around. How do you know he really saw what he says he saw?"

Gunner shrugged. "Intuition."

Kupchak snickered. "Shit. Intuition. Tell me what the guy said. About how Maggie shot the kid."

Gunner recounted the story of Lendell Washington's shooting as Mitchell Flowers had described it, playing the same games of evasion regarding his client's gender he had played with Matt Poole two days before. He outlined the methods of coercion someone had used on Flowers to keep him quiet, and then ex-plained how Flowers's capitulation to them made him feel re-sponsible for McGovern's dismissal from the LAPD, if not his ensuing suicide. The Uncle Tom angle never came up. Somehow, Gunner was sure Kupchak wouldn't be particularly sympathetic to it.

"So your client's on some guilt trip. That what you're trying to tell me?"

"That's what it amounts to, I guess. Yeah." Kupchak was giving him an odd look. "You can't buy that?"

"If it was anybody else but Maggie? Maybe. I don't know. But Maggie . . ." He ended the sentence with a shrug of his own. "Let's just say he was a hard man to feel sorry for. For some people in this community, anyway."

"You mean black people."

"I didn't say that. You did."

"Come on, Kupchak. Let's not pretend we don't both know what kind of nightstick-happy nigger-hater McGovern was, all right?"

"Look. Maggie was no racist," Kupchak said flatly, his face turning crimson again. "He was just . . . *intolerant* of a lot of things. That's all. Drug use. Welfare dependence. Child abandon-ment. You know."

Gunner just looked at him.

"Next question," Kupchak said.

Gunner wasn't really ready to change the subject, but he knew it was the only prudent thing to do. If he pressed the issue of McGovern's bigotry and lost his cool with Kupchak now, consid-ering their surroundings, he could easily find himself having the spit-shined shoes of a dozen peace officers surgically removed from his tailbone tomorrow.

"You ever talk to McGovern about the Washington kid's shooting? One on one?"

"You mean off the record?"

"On or off—whatever."

"Of course I did. Many times."

"And?"

"And his story was always the same, if that's what you're getting at. The kid fired on him first."

"Humor me with the details, will you, Sergeant? 'Once upon a time . . .'"

"He was on morning watch, as usual, breaking in a new partner. A female officer named Lugo, Deanna Lugo," Kupchak said, annoyed at being cattle-prodded along. "Around two, two-thirty, they got a call over the radio that a couple of kids were holding up a liquor store over on Vernon and Third Avenue. Washington and some cousin of his. Something or another Ford; I don't remember the kid's first name. Anyway, Maggie and Lugo, they were just a few blocks away, so they were on the scene in minutes, but the kids took off on 'em soon as they saw the car, so they had to run 'em down. Maggie, he went after Washington, and Lugo, she went after Ford."

"They split up?"

"You mean Maggie and Lugo? Yeah, they split up. I just told you—"

"No, no, no. I'm talking about the kids."

"The kids? Oh, yeah. Yeah, they split up. Maggie said this kid Ford just left Washington standing there. Didn't call out for him or nothin', just took off without him. He was a real sweetheart, apparently. The guy behind the counter of the liquor store said it was him who'd run the whole show. He was the one holding the piece and giving all the orders. All Washington did that night was collect the money and wet his pants, the guy said; he was scared shitless from the time he and his cousin came in the store 'til the time they left."

"Was he holding?"

"Who? Washington?"

"Yeah."

Kupchak shrugged. "Not so the guy could tell. But that doesn't mean he wasn't. He was scared shitless, like I was saying. He'd had a piece on him, he probably would've been too spooked to show it."

Gunner nodded to concede the point.

"Anyway, where was I?"

"Washington and Ford split up."

"Oh, yeah. The way Maggie figured it, Ford must've seen him and Lugo coming and decided he'd carried Washington long enough, so he took off without him. He probably hoped Maggie and Lugo would prefer chasing one kid to two, and would go after Washington alone."

"Only they didn't."

"No. They split up, too. Maggie went after Washington, and Lugo went after Ford. Maggie chased Washington for about six blocks, east, 'til he went into the alley where the shooting took place, between Forty-second Place and Forty-second Street, at Van Ness. Maggie said the kid just disappeared, the fucking alley was so dark, so he didn't go in after him. He just stopped where he was and called for the kid to come out, and that's when the little bastard opened up on him. Two rounds, Maggie said, one right after the other. He said he could hear the second slug go by, it came so close to his head."

"And that's when he returned fire."

"Yeah. You don't think he was entitled?"

"How many rounds did he fire?"

"Three. That's what he told the IAD guys, and that's what he told me."

"What about Officer Lugo? She count it as three rounds, too?"

Kupchak started to speak, stopped, then said, "Officer Lugo said she couldn't say how many rounds Maggie fired. She and Ford didn't arrive at the scene until after the exchange of gunfire was over, she said."

It seemed to pain him to have to relay this information. One side of his face had appeared to grow harder than the other as he spoke.

"But the kid was only hit once," he went on. "That's all. He took one round high on the right shoulder, up near the collarbone. The doctors said he should've made it, that he *would've* made it, he hadn't been a bleeder. Maggie got a lousy break there."

Gunner started to point out that the break Washington got was even worse, but instead just asked, "What about the gun?"

"The gun?"

"Yeah. The gun. The one the counter guy at the liquor store didn't see, but that McGovern said he found on the body. He find it just like he said, or was it a plant?"

Kupchak tried to smile, but he was too insulted by the question to put much behind it. "You really expect me to answer a stupid question like that?"

"Look at it this way. I think you just did."

Kupchak fell silent.

Gunner tried to wait for the cop's recalcitrance to play itself out, but it soon became obvious that he was waiting in vain. Struggling to keep his growing impatience out of his voice, he said, "Look, Sergeant. This isn't 'Sixty Minutes,' and I'm not Ed Bradley. I'm not asking you these questions because I'm out to bury anybody, I'm asking them because I need to know the answers to them. McGovern's ass was going to be in a sling if he couldn't find a weapon on Washington, and he knew it. You think I need you to tell me he might have placed a drop gun on the kid in a spot like that?"

Kupchak ignored the question.

Gunner gave him a few seconds more to speak, then said, "Okay. You win. You can't help me, and I can't help you. Sorry I wasted your lunch hour."

Without another word, the black man started eating again, acting as if Kupchak had stood up to leave and was no longer sharing his table.

Kupchak watched him eat for a long, silent moment, too bewildered and humiliated by his sudden dismissal to say anything. Gunner wouldn't even raise his eyes to look at him.

"So I don't know if the fucking gun was a plant or not, all right? Maggie never told me, one way or the other. Way it looked, I guess it could've been a drop gun, sure. But so what if it was? What does that prove?"

Gunner wiped his mouth with a paper napkin and regarded him again. "Prove? I don't think it 'proves' anything. But it certainly seems to *imply* a number of things. Doesn't it?"

"Like maybe the kid wasn't armed, after all."

Gunner nodded.

"How the fuck did I know you were gonna say that?" Kupchak asked, grinning sardonically again. "You see what the poor bastard was up against? Who the hell was gonna believe there was a weapon, if he couldn't *produce* one?"

"I've got a better question for you. Why would he have found it necessary to 'produce' a weapon if Washington was already holding one?"

"Because he couldn't find the goddamn thing. What do you think?"

"He couldn't find it?"

"No. He couldn't find it. Maggie figured the kid must've tossed it before he got to him. You know, so he'd appear to be clean."

"Tossed it where?"

"I don't know. Over a fence, up on the roof of one of the garages . . . Who knows?"

"The gun was lying around somewhere, Kupchak, somebody would have come across it, don't you think?"

"Look, Gunner, how many times do I have to tell you? The goddamn alley was dark! Maggie and Lugo could've missed an elephant in there that night!"

"Maggie and Lugo, maybe," Gunner said. "But not the bloodhounds from Internal Affairs. The way I hear it, those guys search the area surrounding an officer-involved shooting like their lives depend upon it."

"They search as hard as they wanna search," Kupchak said, with evident contempt for the subject.

Gunner paused. "And the two slugs from Washington's gun? Or the powder burns on his hand? Would they have missed those, too?"

"It wouldn't have been the first time."

He'd said this last with the same note of casual loathing in his voice, and this time Gunner decided to call him on it. "I get the feeling you don't think they did a quality job on McGovern's case," he said.

Kupchak inventoried the faces around them before answering. "I think they did exactly what they set out to do," he said.

"You want to spell that out?"

"No. I don't. I think you know what I'm saying."

"I know what it sounds like you're saying. It sounds like you're saying they fucked him over."

"Does it?"

"But you're not saying how."

"You're a detective. You figure it out. The goddamn gun never turned up, and neither did anything else that might have done Maggie's case any good. That doesn't sound like a rear-ender to you?"

"It might. If I thought the people you're talking about had something against him."

"Oh, they had something against him, all right. The same thing they have against a lot of good cops: he wasn't their cup of tea. He was too much his own man, too independent a thinker." He shook his head. "But that's not what cost him his badge."

Gunner gave him all the time he needed to elaborate.

"The assholes in IAD, they may be bloodsuckers, but they don't generally make a celebrity out of a guy when they take him down unless somebody tells 'em to. You understand what I'm saying?"

"Somebody was pulling their strings on this one."

Kupchak nodded his head.

"You know who that somebody might have been?"

Kupchak shrugged. "I've got a few ideas. But none I'd care to discuss here. Why don't we just say it was somebody with an office downtown, and leave it at that?"

It wasn't an idle suggestion; it was a directive.

Acquiescing, Gunner said, "Okay. You don't want to talk about the who, let's talk about the why."

"The why's a gimme, Gunner. They went after Maggie because of the Dexter Hardy thing."

"Dexter Hardy?"

"That's right. Dexter Hardy."

"What did McGovern have to do with Dexter Hardy?"

"Nothing. That's what's so nuts about it. He was nowhere near the scene that night."

"Then how—"

"How could he get blamed for what happened? I'll tell you how. By training three of the four officers who *were* there that night. That's how. Tripp, Benzinger, and Ammolino, they all rode with Maggie when they first came up."

Gunner shook his head. "I don't get it," he said.

"Maggie was their probationary officer, Gunner," Kupchak said. "He was the one who taught 'em to be cops. Get it?"

Now Gunner understood. Dexter Hardy was a thirty-eight-year-old garage mechanic and part-time armed robber who had had fame beaten into him by a small army of LAPD officers during a routine traffic stop in Carson eighteen months earlier. Because a neighbor with a camcorder had taped the entire incident, Hardy was today a maimed celebrity rather than a corpse, the star of a horrific home video depicting four Caucasian policemen—among them, three officers named James Tripp, Alan Benzinger, and Joseph Ammolino—clubbing an unarmed black civilian in the street like children attacking a piñata, as six other officers stood around and watched. The riots that had decimated South-Central Los Angeles and titillated the nation six months later had started within minutes of the four principal officers involved in Hardy's beating being acquitted of assault charges in a Simi Valley courtroom.

All in all, it made for the most humiliating and damaging public relations fiasco in the LAPD's 210-year history.

"Maggie was fifteen miles away when the Hardy arrest was made, but he may as well have been right in the thick of it, for all the shit they laid on him," Kupchak said. "Some people said Tripp, Ammolino, and Benzinger were just the tip of the iceberg, that Maggie had been building cops like them for years, and was still doing it."

"Who are you talking about, Kupchak? Stop saying 'they' like I'm supposed to know who you mean."

"I'm talking about the members of the new regime. Okay? Chief Bowden and his appointees. With all their promises of a new order, and better community relations, and all that shit, cops like Maggie were on their shit list from day one. They were just waiting for somebody like him to fuck up."

"And of course, he did."

"The second he drew his weapon on that kid. Self-defense or no self-defense."

Kupchak's fellow officers were suddenly leaving the tables surrounding them one by one, trays full of trash in hand, signaling the end of lunch hour. Before Kupchak could follow suit, Gunner asked him to try to remember Lendell Washington's buddy Ford's first name, and where Gunner might start to look for him.

"His first name? I wanna say Moses, but I don't think that's right. No. It was Noah. Noah Ford, yeah." His eyes narrowed as he pictured the kid in his mind, not enjoying the memory. "They gave the little punk two years, as I recall, and I think he served all of six months. Bein' fourteen years old has its advantages, I guess."

"Then he's out now?"

"He was for a quick minute. But you know kids like that. Soon as they pull one foot out of the shit, they step in some more with the other."

"Meaning?"

"Meaning he's right back in the can, I think. At least, I saw him go through booking just a couple of months ago. Check with the Department of Corrections, I bet they can tell you where to find him."

Gunner nodded. "You happen to remember who the Internal Affairs officers were who worked McGovern's case?"

Kupchak's face grew rigid again. "Couple of guys named Jenner and Kubo. Why do you ask?"

Gunner only barely heard the question, his mind having suddenly turned to something else. "Because I'm going to have to talk to them, too," he said, plainly distracted. "You say their names were Jenner and Kubo?"

Kupchak nodded.

"That wouldn't be Daniel Kubo, would it?"

"Yeah, that's right. You know him?"

Gunner nodded, not sure if he'd just received good news or

52

bad. "If it's the guy I'm thinking about, we entered the police academy together. We used to be fairly close, but . . . I haven't seen or heard from Danny in years, now."

"The police academy? *Our* police academy?"

Gunner nodded his head again.

"Don't tell me you used to be a cop."

"Not quite. I spent six weeks at the academy, and that's about as far as it went."

"They dropped you out?"

"You might say that."

"How long ago was this, you don't mind my asking?"

Gunner got to his feet and said, "Twenty years ago, give or take a few. Too long ago to remember, really." He handed Kupchak one of his business cards. "You think you could get this to Deanna Lugo for me? And ask her to give me a call when she gets a chance?"

Kupchak got to his own feet, feeling somewhat awkward, and said, "I guess I could do that." He put the card in his breast pocket with his left hand and shook the hand Gunner was offering him with his right.

"You've been a big help, Sergeant. Thanks," Gunner said.

"Forget it. I didn't do this for you or your client, Gunner. I did it for Maggie. Because I don't give a fuck what anybody else thought about him, I considered him a friend. That straight up enough for you?"

He wouldn't let go of Gunner's hand. He was trying one last time to pick a fight, to goad the black man into exposing himself as a liar and a cop-hater, but Gunner would have none of it. He had played this game before, with other men who thought it proved something about both the winner and the loser, and so he knew the vacuousness of it all too well.

He stared Kupchak down and waited.

It took a few minutes, but eventually the older man grew tired of his own childishness and surrendered Gunner's hand, laughing a laugh as thin as paper to cover his embarrassment. Then he walked quickly away, without so much as a backward glance in Gunner's direction.

It was all the good-bye his pride would let him say.

5

Gunner called Danny Kubo from the office immediately after his lunch with Harry Kupchak, but not before stopping in at home to stare at the lifeless message light on his answering machine like an old friend that had let him down. Claudia had given him no reason to think she would call, now or ever, but that hadn't stopped him from hoping she would, anyway. Rejection was relatively foreign to Gunner, and he didn't know how to take it seriously. That her commitment to their separation could be strong enough to enable her to cut him adrift as promised, however temporarily, truly amazed him.

It only made matters worse that he was starting to believe she was doing the right thing. The distraction of his work over the last twenty-four hours had forced him to think about the trial separation she was insisting upon economically, without emotion, and in that light he could see the obvious wisdom in it. She wanted to know that her feelings for him were real, and until she was satisfied that they were, she wasn't really doing him any favors by letting him hang around. It wasn't her fault that he had already answered for himself the same question regarding his feelings for her; that was just the way these things often worked out.

"That don't look right, Mickey. That don't look right."

"Shut up and hold the goddamn picture still!"

"Lookit them legs, man! They all crooked an' shit. Damn!"

Weldon Foley cracked up laughing. He was holding the pages of a copy of *Sports Illustrated* open for Mickey Moore's perusal, watching the barber shape the back of a black teenager's head, as Gunner walked into the shop, sending the little brass bell above the door into a frenzy. Foley himself had had no use for barbers for some time now, as the last gray hair had fallen out of his head more than a decade ago, but he was a regular visitor to Mickey's establishment nevertheless. He was a retiree with nothing but idle time on his hands and he couldn't seem to find a hangout in the world more consistently amusing.

"Hey, Gunner. Come over here, man. I wanna show you somethin'," Foley said between convulsions.

"Nobody asked for his opinion. He's just as blind as you are," Mickey snapped, scowling at Gunner as the younger man moved toward them.

The tall, dark-skinned kid in the chair looked worried, but all he did was watch as Gunner walked around him to see what it was that had Foley so broken up. Mickey had crowned the kid's head with an eight-inch cylinder of hair, sheared the top of it flatter than the green on a miniature golf course, and shaven him bald from the top of the ears down—but there was nothing particularly unusual about any of these things. The barber had done the same to hundreds of customers over the last few years; such a cut was actually the popular debauchery of the moment. But the clump of dark hair Mickey had left uncut at the base of the kid's skull was . . . *what*?

Foley held the *Sports Illustrated* open again to give Gunner a hint. Inside was a full-page ad for Converse shoes, featuring a photograph of Magic Johnson in uniform and in midflight, basketball cradled lovingly in both hands, legs tucked up underneath him as he ascended to the basket for a lay-up.

"You've got to be kidding," Gunner said.

Foley turned to Mickey, grinning. "See? What'd I tell you? You done jacked this boy's head all up!"

He fell out laughing again, tears streaming from both eyes, as Mickey took a swipe at his head and missed. The kid in the chair spun around and said, "Say what?" but Mickey glared him back into place and told him to shut the hell up. The kid looked like he wanted to cry. Gunner took the magazine from Foley's hands and gave Mickey's handiwork a second look, only to conclude that time was not going to improve it. Foley was right: the kid was doomed.

He had wanted Magic Johnson making a lay-up, and what he'd gotten was William "The Refrigerator" Perry taking a crap.

Gunner handed the magazine back to Foley and started out of the room, head down, trying to get away before he and Foley were both out of control, but Mickey saw the smirk on his face in passing and said, "That's right. Get the hell on out of here, 'fore your mouth gets you in trouble. I told this junior flip when he came in here, I'm a barber, not an artist!"

"You got that right," Foley said.

"I wanted to draw pictures of people slam-dunkin' for a livin', I would've gone to *art school,* not to barber college! People got some nerve, bringin' their nappy heads in here, askin' me to cut the goddamn Mona Lisa into hair they ain't washed in six weeks!"

Gunner pushed through the curtained doorway at the back of the shop and stepped into the dark austerity of his office, rushing to get outside the range of Mickey's vitriol. He had a sweet arrangement here—low rent, free utilities, and a semireliable answering service—and he didn't want to ruin it by doing anything his landlord could falsely take for ridicule.

Turning on the table lamp atop his desk, Gunner flipped through the short stack of mail waiting there as he dialed the phone. It looked as if every collection agency in town was in line to sue him for the same overdue $119.97. The letters were all from companies with names like Financial Resource Developers and Professional Credit Associates, but Gunner wasn't fooled; he could smell a bloodsucker a mile away.

"Internal Affairs. Fowler."

Gunner asked for Danny Kubo, but Fowler said he wasn't in. Kubo wasn't his partner, Fowler said, so he had felt no obligation to keep tabs on him this afternoon.

"How about messages?" Gunner asked.

"Excuse me?"

"You feel any obligation to take messages for him, at least?"

Fowler actually laughed. "You're missing the point, pal," he said. "Dick Jenner is Kubo's traveling secretary, not me. And he's out, too."

"All I want to do is leave a name and a couple of numbers," Gunner said.

Fowler hesitated, then said, "Okay. Let's have 'em."

Gunner told Fowler his name, spelling his last one, then recited both his home and office phone numbers. Fowler was able to repeat it all afterward, but that only proved he had a good memory, not that he'd actually written anything down. Still, Gunner thanked him for his time and hung up, then drew a copy of the local phone directory out of a desk drawer and began scanning through a page and a half of Washingtons until he found the one he was looking for.

Harriet T. Lendell Washington's mother.

"This card is a fake. As phony as a three-dollar bill."

His name was Milton Wiley, and he had introduced himself as Harriet Washington's attorney. He was a dark-skinned black man in his middle forties, as lean as an eel and dressed just as slippery. He had a goatee spattered with silver and a thinning pate to match, and as he stood in the doorway of his client's home, barring Gunner's path to the tiny living room beyond, he examined the business card Gunner had given him with open disgust, not buying the lies printed on its face for an instant.

"You're not from the *Guardian*. And you're not a reporter. But nice try." He started to close the door in Gunner's face.

"Who is it, Milton?" someone behind him asked.

Wiley turned to find a short, wiry black woman peering anxiously over his shoulder, trying to see past him to the man at the door. She was not an attractive woman, particularly—her mouth was overly large and her eyes were set too far apart—but even from where he stood, Gunner could see there was an aura of strength and intelligence about her that seemed to render her physical shortcomings moot.

"It's a spy for the police," Wiley told her, turning to glare at Gunner again. "I was just telling him good-bye."

He tried to close the door again, but the woman said, "You

don't have to do that. I've got nothing to hide from the police. Let him in." She moved forward before Wiley could stop her and ushered Gunner into the house, smiling gamely and offering him her hand. "I'm Harriet Washington. Please come in and sit down, won't you, Mr. . . . ?"

"Gunner. Aaron Gunner." He shook her hand.

"Harriet, please," Wiley said.

But Washington wasn't listening. She was moving into the living room now, showing Gunner to a seat on the small, floral-patterned sofa sheathed in clear plastic that was the room's modest centerpiece. Two matching armchairs waited on either side, turned toward the sofa at opposing angles, and Washington sat down on the one to Gunner's right. Wiley closed the front door and eventually joined them in the room, but insisted on standing, apparently determined to maintain some semblance of a supervisory attitude over the proceedings.

"Harriet, you didn't hear what I said. I said that this man works for the *police*. He tried to pawn himself off as a reporter for the *Guardian*, but his business card is a fake. I call that paper regularly, the phone number on the card is a complete fabrication."

Washington looked at Gunner expectantly. "Is this true, Mr. Gunner?"

There wasn't much point in lying. They were going to be guarded in their dealings with him now, no matter who he claimed to be.

"In part, yes."

"In part?"

"I'm not a reporter for the *Guardian*, Mrs. Washington." He glanced over at Wiley as he offered Washington a glimpse of his license. "But I'm not working for the police, either. As you can see, I'm a private investigator."

"Uh-huh." Wiley's head moved up and down, his mouth turned up in a self-satisfied grin. "What did I tell you?"

"It's the truth. I only tried to run the reporter line on you because I thought you'd be hesitant to talk to me otherwise."

"And you thought right," Wiley said.

To Washington, Gunner said, "My client and the LAPD may appear to be on the same side in this thing, Mrs. Washington, but I can assure you they're not."

"Your client?"

"A neighbor of yours who claims to have witnessed your son's shooting. Someone who says the cop who shot him that night was fired upon first, just as the cop had always insisted."

"All right, Harriet. Enough is enough," Wiley said angrily. "Whoever this man is, whoever his client may be, his intentions are to sabotage our case against the police department, and he's got to go. Now." He crossed his arms across his chest and waited, fully expecting to be obeyed.

"I want to hear what this client of his has to say," Washington said.

"No. No! I strongly urge against it!"

"Sit down, Milton." She fixed him with a stare that could have sliced through tempered steel; Wiley had no choice but to do as he was told. When she turned her attention to Gunner again, she said, "You'll have to forgive Milton, Mr. Gunner. But the police have done everything in their power to see that our case against them never gets to court, and for all we know, they sent you here in the hope I'll say something they can use against us later."

"Of course that's why they sent him," Wiley snapped. "All this business about a client who witnessed Lendell's shooting is nothing but a false pretense."

"No, Mr. Wiley. It isn't," Gunner said, finally getting a little fed up with the attorney's endless attempts to slander him.

"Then what's this client's name?"

"I'm not at liberty to say."

"Oh. I see."

"Let's just say the person who hired me is a private citizen trying to correct an unfortunate mistake. Somebody who was pressured into keeping quiet about what they saw the night Mrs. Washington's son was killed, and who now regrets having done so. Granted, they may be a little late getting around to it, but—"

"Damn right, they're a little late. Why the hell didn't they feel the need to correct their 'unfortunate mistake' six months ago, *before* Mrs. Washington filed suit?"

"Because Jack McGovern didn't commit suicide until last Friday," Gunner said bluntly, almost immediately wishing he hadn't.

"Ah. Officer McGovern." Wiley smiled, thinking Gunner had slipped up and told him something he wasn't supposed to know. "Now we're getting somewhere."

"I hope so."

"You're working for the family. His wife or his kids, somebody like that?"

"I told you who I'm working for."

Wiley shook his head. "I don't think so. Officer McGovern terrorized the people of this community for over twenty years, there's no way any neighbor of Mrs. Washington's would pay you five cents to do anything but dance on his grave."

"My client's motives for coming forward now have nothing to do with Jack McGovern, per se. I told you. They're strictly personal."

"Perhaps you should explain what that means."

"I already did. You weren't listening. My client's been quiet all this time about what he saw because he was *told* to be quiet, by someone who knew all the right things to say in order to scare the living daylights out of him. Not because the cat caught his tongue."

There. Gunner had finally said it, tired of being secretive about something only the police could possibly think to use against him: his client's gender.

"He was blackmailed?" Wiley asked, apparently oblivious to Gunner's generous disclosure.

"Yes."

"By whom? And for what purpose?"

"If I could answer those questions, Mr. Wiley, this conversation wouldn't be necessary. Would it?"

He was suggesting that Wiley had asked a foolish question, and Wiley was duly insulted. Scowling, the attorney said, "I don't think it's necessary in any case, Mr. Gunner. So, if you don't mind, we'll end it right here and now." He turned to face Washington. "Tell Mr. Gunner good-bye, Harriet, while I show him to the door."

He was nearly on top of Gunner when Washington asked, "What is it you want to know?"

She had meant the question for her guest, and had asked it without giving Wiley so much as a sideways glance. The insult froze Wiley in place like a blast of cold air, and he turned to her, his face flushed red with embarrassment.

"Harriet, I am advising you not to talk to this man. We have nothing whatsoever to gain by answering his questions, and everything, quite literally, to lose."

"I can't tell him anything but the truth, Milton. And the truth is what we want the world to know, isn't it?"

"Yes, but—"

"What happened to my son was a sin, Mr. Gunner," Washington said, turning away from Wiley again. "And when you learn the facts, I know that you'll agree. That's why I'm not afraid to talk to you."

"Harriet," Wiley pleaded, "please listen to me. Before you say another word—"

"Tell me what you want to know," Washington said to Gunner, still treating her attorney like an apparition only Gunner could see and hear.

And that was it for Wiley. She had shamed him not once, not twice, but three times now, and it seemed to take everything he had just to find his chair again and sit down in it, seething. Gunner waited to see if he was really going to leave it at that, but all he got for his trouble was a look down the cold, dark mine shaft that had suddenly become visible behind Wiley's eyes.

"Mr. Gunner?"

Washington was eyeing him expectantly.

"All right, Mrs. Washington," he said, giving Wiley one last look before going on. "I guess I'd like to know what your son was like, for starters. The kind of company he used to keep, how he did in school. That sort of thing."

"You want to know if he was the kind of boy who could have tried to murder a policeman."

Gunner should have seen that coming, but it had caught him unawares, all the same. "That's putting it rather indelicately, but I guess that is what I'm asking, yes."

"Then my answer to you is no. Lendell was not that kind of boy. He was a weak child, Mr. Gunner, not a bad one. I know all mothers say that about their sons, but this time it's true. Lendell could be talked into all kinds of trouble—but no one could have made him fire a gun at somebody. No one."

"How about just carrying one around? Could he have been talked into that?"

"No."

"Not even by Noah Ford?"

"No. Not even by Noah." She paused. "Those boys were very close, of course. Lendell loved Noah like an older brother. But . . . there are many things that come natural to Noah that Lendell was simply incapable of. Even my sister will tell you that."

"Your sister?"

"Noah's mother. Charlene. You didn't know the boys were cousins?"

Gunner shook his head. He vaguely remembered Harry Kupchak mentioning it, but he didn't know that the fact was supposed to be common knowledge.

"Noah is a devil, Mr. Gunner. He's my nephew, and I hate to talk about one so young that way, but it happens to be the truth. He was a bad influence on Lendell from the beginning, and I had no business allowing them to become so attached to one another. I always thought, because Lendell was an only child, he needed a friend like Noah, that their friendship would do him good. So I let them be. But even Pervis knew I was asking for trouble, letting them run the streets together like I did. He warned me many times against it. I just never took him seriously."

"Pervis is . . . ?"

"Lendell's uncle. Charlene's and my little brother. He lives here in the house with me, so naturally he and Lendell were also very close. Pervis used to tell me how he felt about Noah, and I'd just say he was being overprotective of Lendell. But he was really just being smart. I can see that now."

"Lendell and Noah had been in trouble before, then."

"Oh, yes. Many times."

"Harriet, for God's sake!" Wiley was on his feet again. "Will you listen to what you're saying? You're establishing the fact that Lendell was a *problem child*—precisely what the police will attempt to do in making their defense. You're building their case for them!"

"Lendell was not perfect, Milton," Washington said, "and I'm not going to pretend that he was. I've told you that." She looked at Gunner again, forgetting to dismiss Wiley officially, and said, "Lendell and Noah had been in trouble before, of course. For fighting in school and defacing public property. Things like that. Even shoplifting, once. But never for anything like that liquor store robbery, Mr. Gunner. Never anything like that."

"As far as you know, you mean."

"No. That's not what I mean. I mean that it never happened."

She said it with the kind of confidence people generally had only in reality, not in the stuff of their dreams. That in itself only proved how desperately she believed it, Gunner knew—but it was also a fair indication of how futile it would be to challenge her on the subject.

"Where is Noah now, Mrs. Washington?"

Wiley's client shook her head. "I'm not sure. His mother and I don't talk as often as we used to, for obvious reasons. But it seems to me the last time we spoke, she told me he was in jail again."

"You wouldn't happen to know which jail, in particular, would you?"

"No. I wouldn't."

"Haven't you been listening?" Wiley asked. "She told you. The boy's a devil. Certainly no one to look to for the truth. If you're thinking about talking to him, you'd just be wasting your time."

"I'll keep that in mind, Mr. Wiley. Thanks."

"No, you won't. You're going to talk to him anyway. Aren't you?"

"I thought it might be a good idea, yes."

"To ask him what? He wasn't a witness to Lendell's shooting. What could he possibly tell you that would be relevant to anything?"

"I won't know that until I talk to him, Mr. Wiley. But, if nothing else, I would think he should at least be able to tell me why."

"Why?"

"Why they did it. The liquor store robbery. Did they do it for the kicks, or just for the money?"

"Lendell didn't do it for either," Harriet Washington said sharply, clearly infuriated by the question. "He did it because he was forced to."

"That's right," Wiley agreed. "The boys' history together proves that."

"But that's not the way Noah tells the story, is it?" Gunner asked him, just to see what would happen.

Wiley and Washington each stole a glance at the other, filling a short silence with a shared unease. "As I told you before, Mr. Gunner," Wiley ventured bravely, "Noah is not the best person in the world to consult for the truth. Especially when he's in trouble. Naturally, then, it isn't surprising that he has always insisted the liquor store robbery was Lendell's idea, and not his. It's what any liar would say, under the circumstances."

"And what does he say about Lendell being armed that night?"

"Oddly enough, on that point he agrees with us. He says Lendell never had a gun. Of course, he also says the same thing about himself. Never mind that the counterman at the liquor store swore that he had one."

"He have a gun on him when the police took him into custody?"

"No. But what does that prove? He had the same opportunity to dispose of a weapon the police say Lendell had. My feeling is, he tossed the gun somewhere as he ran and it just never turned up. Or no one bothered to look for it."

"Mr. Gunner, my son did not deserve to die," Washington said, stating what was to her a simple fact. "If you had known him, you'd know that. He was there that night with Noah, yes, but he wasn't the one holding a gun, and he certainly never used one to shoot at that policeman. He simply could not have done such a thing."

Gunner nodded, trying to show some sensitivity for her position, and said, "I'd like to believe that, Mrs. Washington. But I'm afraid it's difficult to reconcile with my client's account of your son's death. My client says he saw Lendell fire two shots at Jack McGovern before McGovern fired three shots back, and frankly, I believe him. I wouldn't be here otherwise."

"Then your client is mistaken."

"Or as big a liar as Noah," Wiley added.

Gunner looked at him. "He may be mistaken," he said evenly, "but I don't think he's a liar. He has no reason to lie."

"Unless the police are paying him to. Is that what you mean?"

It hadn't been, of course, but now Gunner wondered if it shouldn't have been. Mitchell Flowers seemed genuine enough, but Gunner really knew next to nothing about him, and he'd been fooled by competent actors, and actresses, before.

"If that were the case, he wouldn't have hired me," Gunner said, defending his judgment of character as best he could.

"On the contrary," Wiley countered. "It looks infinitely better this way. If the police had produced this 'new witness' of yours on their own, claiming to have found him quite by accident, do you think anyone—especially Mrs. Washington and I—would have taken him seriously for a moment? Of course not. People are not that gullible. However—if he were to come to their attention through someone like yourself, someone with no personal or professional interest in the outcome of Mrs. Washington's case against the department, it's likely he would be looked upon in an altogether different light. Isn't it?"

Again, Wiley was making a lot of sense, considering possibilities Gunner should have considered himself long ago.

"I don't think that's the case, Mr. Wiley," Gunner said. It was the only retort he could come up with.

"Well, I do," Wiley said firmly. "And if I'm forced to, I'll prove it in court. Relay that message to your client for me, will you, Mr. Gunner?"

He was saying good-bye, and by her silence, so was Washington. Gunner regarded them both, feeling not unlike a house pet being shooed outside, and stood up to offer Washington his hand again.

"Thank you for seeing me, Mrs. Washington. It was a gracious thing to do."

Washington shook his hand, wearing the least convincing smile she had shown him all day, and said, "You're quite welcome, Mr. Gunner. Even if you are all wrong about Lendell."

The three of them went to the door together. Wiley moved to open it for Gunner just as someone out on the steps wiggled a key in the lock and stepped into the house, nearly knocking Wiley over in the process.

"Pervis," Washington said to the new arrival, sounding a bit uneasy, "this is Mr. Gunner." She waited for Pervis to comment, but all he did was stand there. "He's a private investigator who came to ask me a few questions about Lendell's shooting."

Pervis didn't appear to approve. He was a slender young black man in a gray silk suit, with an angular, clean-shaven face and a diamond in his left ear. He turned the same disapproving stare toward Wiley he had shown to Gunner, then stepped right past both men without saying a word to either.

Washington was appalled.

"Pervis!"

The young man stopped and turned around. "So another clown's joined the circus. What is that to me?"

"I don't know what you're talking about," Washington said.

"Yes you do. You know exactly what I mean." His eyes turned soft as he looked at her. "Do yourself a favor and give it up, Sis. The boy's dead." He waved his hand before him, gesturing toward Gunner and Wiley, and suddenly his gaze was ice cold again. "None of this shit is going to bring him back."

He turned and disappeared into the rear of the house.

6

The next morning, after learning from the California Department of Corrections that Noah Ford was presently serving a two-year term out at Central Juvenile Hall in East Los Angeles for possession of cocaine with intent to distribute, Gunner got in his car and drove out to see him. Or, at least, to make an attempt to see him.

He hadn't called ahead to tell anyone he was coming, and Ford wouldn't have known who he was if he had. This wasn't the way an organized professional was supposed to operate, but he couldn't think of anything better to do with his time. He had wanted to talk with Danny Kubo before he tried talking with Ford, but Kubo still hadn't returned the phone message Gunner had left for him the day before. Nor had he been around to answer his phone this morning when Gunner had tried to reach him again, only to be greeted by a tinny voice-mail message that had sounded even less reassuring than Kubo's office-mate Fowler.

Gunner wondered what was going on.

Central Juvenile Hall was a sprawling collection of brick bungalows and dormitories that dated back to the 1940s, situated along a meandering stretch of Eastlake Avenue near the County/ USC Medical Center. Its exterior was so nondescript one could pass right by it and never recognize it as the largest youth correctional facility in the country, housing as it did more than six hundred inmates daily.

Gunner had to engage in some more minor misrepresentation before the guards would grant him entrance to the facility, but other than that things couldn't have gone more smoothly. He told them he was an investigator under the employ of Ford's "newly hired" attorney—an attorney whose name had probably not been reported to them, yet—and rather than go to all the time and trouble of proving him a liar, they just opened the gate and let him in. A young, all-business correctional officer named Bevins escorted him through a metal detector and onto the grounds, making small talk as they walked.

Bevins unlocked one of two doors in the massive, wrought-iron fence that separated the inmates from the free world beyond, and Gunner soon found himself facing what looked like a school playground at recess time. Scattered across several giant fields of lifeless grass, teenage boys in bright orange uniforms were playing ball games of every kind, looking for all the world like kids at a church picnic. Almost all were black or Hispanic. The only hint that these were in fact underage thieves and rapists, extortionists and murderers, was the sad austerity of the dormitory buildings surrounding them, and the steely-eyed observation of the correctional officers, like Bevins, who wandered among them, waiting to extinguish the first ember of discord or defiance.

"Rec time," Bevins said dispassionately. "Looks like we're going to have to find him."

Gunner nodded, already scanning the yard for kids who looked the right age. In the process, he stumbled upon a familiar face.

Playing in the outfield in one of the two softball games presently in progress was a gangbanger Gunner had met the year before named Donnell Henderson, an eighteen-year-old pretty boy with pale skin and a full head of hair. Gunner had dealt with Henderson only briefly, in the course of working the same case that had introduced him to Claudia Lovejoy, but he'd nevertheless been impressed enough with the kid's intelligence to hope that he would never end up in a place like this, despite his gang affiliations.

To see him here now was a genuine disappointment.

"Somebody you know?" Bevins asked.

Gunner shook his head. "I thought so at first. But no. That's not him."

Bevins didn't believe him, but he looked off in the direction of a crowded basketball court to their left and said, "I think that's Ford over there. See him?"

Of course, Gunner didn't, but that mattered little, because Bevins didn't really want an answer. He was already moving toward the court, taking it for granted that Gunner had enough sense to follow. As Gunner watched from the edge of the court, Bevins pulled Noah Ford from the game, chose a substitute for him from a group of kids sitting on a bench nearby, then marched Ford to Gunner's side, all with the efficiency and brusqueness of a USMC drill sergeant.

"You want him inside in an interview room, or you gonna talk to him out here?" Bevins asked.

"Out here will be fine."

"Okay. I'll be right over there if you need me." He started backpedaling toward the basketball court. "You want back in this game, Ford, you better act right. I'll be watching you, understand?"

Ford never even turned around.

Looking him over, Gunner realized he wasn't at all what Gunner had expected. All the fourteen-year-old sociopaths he had known in the past had looked like thirty-year-old sociopaths reduced to scale, exact replicas of the larger models right down to the scowls on their faces and the threat in their walk. You saw them coming and you knew the trouble you were inviting, not getting the hell out of their way. But Ford just looked like a fourteen-year-old kid. He was baby-faced and scarless, dwarfed by the prison uniform that engulfed him, and his eyes were all but devoid of resentment.

"Mr. Bevins says you wanna see me," he said to Gunner, with seemingly benign curiosity.

"I do if your name's Noah Ford."

"How come you know me, but I don't know you?"

Gunner answered that by explaining who he was and why he was here, simplifying the details wherever possible. Ford listened attentively, but showed little sign of understanding, let alone actually giving a damn.

"So?"

"So I want to talk to you. About what happened to Lendell."

Ford shrugged. "Cops shot him, man. That's what happened." The basketball game behind him was getting noisy now, and he was having a difficult time ignoring it.

"That's what I want to talk about. How Lendell got shot," Gunner said.

"My lawyer said I ain't gotta talk about that no more. He said that's all over with."

"He's right. It is. I just need to ask you a few questions about it, that's all."

"Questions? What questions?"

He turned his body toward the court, ever so slightly.

Gunner said, "I need to know if Lendell had a gun on him that night, Noah. And if he did, whether or not he fired it at the cop who killed him."

Ford didn't say anything.

"Noah. Listen up."

Ford stopped trying to sneak a peek at the game and turned all the way around again.

"You told the police he had a gun. Remember?"

"I did?"

"Yeah. You did. You told them he was the one who wanted to do the liquor store, and he was the one carrying the gun. Now, was that true, or not?"

"I don't know."

"You don't know?"

"No, man. I don't know."

"You don't know *what*?"

"I don't know whose idea it was. To do the liquor store. 'Cause, like, it wasn't his idea, an' it wasn't my idea. Right? We just"—he shrugged—"*did* it."

"And the gun?"

Ford glanced over at the basketball court yet again, unable to help himself, and said, "Man, I gotta go."

70

"Just tell me about the gun, Noah," Gunner said forcefully.

Ford looked at him, surprised by the sudden shift in his tone, and laughed, sounding just like the little boy he was.

"Fuck you, man. I gotta go," he said.

And then he turned around and sprinted off, answering the call of a child's game the way children so often did.

Gunner cursed his poor planning all the way to Mickey's.

Trying to get Ford to talk to him without giving the kid some time to get used to the idea had been dumb. He'd had the *fuck you* Ford laid on him coming. What he should have done was get a phone number for the kid's mother from Harriet Washington when he'd had the chance, and arrange a visit through her. Getting past both her and Ford's lawyer would probably have required the same kind of effort and patience he'd had to expend on Harriet Washington herself, but it would have been worth it if it had meant coming away from Central with a few straight answers to his questions, rather than the handful of nothing he had now.

He called Information to get the number of a Charlene Ford as soon as he arrived at his office, but there was no listing for anyone by that name. He hadn't really thought there would be—childbirth out of wedlock being as tragically endemic as it presently was—but he'd taken a stab at it, anyway, hoping against hope he could avoid asking Harriet Washington for any more favors. Putting off calling her even further, he left yet another voice-mail message for Danny Kubo before trying to reach Claudia Lovejoy at home, only to learn she was still making herself as scarce as Kubo was. She didn't even have her answering machine on anymore.

When Gunner finally did call Washington, she refused to give him her sister's number, though she did agree to call her in his stead to leave his number with her. She didn't know what the chances were that Charlene, last name Woodberry, would want to talk to him, she said, but she'd make the call, anyway.

Gunner hung up, made a fresh pot of coffee for himself and Mickey, and waited around for the phone to ring.

Nearly an hour later, it did.

"I had a feeling I'd be hearing from you," Danny Kubo said.

"Yeah? How intuitive."

"Intuition's got nothing to do with it. I'm just not stupid. I see things, I hear things, I put two and two together. It's really not that complicated."

He sounded irritated, but that was to be expected. He was calling under duress. When Gunner had left his third message in two days on Kubo's voice-mail an hour ago, it hadn't been just to say yet again that he would appreciate a call back. This time, Kubo's old friend had issued a thinly disguised threat, in the form of a cheerful announcement: Gunner would be coming to visit him tomorrow. Downtown. He was going to walk into Parker Center, drop Kubo's name with every high-ranking officer he stumbled into, and generally roam the halls of the LAPD's inner sanctum in search of Kubo's office like a tourist traipsing about Disneyland.

Kubo knew better than to think he was bluffing.

"So how are things?" Gunner asked him.

"Things are things. You want to talk small talk, or do you want to talk business?"

"I think you already know the answer to that. Otherwise, you'd have called me before now."

"Hey. I was busy."

"Yeah. I can imagine."

Both men fell silent, listening to the phone line click and hum as they waited for someone to get to the point.

"Look, Aaron. I'll tell you up front," Kubo said finally. "I'm not going to be able to help you. It's just not possible."

"You don't think you should maybe hear what kind of help I need before you tell me that?"

"I don't need to hear. It's just like you said. I already know. Word is, you're digging around in the Jack McGovern case, trying to prove he got a raw deal from the department. Isn't that right?"

"I'm trying to prove the department may have made a mistake when they dismissed him, yes."

"For the sake of some guy off the street who claims to have witnessed the Lendell Washington shooting."

"Yes."

"Eight months after the fact."

Gunner left that one alone.

"And this guy says the kid fired on McGovern first?"

"Yes."

"So you figured you'd look me up to ask if I'd care to compare notes, right?"

"Somebody said you were one of the IAD guys who investigated the case. Why shouldn't I ask you about it?"

"Because I can't tell you anything, that's why. The work I do is strictly interdepartmental, I couldn't talk to you about it if I wanted to."

"And you don't want to."

"No. As a matter of fact, I don't. We closed the books on McGovern months ago, and as I'm sure you already know, he closed the book on himself over the weekend. Permanently. What's the point in second-guessing the fucker's dismissal now?"

"If he was guilty? Not much. But if he was innocent—if he killed the Washington kid in self-defense, the way he always said . . ."

"He didn't. Believe me."

"I want you to hear my client's version of things, Danny. Before you make any final judgments."

"Forget it."

"It'll only take five minutes of your time."

"I said forget it. Aren't you listening?"

"Okay. See you in the morning, huh?"

Gunner hung up the phone.

He had to wait a solid hour for Kubo to call back, but call back Kubo did. And this time, he was ready to name a time and a place.

They ended up at the Pacific Design Center in West Hollywood, the jolly blue and green giant of Los Angeles landmarks that blotted out the sun at the corner of Melrose and San Vicente. Resembling a seven-story construct of giant blue and green building blocks, the center was a glorified shopping mall for licensed interior decorators, where everything from George II mahogany writing desks to wall-sized, marble-encased aquariums could be found at preposterous prices. Million-dollar homes and offices required million-dollar appointments to make their extravagance complete, and there was no better place in Los Angeles to look for such appointments than here, the Neiman-Marcus of the *Architectural Digest* set.

"I suppose you come here often," Gunner said after he had finished filling Kubo in, offering him a brief and sketchy outline of his work for Mitchell Flowers to date. The two men were wandering from floor to floor, peering through all the display windows from a safe distance, trying not to laugh at the unbelievable decadence of it all.

"Every chance I get," Kubo said, examining a two-foot-tall ceramic flamingo that had a four-figure price tag dangling from one of its spindly legs. "But I figure I'm the only cop in town who does, so we shouldn't have to worry about bumping into anyone I know."

It had been twenty-two years since he and Gunner had been wet-nosed recruits of the LAPD, the scourges of the cadet academy up in the Dodger Blue hills of Elysian Park, yet Kubo didn't wear the time at all noticeably. He was a smooth-skinned Japanese-American with the face of a kid and the energy to match, and his body still looked like something out of a male wish-fulfillment catalog. Habitually dressed like a commodities broker out to impress the boss, his only discernible flaw was a segmented and misaligned right eyebrow, a souvenir from the day back at the academy that a maniac cop and martial arts instructor named Phillip Adler split his forehead open with the heel of his left foot. Deliberately. Adler had let his peculiar dislike for Orientals get the better of him that day, and was well on his way to seriously maiming one . . . until Gunner stepped out from the crowd of terrified cadets watching the scene to shatter Adler's jaw with a solid right hand.

They gave Gunner his walking papers two days later.

"You think I'm being paranoid, but I'm not," Kubo said.

"Word gets around I've been talking to you, I'm never going to hear the end of it. Whether I actually tell you anything or not."

"Word's not going to get around," Gunner said.

"Yeah, right. Like it didn't get around that you had a black linebacker in a go-go dress leave flowers for Harry Kupchak with the desk sergeant at Southwest yesterday."

Gunner started to grin, but Kubo wasn't having any.

"You think it's funny, making a cop look like an ass in front of his fellow officers, but I've got news for you. You're playing with his life. Once a cop loses the respect of the men he works with, he's finished. Dead and buried."

"If I could have gotten the man to talk to me any other way, I would have," Gunner said.

"Maybe he had more important things to do than talk to you. You ever think of that?"

"I didn't ask him to do it for me. I asked him to do it for his friend McGovern."

"It doesn't matter who you asked him to do it for. You were wasting the man's time—just like you're wasting mine now. Because you're never going to prove what you're trying to prove. What your client says he saw never happened."

"Says who?"

"Says *me*. We took that alley and the yards on either side of it apart. If the Washington kid had lost a gun that night, we would've found it. Either that, or some slugs."

"Depending on how long you looked, you mean."

"We looked until we were satisfied," Kubo said.

"Satisfied of what?"

"That we weren't going to find anything."

"And that took what? Two hours, three hours . . . ?"

Kubo frowned, realizing he had already said more than he had planned to. "It's none of your business how long it took. I'm telling you Washington was clean, and that's all I intend to say about it. Now, or ever."

"Shit. Are you starting that again?"

"I'm not starting anything. I'm just telling you how it is. You're chasing your own tail with this McGovern business, and

I'm not going to risk my career trying to help you. What does it take to get that through your head?"

He was visibly angry, which was not a common state for Kubo. Unflappability was as much a Kubo trademark as the latest and greatest in menswear.

"McGovern shot that kid without provocation," Kubo said. "The little bastard made him run six blocks and was about to lose him for good, so McGovern put a bullet in him to keep him from getting away. That's just how the sonofabitch was."

Gunner was shaking his head. "That's not how my client says it happened, Danny."

"Then your client must be crazy. Or blind. Or both."

"I don't think so."

Kubo looked at him like he was dense. "You don't think so?"

"No. I don't. There's probably more to his story than he's been telling me—like what his interest in all this really is, for instance—but I believe he's telling the truth about the gunshots. Or whatever it was he saw in that alley the night Lendell Washington was killed."

"He didn't see anything. I told you."

"Yeah. I remember."

"But you don't believe me."

Gunner shrugged. "You haven't given me any reason to believe you—yet."

"If you read the papers eight months ago, you should have all the reasons you need."

"Such as?"

"Such as the fact McGovern tried to plant a gun at the scene, number one. And he tried to lift some of the money Washington took from the liquor store, number two. Do I need to go on?"

"Only if you think you owe it to me," Gunner said.

He fixed his eyes on Kubo's and kept them there, waiting for an answer. It was an unfair twist of the knife, but it got the job done.

"I'll give you five minutes. Take it or leave it," Kubo said.

Without missing a beat, Gunner said, "You said McGovern

tried to take some of the money Washington had stolen from the liquor store?"

"That's right."

"What made you think so?"

"What made us think so? Some of the money was missing, Sherlock. What else? The counterman at the liquor store said Washington and Ford got away with in excess of two hundred bucks, but we only recovered a little over a hundred at the scene."

"And you figured McGovern had pocketed the rest."

"Yeah. Assholes like him do that kind of shit all the time."

"Washington couldn't have just dropped the money in the street? While he was running?"

"You mean, like McGovern said he did?"

"Yeah."

"He could have. Sure. But he didn't."

The way Kubo had said it didn't invite any further discussion of the subject, so Gunner decided to move on, at least for now. "All right. We'll have it your way. We'll assume for the moment that my client's eyes are bad, and he didn't really see what he thinks he did. Okay?"

Kubo just stood there.

"Okay. So explain what he *heard,* then. Five shots in all, two distinct firing patterns. Two shots first, three shots afterward."

"You mean three shots first, and two shots afterward. The three McGovern fired at Washington, and then the two he fired into the ground with his drop gun."

"No."

"Yes."

"Goddamnit, Danny, the man heard—"

"I told you what he heard. If he thinks he heard something different, it was only because of the echo effect. The echo effect confuses people like that all the time."

"The *'echo effect'*?"

"That's right. The acoustics in that alley were perfect for that sort of thing, those five rounds would've sounded like a hundred in there."

"Except my client didn't hear a hundred. He just heard five."

"Five, ten, fifteen, twenty—it makes no difference. The principle's the same. What your client thinks he heard didn't happen. It was three shots, then two. Not the other way around. Trust me."

He had a curious look on his face that Gunner wasn't sure how to interpret. It was either a sign of supreme confidence in what he was saying—or supreme indifference toward it. One or the other.

"What about your other witnesses? They hear this 'echo effect,' too?"

Kubo shrugged. "A few did. Naturally. I told you, it's a common phenomenon."

"And what did they say they heard?"

"Off the top of my head? Beats the hell out of me."

"Try to remember, Danny."

"Hell. One lady said four shots, then two, another said three and three. Something like that."

"But nobody said two and three."

"No. Nobody said two and three. But we had a half-a-dozen people say three and two. No ifs, ands, or buts."

"What about Officer Lugo?"

"What about her?"

"What kind of firing pattern did she say she heard?"

"Officer Lugo was away from the scene at the time of the shooting," Kubo said stiffly.

"I know she was. But she was what, four or five blocks away? She must have heard something."

"She was twelve blocks away. And she did hear something. She heard gunfire." He shrugged again, seemingly commiserating. "She just couldn't say how much. She was too far away to make an accurate assessment, she said."

"Too far away?"

"That's right. That's what she said."

"What about how many weapons had been fired? Was she able to ascertain that?"

"No. She said the shots were all clumped together, that there was no way to distinguish one from the other from where she was when the shooting occurred."

"Jesus."

"You asked what the lady said, I'm telling you. What's your problem?"

"Me? I don't have a problem," Gunner said. "But I bet poor McGovern sure did. You guys had him by the short hairs, and all his partner did to help was take a walk on him."

"She didn't take a walk on anybody. She told the truth. Cops do that sometimes," Kubo said.

"Sure they do. The same way Siamese twins go to the can. In pairs."

"Look. Lugo's a good cop. McGovern wasn't. If I'd been in her shoes, I probably would've let the bastard sleep in the bed he'd made, too."

A uniformed security guard with a freckled face and a flaming red crew cut sauntered past them at a snail's pace, ignoring the squawking two-way radio clipped to his belt to openly look them over like the riffraff they were. They had forgotten to keep walking at some point and were just standing in the middle of the second floor landing, making their complete lack of interest in the wares surrounding them obvious to everyone. Kubo could have easily made the kid disappear with a flash of his badge, but he wasn't going to do that. Instead, he just let the kid look, until looking wasn't fun anymore and the kid decided to take his suspicions elsewhere.

"I think your five minutes are about up," Kubo said to Gunner when they were alone again, eyeing his watch critically.

Gunner nodded without argument and said, "After we talk about Noah Ford."

"Noah Ford? What's he got to do with anything?"

"I understand it was his contention that Washington was the one armed that night, not him. And that he was in fact clean when Lugo took him into custody."

"So?"

"So what happened to *his* weapon? If he was lying about not having one, it should have turned up somewhere, right?"

"It should have, yeah. But—"

"But it didn't."

"No. It didn't. Ford ran Lugo a lot farther than Washington ran McGovern, we had a lot more ground to cover searching for his weapon than for Washington's."

Gunner nodded his head thoughtfully and said, "Sure."

Kubo glared at him. "You don't believe we could've missed it, is that it?"

"On the contrary. I think you could've missed it very easily. The same way you could've missed Washington's."

Kubo didn't say anything.

"Providing, of course, you were trying just as hard to find one gun as you were the other."

"You trying to say we weren't?"

"I'm not trying to say anything. I'm just saying your explanation of things seems a little odd to me, that's all. You don't find one gun, and you say it's because it never existed; you don't find another, and you say it's because you had too much ground to cover. It makes a person wonder, Danny."

"It makes a person wonder what?"

Gunner jumped in with both feet. "How motivated you were to get McGovern off," he said.

Kubo's eyes went cold and his face hardened, instantly divesting itself of all its boyish charm. "What the hell are you talking about?"

"For lack of a better word? A lynching."

"You mean a fix."

"Like I said. For lack of a better word."

"I think you've been talking to too many idiots like Harry Kupchak, partner."

"It adds up, Danny. Even I can see that."

"Yeah?"

"Yeah. Jack McGovern was a bigot and a bully, a wrongful-death suit waiting to happen, and apparently that was news to nobody. He'd worn out his welcome with the department even under the old boys-will-be-boys administration; with Chief Bowden at the helm, he couldn't have been a bigger embarrassment to you if he'd worn a clown suit to work every day."

"So you think we stacked the deck on him just to get him out of everybody's hair."

"Let me just put it this way: The idea's not all that farfetched, once you stop to think about it."

"Unless you're stupid enough to believe we IAD jerks are too scrupulous to have taken part in such a thing. That what you mean?"

A wry smile might have taken the edge off the crack, but the IAD man was fresh out. He fixed Gunner with another icy stare and said, "I owed you a favor once. I don't anymore. Have a nice life, Aaron."

He started for the escalator nearby.

Rather than follow after him, Gunner stayed where he was and said, "I wasn't necessarily talking about you, Danny."

Kubo reached the escalator but stopped and turned around before getting on. "What?"

"You heard me. Maybe *you* wouldn't have anything to do with a frame-up, but some of the people you work with . . ." He shrugged. "Well . . ."

Kubo started back toward him, slowly, moving with a deliberateness that Gunner didn't like. "You don't know what the fuck you're talking about," he said. Less than a foot of breathing space stood between the two men when he stopped to poke a rigid finger in the black man's chest, using it for punctuation as he spoke. "So let me offer you a last piece of advice: Shut up. Before somebody shuts you up."

Gunner held his ground, trying to give Kubo the impression the warning hadn't shaken him. "Somebody like who?"

"If I have to answer that for you, I've been talking to a moron."

"You mean a cop. Like your pal Jenner, for instance."

Gunner was flat on his back before he knew what hit him, blinking water out of his eyes as Kubo stood over him, massaging the knuckles on his right hand with his left.

"That better be the last time you drop my partner's name to anybody. You understand? Leave him the fuck out of this."

A female salesclerk poked her head out of an oriental rug

shop to watch Gunner knead his nose back into shape, making no attempt to get up off the floor.

"Is that a warning, Danny?"

Kubo nodded. "Yeah. That's exactly what it is," he said.

He went back to the escalator behind him and disappeared for good.

7

Gunner didn't even know the woman's name.

She was a heavy-set black woman in her late forties, with shiny high cheekbones and an incomplete set of lower teeth, and she lived in a mustard-colored house on Van Ness Avenue, only yards from the alley in which Lendell Washington had died. Gunner had hoped he could get the names of all three people who had claimed to have witnessed Washington's death the year before from Danny Kubo, but pissing Kubo off the way he had had left him with no other recourse but to ask his client for the information, instead. Predictably, Mitchell Flowers hadn't been able to identify any of the witnesses by name, but he had been able to send Gunner here, to the home of one witness Flowers had recognized only as someone he often saw watering her lawn during his late evening strolls.

Gunner had only had to ring her doorbell once to bring her to the door.

"Can I help you?" she asked, openly suspicious, but making a conscious effort to be pleasant about it.

Gunner flashed his ID at her and introduced himself, saying only that he was a private investigator looking into the circumstances of the Lendell Washington shooting. She told him her name was Helen Church, and agreed to answer his questions without much in the way of hesitation.

"I understand you saw it happen," Gunner said.

"Yes. I did." She nodded.

"Can you tell me about it?"

"What's there to tell? That police officer shot that boy down in cold blood. It's as simple as that."

"By 'in cold blood,' you mean that he did it without provocation."

"That's right. That's exactly what I mean. Without provocation. That boy didn't have any gun. That was just something the police tried to say afterward, to make it look like the boy had it coming."

"Do you mind if I ask where you were when the shooting occurred, Ms. Church?"

"No. I don't mind." She pointed three houses north down the street, indicating a spot along the west side of Van Ness, directly opposite the mouth of the alley Jack McGovern had allegedly chased Lendell Washington into. "I was right there. I was standing right over there."

Nodding, Gunner looked the spot over, then turned around again. "And you happened to be over there because . . . ?" He smiled, hoping to make the question seem innocent.

"Because I saw a policeman chasing a little boy down the middle of my street," Church said, angrily, "and I wanted to see what the hell was going on."

"At two-thirty in the morning."

"Yes. What's wrong with that?"

"I didn't say there was anything wrong with it."

"No. But you were thinking it. Weren't you?"

"Ms. Church—"

"Listen. If you lived around here, you'd know things like this happen all the time. Kids getting shot by policemen, I mean. It's nothing new. A black person can't step on the sidewalk these days without getting hassled or attacked by the police. That's just the way they are down here.

"More people like myself stood up to them, let them know we aren't gonna stand for the way they've been treating us, there'd be a lot more cops like that one—" She stopped, catching herself before she could say something she clearly did not want Gunner to know.

"I'm sorry, Mr. Gunner, but I don't think I want to talk about this anymore. It disturbs me too much to discuss it," she said.

Then she closed the door before he could offer her an argument.

Gunner walked down to the alley itself before leaving, just to look around, but without really knowing what he was looking at—or what he was looking *for*—the effort didn't buy him much. Scanning the oil-stained and rubbish-strewn alley for clues now was like trying to read a book long after the words had been bleached by time from its pages.

Gunner invested a full five minutes in the effort, then left to find something more constructive to do with his time.

Just as her sister had predicted, Charlene Woodberry didn't really want to talk to Gunner. She claimed to have called him only because she felt so bad about the fate of her nephew Lendell, and it had seemed it might please her sister to do so. Gunner had no trouble believing the former, because Woodberry sounded wounded over the phone, like a mouse with its tail caught in a trap. He had to cup one hand over his free ear and the other over the payphone earpiece just to make sense of her whimpering.

As it happened, she was going to visit her son, Noah Ford, late that afternoon, she said, and she would take that opportunity to see if she could persuade him to meet with Gunner again. She couldn't promise what he would say, as she had lost her power to seriously influence his actions long ago, but she would do what she could to encourage his full cooperation.

Had Deanna Lugo not also called him at Mickey's while he'd been out getting beaten senseless by Danny Kubo and perhaps lied to by Helen Church, Gunner would have been at a loss trying to figure out what to do with the last few minutes of his day. He had already spoken to all the other principals of the case at least once, and there was no one left to question about Lendell Washington's death other than Lugo and Danny Kubo's partner, Jenner, whose cage Gunner was at the moment hesitant to rattle, for obvious reasons.

Finding Lugo at Southwest immediately after returning

Charlene Woodberry's call, Gunner asked her if she'd be willing to return with him to the alley in which the Washington shooting had taken place, and Lugo graciously consented.

Gunner was sitting behind the wheel of his own parked car when Lugo appeared around three-thirty, bringing a black-and-white Ford cruiser up to the curb on the alley side of Van Ness behind him. Her partner was nowhere in sight. Gunner watched her get out of the car in his rearview mirror, and one thing, at least, became immediately clear to him: she was the most attractive cop he had ever seen.

He stepped out of the Cobra and moved to join her.

"Mr. Gunner?"

"Officer Lugo. Thank you for coming." He shook her hand, trying not to let the smile on his face betray too much of what he was thinking.

She was a dark-skinned Hispanic with straight, short-cropped black hair and piercing brown eyes, and her uniform fit her supple frame like a glove. There was nothing sexual about the way she smiled at him, but it held a tiny charge just the same.

"Sergeant Kupchak said I should hear you out. That's the only reason I'm here," she said.

"Okay."

"He says you're trying to prove Maggie got the shaft. That right?"

"I guess that's one way of putting it."

"What does that mean?"

"It means I've been hired to prove Lendell Washington took a couple of shots at McGovern the night Washington was killed. That's all."

"Just like Maggie always said he did."

"Yes."

"You mind if I ask who hired you?"

"No. I don't mind."

She waited for him to go on, until it dawned on her that he wasn't going to.

"You don't want to tell me, is that it?"

"My client is someone who claims to have been here when the shooting took place. What else do you need to know?"

"Well, for starters, I'd like to know where the hell this client of yours was last November, when his testimony might have done Maggie some good."

"That's a fair question. Unfortunately, all I can say in answer to it is, my client didn't feel it would be appropriate to come forward at that time," Gunner said defensively.

"No shit. Some hero, your client."

Gunner just shrugged. "I'm only working for the man, officer. Not nominating him for president."

Lugo fell silent, obviously trying to decide how badly she wanted this conversation to continue.

"So. What do you want to know?" she asked after a while.

Gunner had her give him the complete tour, from the spot where McGovern claimed to have been standing when he'd opened fire on Lendell Washington, to the spot where Washington's body had been found. The first was a point less than five yards from the alley's entrance, while the second was about twenty yards farther into the alley than that. The alley itself was lined with dilapidated fences and tiny garages, and trash cans crumpled by time and misuse into grotesque sculptures of aluminum and plastic. The fences ranged in height from four to six feet; some were chain link, most were wooden slats. None stood particularly erect. The yards beyond were small, but for the most part well kept; tall grass was a rarity. There were outdoor light fixtures attached to two of the garages, but only one actually held a bulb, and all but a few of the garages had sloping, tar paper roofs, which meant that anything tossed atop them would have likely slid right back down to earth, or at least been easily detected by anyone standing below.

According to Lugo, Washington had breathed his last about halfway down the alley, in front of the graffiti-marred door of a lemon yellow garage. The low picket fence beside it allowed for a good view of a backyard someone obviously tended with great care. The lawn was green and well manicured, and the shrubbery arranged around it looked trim and healthy. Unless it had looked substantially different the previous November, there would have been no place in this yard for a gun to hide.

Lugo's version of the events leading up to and following Washington's death held no particular surprises. It was essentially the same story Harry Kupchak had told. McGovern and Lugo had shown up at the liquor store six blocks away just in time to scare Washington and Noah Ford off. The two robbery suspects had split up, and McGovern and Lugo had done likewise, McGovern chasing Washington here, Lugo chasing Ford a dozen blocks farther south. It was during her pursuit of Ford that she heard the shots emanating from the alley, Lugo said, and just as both Kupchak and Kubo had reported, she was nonspecific about the number of shots she had heard. She tried to contact McGovern on her handset radio to find out what, if anything, had happened, but McGovern was not responding to her calls at that time. In fact, he didn't make contact with her until she and Ford had returned to the liquor store to retrieve the patrol car waiting there, after Ford had tried to sprint across a busy intersection against the light and was knocked off his feet by a passing car. McGovern gave Lugo his location and reported that Washington had been shot. She tossed Ford into the back of the patrol car and the two of them arrived at the alley minutes later, but by that time Washington was already dead and a host of witnesses were lingering about the alley, ready to seal McGovern's fate.

That was about all she could remember, Lugo said.

Going back to the beginning of her story, having held all his questions until now, Gunner said, "You never saw the gun Ford allegedly used in the robbery?"

Lugo shook her head. "No."

"What do you suppose happened to it?"

"I don't know. He must have chucked it somewhere, I guess. You know—when he was running."

"Or given it to Washington before they took off."

Lugo shrugged. "Possibly. It's hard to say what he did with it. The little jerk ran me halfway across town, I couldn't keep him in my sight every moment."

Gunner nodded, seeming to buy that. "Why do you suppose

they split up in the first place? Washington was supposed to be pretty weak in the knees, and he was the one holding the cash. Doesn't it seem odd he would take off on his own, rather than stick with his cousin, Ford?"

"Not if Ford was running the wrong way," Lugo said.

"The wrong way?"

"Yeah. The wrong way. That was the first thing we heard Washington say when Ford took of: 'You're goin' the wrong way!' Or words to that effect."

"What did he mean, the wrong way?"

"Well, it's only a guess, but he probably meant Ford was running south, when they both lived to the north. Washington's mother's place is on the sixteen-hundred block of Leighton, and Ford's is on the thirty-nine-hundred block of Dalton." Lugo pointed to the north, just in case Gunner needed the help. "That way."

"Then Ford was running *away* from home, not toward it."

"Yeah."

"And you think that was why Washington let him go."

"Sure. Wouldn't you have done the same thing, if you were him?"

"How did Ford explain himself later?"

"He didn't. He wasn't talking, except to say he didn't do anything. You know, the usual denials. Washington did it all, he said." She paused. "At least, that's what he was saying at first. Until his lawyer got ahold of him."

"And then?"

"And then he changed his story."

"Yeah? How's that?"

"Well, he took the rap. Pleaded guilty to everything but carrying the gun. Since we never could find a weapon we could connect him with, his lawyer cut him a deal and he was back on the street in six months."

"You wouldn't happen to remember this lawyer's name, would you?"

"No. But I've seen him around. He's the same guy Washington's mother's hired to handle her case against the department, I think."

"Milton Wiley," Gunner said, nodding his head.

"Yeah. That's him."

Well, what do you know, Gunner thought to himself.

Changing the subject, he said, "The gun McGovern said Washington dropped. You ever see it?"

Lugo paused conspicuously before answering. "Yes."

"When?"

"When I first arrived at the scene. And later, when the IAD team asked me to look it over."

"Describe it for me, if you can."

Lugo shrugged again and said, "It was a thirty-eight–caliber Charter Arms. A Pug, I think. Black finish. No handgrips, no serial numbers. Just your typical piece of street iron."

"And that fit the description the counterman at the liquor store gave you for the gun Ford was supposed to be flashing around?"

"No. The counterman at the liquor store couldn't give us a description of the weapon he saw. All he was able to tell us was, it was a revolver of some kind. Not an automatic."

"Then it could have been the same gun. Is that what you're saying?"

"It could have been. Sure."

"Except that Ford's prints were never found on it."

"That's what I understand."

"And the prints on the gun that belonged to Washington came from his right hand. His off hand."

"Yes. At least, that's what they said."

"And you don't find that a little strange?"

"What's that?"

"That the prints on the gun came from Washington's off hand."

"Strange? No. I don't find it strange."

"Why not?"

"Because I gave up trying to understand everything that happens on this job a long time ago, Mr. Gunner. You live longer that way."

She was looking him straight in the eye, daring him to call her a liar.

"Just for the sake of argument, let's say the Charter Arms was a drop gun McGovern placed at the scene. Can we do that, Officer Lugo?"

"Just for the sake of argument? Sure."

"Good. Now let's go a step further and say that the reason McGovern planted the Charter Arms was because he couldn't find the gun Washington really had. All right?"

Lugo shrugged.

"Okay, then. Question: What happened to Washington's gun? How is it nobody ever found it?"

Lugo shrugged again. "I don't know. I know Maggie always said it was pitch black in here that night. At least, it was before all the shooting started. That's why alleys like this are so popular with the drug trade. They're all dark as hell. Nobody has the money to keep their garage light on all night, and the few that do just get their light bulbs busted out for their trouble. On an overcast night like that one, Maggie probably wouldn't have been able to see three feet in front of him in any direction."

"But it wasn't that dark later that evening. Is that what you said?"

"You mean, when Ford and I got here?"

"Yes."

"No. It wasn't that dark by then. By that time, half the neighborhood was up and awake, and there were lights on over that garage there"—she pointed toward the one garage Gunner had found to have a bulb installed in its floodlight—"and in several of the yards on both sides."

"Then Washington's gun *should* have been visible to someone from that time forward."

"Yes. Except that no one was looking for another gun then. We all thought the gun Maggie turned in was Washington's. There was no reason for anybody to go looking around for

91

another one until the lab boys came back and said the so-called 'wrong' set of Washington's prints were on the Charter Arms."

She was right, of course. Gunner could have kicked himself for not seeing the same point sooner.

"Let's talk about the money for a minute," he said, groping for the upper hand in their conversation again.

"The money?"

"The money that was missing from the liquor store cash. The hundred dollars or so McGovern was supposed to have lifted off of Washington's body."

"Yes?"

"That sound like something McGovern would have done to you? Was he into that kind of action?"

"You mean stealing?"

"Yes. That's the word I'm looking for, I guess. 'Stealing.' "

He said it while meeting her gaze head-on, to let her know she could bullshit him here if she wanted, but it wasn't going to wash if she did.

"Let's just say that Maggie hated to see a good dollar go to waste, Mr. Gunner. All right?"

She hadn't intended for the line to get a laugh, but Gunner found it amusing, nonetheless. Wisely, however, he allowed himself only the slightest of grins and moved on, not caring to test the limits of Lugo's tolerance for insult.

"You said Harry Kupchak told you that I'm trying to prove McGovern got the shaft. Is that right?"

"That's what he told me, yes."

"Were those his words, or yours?"

"What? That Maggie got the shaft?"

"Yes."

"Those were his words. Not mine."

"Meaning that you don't see it that way."

"I didn't say that. I think Maggie got the short end of the stick in a lot of ways, sure."

"Yeah?"

"Yeah. At least, he sure as hell didn't get as many breaks as he could have. Did he?"

"Breaks of what kind? From who?"

"From everybody. IAD, the department brass, the media people—you name it. From the moment the Washington kid's body hit the ground, Maggie didn't get an inch of slack from anybody."

"And you think he deserved one?"

"I think he should have gotten a little more support from some people. Yes."

"You don't include yourself in that group, I take it."

"Me? Why should I?"

"I don't know. Maybe because you were so vague about the number of shots you heard fired that night, for one thing. I mean, while McGovern had insisted there'd been five—Washington's two, followed by his three—you've always been relatively uncertain about it. And that's a somewhat unusual stance for a cop's partner to take under the circumstances, don't you think?"

"I couldn't tell how many shots had been fired. I was twelve blocks away," Lugo said forcefully.

"I know. You said that."

"Then what's the problem?"

"The problem is, that wouldn't have stopped some cops from saying they heard five, anyway. You know that, and I know that."

Lugo was about to dispute that when a loud noise from the far end of the alley caused both of their heads to turn. A black man in a soiled and tattered black tuxedo was rummaging through the trash cans several yards down, tossing the aluminum lids over his shoulder as he went from can to can. He had a beard full of dust and lint obscuring his face, and a shopping cart loaded with clothes and refuse standing at his side.

It wasn't anything Gunner and Lugo didn't see every day.

"Look," Lugo said, turning back around. "If you think I should have lied just to make things go a little easier for Maggie, you're crazy. The second I saw that kid lying there, I knew Maggie's fate was out of my hands. It wouldn't have mattered what I did or said to save him."

"How could you know that?"

"Because I was his partner. You think I could be the man's partner and not know what everybody thought of him? How much some people wanted to see him dead, let alone drummed out of the department? He was old school, Maggie. He was hot-tempered and pigheaded, and his ideas about some things were downright ignorant. Maybe qualities like those didn't mean much at one time, but these days they mark you for extinction. Not to mention make you as safe to be around as a stick of lit dynamite.

"So I told it the way I saw it and let the chips fall for Maggie where they would. It was all I could do, considering."

"Considering what?"

"Considering they would have taken me down with him, if they'd been forced to. I told you."

"Who are you talking about? The IAD guys?"

"Yes."

"Kubo and Jenner."

"Yeah. Them."

"You think they set McGovern up?"

"I don't know about a setup. It just seemed to me they were going about their work building a case against him with an awful lot of enthusiasm. More than the usual amount, anyway. Jenner, especially."

"You ever meet either man before?"

Lugo shook her head. "No. And I don't plan to again. I like being a cop, Mr. Gunner. And I intend to be one for a long time. If that means I'll have to do things differently from time to time than another cop might under similar circumstances, so be it. I apologize to nobody." She waited to see how Gunner would take that, but the investigator had no reaction to it, as near as she could determine. "Any more questions?"

"Just one," Gunner said.

"Let me guess. Am I free tonight? What's my sign? Something like that?"

It was hard to tell how much cynicism was hidden in the question. Smiling despite himself, Gunner said, "Actually, I was going to ask you to give me your gut feeling about what happened here that night. Regardless of what you saw or didn't see, heard or didn't hear. All things considered—"

"Do I think Maggie shot the Washington kid without due cause?"

"Yes. That's my question."

Lugo thought about it for a moment, then nodded her head almost despondently. "Yes. I do." She shrugged. "So I guess it doesn't matter what kind of job they did on the poor bastard, does it?"

"Not unless you're the kind of cop who'd take offense at that sort of thing."

"You mean having the men upstairs come down on your partner like a load of bricks?"

"Yes."

"I should be more outraged than I am, I guess."

"Let's just say, I find myself wondering why you're not."

"Okay. I'll give you a hint. Know how many of Maggie's old partners showed up at his funeral yesterday morning? Two. Me and some detective out of Harbor who used to ride with Maggie back in the early eighties. I don't remember his name. Maggie must have broken in close to fifty rookie partners over his lifetime, and only two of 'em cared enough about him to say goodbye. That tell you anything?"

Gunner didn't answer, preferring to wait for her to answer the question for him.

"He was bad news. That's what it should tell you. And every cop who ever rode with him has the scars to prove it. Whether they realize it or not."

Suddenly, she was in a hurry to leave. The cool, unshakable professionalism she had exhibited up to now was fading fast, and Gunner was starting to get a good look at the angry young woman she really was.

"Look, Mr. Gunner. I hate to cut this short, but . . ."

"You have to be going."

"Yes. I'm sorry."

"Don't be sorry. Thank you for coming." The investigator reached out to shake her hand again. "On the off chance I might need to talk to you again, would it be all right if I called you? Or have you said all you have to say on the subject of your ex-partner?"

Lugo produced one of her business cards and handed it to him. "You want to call, call," she said. "But do me a favor. Don't try to tell me that when you do, the only thing you're going to have on your mind is Maggie. All right?"

"I'm not sure I follow you."

"Come on, Mr. Gunner. That goofy look you've been giving me for the last fifteen minutes hasn't had anything to do with business. Obviously, I've got something you need—or at least, something you can deeply appreciate—and it could be the feeling is mutual. I don't know. It's a little early to tell, yet."

Gunner kept expecting her to grin, but she never did. She was deadly serious.

"Wait a minute," Gunner said, thoroughly caught off guard.

"Look. Forget I said anything. You think of any more questions you'd like to ask about Maggie, just give me a call down at the station, all right?"

Lugo turned and started out of the alley.

For a brief moment, Gunner thought about going after her. But then it occurred to him that he'd have to *say* something to her if he did—and his mind had just become a total blank.

Getting caught with one's libido showing could do that to a man.

8

Gunner was only three blocks from home when they put the lights on him.

He had just spent the greater part of Friday night at the Acey Deuce, the neighborhood bar and night club in which he did the vast majority of his drinking, and he still had a light buzz on. Having Deanna Lugo come on to him this afternoon had put him in a somewhat celebratory mood, and he'd wanted to put the day to rest in the company of some friends, rather than with a bottle of Wild Turkey and a few fond remembrances of Claudia Lovejoy back at home. Up until now, it had seemed like the right thing to do.

On his way home, he had stopped for a brief moment back at the alley behind Forty-second Place, just east of Van Ness, to see for himself what the scene looked like at night. Lugo had been the second person to mention, after Harry Kupchak, how impossible Jack McGovern had found it to see inside the alley on the night of Lendell Washington's shooting, and Gunner had decided he didn't like not knowing how much truth there was to the claim. A lot of time had passed since the night in question, and how things were today did not necessarily have any bearing on how they had been then, but tonight, the alley had been dark.

Very dark.

And Gunner found that problematic.

It was almost midnight. Traveling east along 108th Street, enjoying the cold night air that the topless Cobra afforded him, he couldn't remember doing anything special or reckless, had made no sudden lane changes nor abruptly increased his speed—and yet there it was: a blazing red light bar blinking in his rearview mirror.

The neon calling card of the Man.

Gunner pulled the Cobra over to the curb just on the other side of San Pedro and waited for instructions. Depending upon who he was dealing with, he could be ordered to show his hands, or to step out of the car—or be greeted by silence, which in its own way was more disconcerting than anything else.

The Cobra's engine hadn't completely died when a wave of white light washed over its and Gunner's back, as the driver of the black-and-white behind them hit the search light mounted above the sideview mirror on the driver's side of the car. Gunner could hear the patrol car's doors open and close, but the light in his eyes when he glanced in his mirrors gave him nothing to see of the two men approaching but silhouettes, one on his right, one on his left.

Gunner knew better than to turn around for a better look.

The uniform on his right came as far as the Cobra's rear quarter panel and stopped right there, his right hand resting on his weapon. Gunner could actually hear the pop as he unclipped the safety strap securing the revolver to its holster.

The uniform's partner, meanwhile, came all the way forward to Gunner's side and said, "Good evening. May I see your driver's license and registration, please?"

A narrow-framed white man with a pockmarked face, he'd made the word *please* sound like a vulgarity he found personally offensive.

"What seems to be the problem?" Gunner asked.

There was a slight delay before the question received an answer. "There's no problem. Your driver's license and registration, please." Before Gunner could argue, the officer said, "Use your right hand only, and keep your left hand up near the top of the wheel, in plain sight."

Okay, Gunner thought. *It's going to be like that.*

He produced the requested documents in the manner prescribed and watched as the stone-faced officer held a flashlight to them, looking each over carefully. He was in no hurry. Even his partner was starting to show signs of impatience when he finally looked up and said, "Step out of the car for me, please, Mr. Gunner."

Gunner looked at him, tempted to protest, but kept his mouth shut and did as he was told.

"Step around to the other side of the car and wait. I'll just be a moment," the officer said.

He didn't move until Gunner had joined his partner on the sidewalk. Then he moved back to the patrol car and got on the radio to run a check on the Cobra and the black man he'd found driving it.

The young black patrolman sharing the sidewalk with Gunner studied his face skeptically.

"You look like you've been drinking," he said.

Gunner shrugged, knowing how little good a lie would do him. "Some."

"What's that mean, 'some'?"

"It means I had a pretty good buzz on about two hours ago, but now I hardly feel a thing."

The officer fell silent, no doubt trying to decide whether or not the subject was worth pursuing. Then he nodded in the direction of the Cobra and said, "That's a lot of car to be driving around drunk in, don't you think?"

Gunner didn't say anything.

"It's a Cobra, right?"

"Yeah."

"Yours?"

"Yes."

"Is that right?" That seemed to throw him for a minute. "You put it together yourself?"

Gunner had been expecting the question; he heard it all the time. "It's not a kit car," he said.

"What?" The cop stepped closer to the car for a better look. "You're kidding. This is the real thing?"

Gunner nodded.

"You mind if I ask how you got it?"

"A buddy in Nam left it to me," Gunner said tersely.

"A buddy? What kind of buddy?"

"A dead one."

The cop looked at him, finally at a loss for words.

Here and there along both sides of the street, people had stopped to gather and gawk, and Gunner was beginning to grow weary of all the attention. He watched as the officer at the car started back toward him, his clipboarded ticket book in hand.

Showing his partner a little nod Gunner was meant to miss, the cop offered Gunner his clipboard and a pen and said, "Sign there at the bottom, please, Mr. Gunner."

"What's it for?" Gunner asked, irritated.

"Your left taillight is out. Just like it says."

He stood there grim-faced, waiting for Gunner to either sign the ticket or give him an argument.

Gunner signed the ticket.

The cop pulled Gunner's copy of the citation out of his book and handed it to him. "Have a good night, sir," he said.

Even though he knew there was no chance now that Gunner would.

"Mr. Gunner. It's good to hear from you," Mitchell Flowers said. It was barely nine o'clock on a Saturday morning, yet he sounded like someone who had been awake for hours.

Gunner could picture him standing at his living room phone, dressed like an urban farmboy, a muddy garden spade in his free hand.

Mr. Black Middle America.

"I'd like to see you this morning, Mr. Flowers, if that would be possible," Gunner said.

"Is something wrong?"

"I'm not sure. Will you be home for the next fifteen minutes?"

Flowers had to think about that for a minute. "This can't be done over the phone, Mr. Gunner?"

"It could, sure. But I'd rather do it in person. How about it?"

Silence.

"I'll come incognito," Gunner promised.

"If you think it's that important," Flowers said finally. "Come on over."

A heartfelt invitation it wasn't.

Gunner was going to try to weasel out of the case.

He realized now that he had been crazy to accept it in the first place. Four days on the job, and all he'd really managed to prove was what he'd known from the beginning: Clearing Jack McGovern of Lendell Washington's murder couldn't be done.

There seemed to be evidence galore that McGovern had been facing a hopelessly stacked deck from the beginning—from the opportunistic Milton Wiley to the overzealous IAD team of Danny Kubo and Dick Jenner, everyone who could have possibly made things worse for him apparently did—but that wasn't the point Gunner had been hired to make. What Mitchell Flowers had paid him to establish was that all the effort McGovern's friends and enemies had spent trying to bury him had been directed at an innocent man—and so far, Gunner had come much closer to proving McGovern's guilt than his innocence.

Gunner didn't really need a more compelling reason for quitting the case than that, but he had one all the same. Getting pulled over by Frick and Frack the night before had reminded him of it, after he had somehow neglected to mention it last Monday night, when he'd fooled both himself and Mitchell Flowers into thinking he could do what Flowers was asking of him.

Cops made Gunner nervous.

He had never gone in for the popular dictum that said no cop was to be trusted and every cop was to be feared, but he had seen enough uniformed madmen in his time to know that his next confrontation with a policeman could always be his last. A run-in with the wrong cop, at the wrong time, was all that it would take. Because many of the men and women who patrolled these streets didn't always see things the way they really were. They didn't think they could afford to. In the interests of staying alive, they had taught themselves to expect the worst of every situation, and to treat strangers like the enemy. It was experience-driven paranoia, coupled with a vast array of preconceived notions about whole groups of people. Notions that could get a man belonging to such a group killed or crippled for life under the right set of circumstances.

Gunner had no reason to believe that either of the officers he had met Friday night fell into this particular category, but he had no reason to believe they didn't, either. And that was the real problem: never knowing. Not knowing how much one could say to whom, or in what tone of voice; how fast you could move your hands, or where you should keep them; what expressions to keep off your face, or what to do with your eyes. Any step could be a false step, in the wrong cop's eyes, and the right false step on any given night could buy you a ticket to the boneyard. All you had to do was be unlucky enough to draw a meeting with a crazy like Jack McGovern.

Ostensibly, Dennis Bowden was out to change all this, but change was going to be a long time coming. In fact, the pressures Bowden was exerting on the troops to clean up their act were only adding fuel to the fire at this point, giving the already angry cop on the street just one more thing about his job to resent. In this, the still smoldering aftermath of the Dexter Hardy riots, the law-men of South-Central Los Angeles were being measured for per-fection as they had never been before, and the stress of such scrutinization was going to break more than a few of them as time went by.

Up to now, Gunner hadn't had anybody snap on him, and maybe he never would. But Russian roulette was still Russian roulette, no matter how many times the cylinder in the chamber turned up empty.

And Gunner had never cared much for suicide.

"I don't understand," Mitchell Flowers said.

They were in his living room, drinking coffee. He had a nice little home on Forty-first Street, between Western and Van Ness, less than six blocks from the alley where Lendell Washington had died. There was a swing out on the front porch, and a chain-link fence surrounding the front yard. A German shepherd yapped playfully out in the back.

Inside, Gunner had never seen so many doilies in his life.

"You're giving up. Is that what you're saying?"

"I'm saying I've been on the case for four days now, and I think you're throwing your money away," Gunner said. "That's what I'm saying. Everyone seems to agree that there may have indeed been some extracurricular activity behind McGovern's dismissal, but since he was guilty anyway, it doesn't really matter."

"But he wasn't guilty. That's my whole point," Flowers said.

Gunner took a deep breath. "You still insist Washington had a gun?"

"Yes. I saw him fire it."

"You mean you saw McGovern fire it. After he'd shot Washington."

"No. I saw the boy fire a gun at McGovern. Before McGovern started shooting."

"You're sure about that?"

"Of course."

Gunner shook his head. "I hate to differ with you, Mr. Flowers, but I don't think you did. I've been told by a number of people so far that that alley was as dark as the bottom of a well that night, and I'm inclined to believe them. I checked the alley for myself last night, and it was like they say: pitch black. Now, I'm not ready to say you've been lying to me, exactly, but—"

"But what?"

"But I wonder why you haven't exactly been telling me the truth, either. Not all of it, anyway."

Flowers fell silent, a sure sign that Gunner was on to something. He had an angry, yet uncertain look on his face, like that of a man who was both insulted and apprehensive at the same time.

"I saw him fire two shots," Flowers insisted.

"You mean you saw the muzzle flashes."

"Yes."

"But you didn't actually see *him*."

Flowers paused, fishing for an answer. It almost looked to

Gunner as if he were making one up on the spot. "No. I guess I didn't. But—"

Gunner lowered his eyes to the floor and shook his head, biting down on a choice vulgarity. "Why didn't you tell me that before?" he asked, looking up again.

"What?"

"That you never actually saw Washington fire a gun. That's what."

Flowers shrugged. "I don't know. I guess I never thought about it. So I didn't actually see him fire the gun. So what?"

"So maybe he wasn't the one who fired it," Gunner said. "You ever think of that?"

If Flowers had ever considered the possibility before, it didn't show on his face. He appeared to be genuinely taken aback. "I don't understand," he said.

"I'm suggesting that perhaps there was someone else in the alley with him, Mr. Flowers. Someone with a gun. Someone you didn't see."

"Someone like who?"

Gunner had come prepared to answer just such a question. All he'd had to do was spend half the previous night mulling it over. "I don't know," he said. "A crack dealer, maybe."

"A crack dealer?"

"That's right. McGovern's partner told me yesterday that that alley's a regular drug lover's bazaar around that time of night. Maybe a buyer or a seller was hanging around in there when Washington showed up, saw McGovern coming, and just panicked, not knowing what the hell was going on. He or she could have fired two shots at McGovern just to discourage him, and then taken off."

Just at that moment, Flowers's wife entered the room with fresh coffee. She was a narrow-hipped woman with an insincere smile, and she hadn't said more than "hello" to Gunner since he'd arrived. Her husband had introduced Gunner to her as an old bowling league buddy, an implausibility she had somehow never questioned.

When she had left the two men alone again, Gunner said,

"The other possibility is, there was another kid besides Washington and Ford involved in the holdup. Somebody McGovern and his partner never saw, and Ford never talked about. Maybe a lookout who spotted the law coming before anyone else and took off without ever being noticed."

"And then what? Washington followed him into the alley?"

"Presumably. Yes."

Flowers shook his head. "But I didn't see anyone else," he said.

"From what you told me, you might not have. You said the first you saw of Washington, he was just turning into the alley, with McGovern half a block behind. If that's true, and assuming Washington had been following someone with any kind of lead at all . . ."

Flowers shook his head again and said, "I don't know, Mr. Gunner. It all sounds reasonable enough, I suppose, but . . ." He shrugged to terminate the thought, in essence admitting he had no faith in Gunner's logic.

"You don't think there could have been someone else in the alley with Washington, is that it?"

"No. I didn't say that. It's just . . . Well, I think it's jumping to conclusions, assuming there was someone else there just because I didn't see the gun in Washington's hand. You understand what I'm saying? I mean, if someone else had been there, I'm sure I would have noticed somehow. I would have heard them, at least, even if I didn't see them. Right?" He waited for Gunner to agree with him, but the investigator passed on the offer. "Besides. Even if there had been someone else there—a drug dealer, or another kid, or whatever—what difference would it make? McGovern was still fired upon first, and that's all that really matters here, isn't it?"

"Technically speaking, yes. But I think you're missing my point."

"Am I?"

"Yes. The point I've been trying to make here, Mr. Flowers, is that an already difficult job has just become even more so, now that I have to worry about the possibility of three people having been in that alley, instead of just two."

"And?"

"And, frankly, I don't know if I'm up to the challenge."

"I see. You're telling me your fee is insufficient, that you're going to require some more money. Is that it?"

"No. That's *not* it. The money's got nothing to do with it!" Gunner heard the tremulous rise in his voice and stopped, giving himself a moment to think things over before Flowers's density could incense him completely. "It's not a matter of money. It's a matter of what it's likely to buy you. And right now, that's nothing."

"Lendell Washington fired that gun, Mr. Gunner, and the police are just trying to cover the whole thing up. Don't you see that?"

"Frankly speaking, I don't. But even if I did, I wouldn't know how to prove it. That's what I'm trying to tell you. The only piece of evidence that could lend any credence to your version of things is the gun you insist Washington fired that night—and I can't produce it. Nobody can, apparently."

"Nobody else has really tried," Flowers said.

"Maybe so. I don't know. In any case, the gun hasn't turned up, and without it, like I say, you don't have a case. *We* don't have a case."

"So you think I should just drop it. Just like that."

"I think you should give that option some serious thought, yes. I mean, hell, I'll take your money for as long as you want to spend it, but I feel like you ought to know at this point how little you're likely to get for it."

"And if I take your advice and just let the whole thing go— what happens to the people who threatened my little girl? Nothing, right?"

Gunner didn't quite know how to answer that one. "Unless you went to the police with the note they sent you—"

"I don't want to go to the police. That's why I hired you, remember? I want *you* to find out who sent me that note, without involving the police."

Gunner shook his head.

"Mr. Gunner, please. Listen to me. These people made me do

something I may regret for the rest of my life, and you're the only hope I have of ever putting that fact behind me. Don't you understand?"

"Mr. Flowers—"

"You said you'd take my money for as long as I cared to spend it. Well, I still care to spend it. For at least another week or so, anyway." He leaned forward in his chair and held his hand out for Gunner to shake. "Stick with me on this, I beg of you. Please."

He pushed his hand further forward and waited, defying Gunner to ignore the gesture forever.

Gunner shook his hand.

"Thank you," Flowers said, gushing and grinning like a game show contestant as both men rose to their feet. "One more week. That's all I'm asking for."

Gunner was about to tell him where he could stick his one more week when a fight broke out in the kitchen behind them.

"I'll open the goddamn refrigerator any time I want!" a male voice shouted.

"I said close that door, Sonny," Flowers's wife ordered.

"Bullshit. I'm hungry."

"You don't spend a cent for the food in this house, you've got no right to be hungry!"

The smile on Flowers's face disappeared like something that had been drawn on it with invisible ink. He looked at Gunner sheepishly and said, "I'm sorry. My brother Sonny . . ." He let a shrug of abject helplessness end the sentence for him.

Moments later, a black man wearing high-water pajama bottoms and a sleeveless white T-shirt left the kitchen to join them, a bowl of cold breakfast cereal cupped in one hand. He had a black patch over his right eye and a San Francisco Giants baseball cap turned rearward atop his head, and he walked with a discernible limp that seemed to favor his left side. He looked to be about ten years his brother's junior, which would have put him somewhere in his early thirties.

"Yo. We got company," he said when he caught sight of Gunner, before digging into the cereal while still on his feet.

"Sonny, this is Aaron Gunner. A friend of mine. We used to bowl league together," Mitchell Flowers said.

"League? Man, you didn't never bowl no league."

"It was while you were away. I guess I never told you." His eyes darted to the kitchen for a moment, then came back. "In any case, Mr. Gunner was just leaving."

"Yeah. I really have to run," Gunner said, trying to help out.

"Later, then," Sonny Flowers said, loading another spoonful of cereal into his mouth. He was spilling milk all over the living room floor.

Out on the porch, his brother found it necessary to offer Gunner a second apology. "Maybe now you understand why I was hesitant to have you over," he said. "He's been staying with us now for almost a month, and he and the wife still haven't learned to get along. It's a constant battle between those two."

Gunner shrugged. "In-laws can be like that."

Flowers shook his head. "No. There's more to it than that, I'm afraid. It's Sonny, not Wanda. He's just nothing but bad news. All you have to do is look at him to know that."

"You mean the eye?"

"The eye and the limp, both," Flowers said. "See them together, and you know all you need to know about the kind of people he associates with, and the kind of trouble he likes to get into. This time, it was supposed to be a woman with a pool cue and an angry boyfriend that nearly killed him. The woman put his eye out, and the boyfriend broke his hip. He's been recuperating here with us ever since."

Gunner shrugged and smiled. "It sounds like he's lucky to have you for a brother."

"Yes. He is."

Flowers watched Gunner get all the way to his car, then turned and walked slowly back into the house.

When Gunner called for his messages fifteen minutes later, Mickey surprised him with two.

"But you're not gonna like one of 'em," the barber said.

"Just give it to me anyway, Mickey."

"Okay. Your friend Claudia called."

"Yeah?"

"Yeah. She said she was calling to ask you not to call her anymore. Is that just like a woman, or what?"

Gunner almost laughed out loud, thinking about how much he'd had that coming. He had tried her number at home again this morning, and let the phone ring a full eight minutes in a pitiful effort to harass her into responding to the call. He knew now that she had been there during the attempt, and had simply waited him out. He couldn't have felt more like a fool if she'd explained this all to Mickey in intricate detail.

"Give me the next one, Mickey."

"Somebody named Charlene Woodberry called you, too. She said she spoke to Noah and it's okay to go see him again, if you want. I asked her if you'd know what that's supposed to mean, and she said yeah, you would."

"She was right. I do. Thanks a lot, Mickey."

He hung up without saying good-bye.

Finding a parking space at Central Juvenile Hall on a Saturday afternoon turned out to be a different proposition from finding one on a Friday morning. Gunner had to cruise the entire length of the lot before he came across a spot for the Cobra that wasn't reserved for nonvisitors.

And one look at the crowd milling about the visitors' entrance explained why. Mothers and sisters, wives and girlfriends, baby sons and baby daughters—they were all here, waiting to see one inmate or another. Gunner had to bob and weave his way around a group of teenagers sitting at the curb just to reach the guard's window.

"Who're you here to see?" the officer behind the security glass asked, yawning.

When Gunner told him, a funny look came slowly over the guard's face.

"D'you say Ford?"

"Yeah. Noah Ford. There a problem?"

The guy just blinked at him. "Hold on a minute," he said, and then got up to disappear down a hallway behind him, without bothering to explain what the hell was going on.

He was back in five minutes, the same strange expression on his face.

"Sir, I need to ask you what your relationship is to inmate Ford," he said politely.

Gunner told the same lie he had told the last time, and it went over just as big.

"I see. I guess it'd be all right to tell you, then."

"Tell me what?" Gunner asked.

The guard shrugged, making a gesture of unmistakable condolence out of it. "Well, that your client's dead," he said. "They just told us he expired over at County about twenty minutes ago."

9

"Hello, Donnell," Gunner said.

Donnell Henderson just looked at him, waiting for the small talk to end. They were sitting alone in a soundproof visitation room, inside the green bungalow Henderson's group of inmates called home. The senior officer in charge of Henderson's unit stood watching their lips move from the hallway outside, through the expansive windows that lined the wall facing him. He hadn't appeared to blink once.

"I want to know what happened to Noah Ford, Donnell," Gunner said, deciding to come right out with it.

"Who?"

"Noah Ford. You heard me the first time."

"I don't know anybody named Noah Ford," Henderson said.

"I think you do."

"Why? Why should I? You think everybody knows everybody in here?"

"No. But I'll tell you what I do think. I think secrets don't last five seconds in a place like this. I think a kid would have to be just as dead as Ford is not to have heard what happened to him by now. And why."

"How'd you know I was here, man? Who told you I was in here?"

"Nobody told me. I was here yesterday, during rec time. I saw you drop a few fly balls out in left field."

"Bullshit. I didn't drop any fly balls," Henderson said.

"That was just a joke, Donnell."

"Yeah? Well, go joke somewhere else, all right? Leave me the fuck alone."

"I'd be glad to. Just as soon as you tell me what I want to know."

"I don't know anything, man. I told you."

"Yeah, you told me. Trouble is, you don't lie any better now than you did when we first met."

"I'm not lyin', Mr. Gunner."

"Bullshit, Donnell."

Gunner slid back in his chair, stretching his legs out in front of him to show the kid he was ready to spend the rest of the day here, if that was how long Henderson wanted to fool around.

Henderson stared at him, gradually getting the message.

"Somebody shanked 'im, all right? He got *shanked*."

"Shanked? With what?"

"With a fork, man. At breakfast. What else?"

"You mean a plastic fork?"

"That's right. Plastic. That's all they give us in here, plastic." He shrugged. "But that doesn't stop some homeboys from usin' the shit, anyway. All you have to do is put a knife or a fork in a cat's throat, and . . ." He shrugged again. "You know. Like that."

"That what happened to Ford?"

"Yeah." He nodded.

"They know who did it?"

"Shit. I told you, man. Homeboy was whacked at breakfast. Of course they know who did it. Their senior was standin' right there, right?"

"So? Who did it? What's the kid's name?"

"I don't know his name."

"Say what?"

"I'm tellin' you. I didn't know him. Homeboy was new, and we were in different units."

"And you don't know his name."

"No. All I know is what they called him. You know. His slob."

"His *slob*?"

"Yeah. His slob. His set name."

"All right. So what was that?"

"Pebbles. Like on the Flintstones."

Gunner took his notebook out and wrote the name down, though he knew the chances of his forgetting it any time soon were nil.

"Okay. Let's talk about motive, now."

"Motive?"

"That's what I said, yes. Motive. This Pebbles character—he must have had some kind of reason for doing Ford, right?"

Henderson shrugged again. "I don't know anything about homeboy's motive," he said. "And nobody else does, either. He just did it, seems like."

"Excuse me?"

"That's right. He just did it. Least, that's what all the homeboys in his unit've been sayin'. They all thought him and Ford clicked up."

"It couldn't have been something gang related? A Blood versus a Crip, something like that?"

"Could've been. Yeah. 'Cept they don't mix gangs up like that in here. They put the Crips in one unit, and the Bloods in another. You know—separate. They'd be crazy if they didn't."

"But they still have to mix 'bangers from different sets within the same gang, right? Like the Wall Streeters and the Tees?"

The Wall Streeters and the Little Tees were both South-Central Blood sets, but they were known to be mortal enemies, just the same.

"Sometimes they have to do that, yeah," Henderson said.

"So maybe that was the problem. Between this Pebbles and Ford."

Henderson shrugged yet again. "I guess. 'Cept Ford, he was just a buster. He hadn't been jumped in with any set yet."

"You mean he was a wannabe."

Henderson nodded. "Yeah. That's what I said."

"Then you did know him."

Henderson shrugged. "A little."

"You ever hear him talk about robbing a liquor store late last year? Over on Vernon and Third Avenue?"

The teenager shrugged again. "I never heard *him* talkin' about it, but I heard some other people talkin' about it. So what?"

"So I need to know who he was with that night. How many kids were involved?"

"I don't know that."

"Was it him and just one other homie, or did he have more help than that? Come on, Donnell. Help me out here."

"I told you, man. I don't know who homeboy was with. I never heard anything about that." He seemed to get a sudden thought. "So what was he to you, anyway? I thought you said you didn't like homeboys who bang."

"I was working for his lawyer," Gunner said, getting all the mileage out of one lie that he possibly could.

"Like you were working for Toby's the last time, huh?"

"That's right. Like that." Gunner was looking at the kid's prison garb disapprovingly, trying to make a point. "You and Toby still hang together, it looks like."

Henderson shook his head. "Not anymore," he said.

"No? Why's that?"

Henderson just looked at him.

"Don't tell me the Blues jumped you out, or something."

"Fuck no. Shit."

"Then what happened? Why don't you and Toby kick it together anymore?"

" 'Cause the motherfucker's *dead,* man. Understand? I don't see 'im around anymore, 'cause the 'Nineties popped a cap on 'im. Him an' Cat both, last Christmas."

Gunner didn't know what to say. He hadn't known either kid well enough to be grief-stricken—in fact, he hadn't cared for either one of them at all—but Toby Mills would have only this year entered his twenties, and LeRon "Cat" Rucker couldn't have been more than seventeen.

Just babies.

"I'm sorry to hear that, Donnell," Gunner said. "Really."

"Yeah. I bet."

Gunner let the teenager stare at him in silence until it got to be too much, then rose to his feet. "Look. If there's anything I can

do for you"—he gave Henderson one of his business cards—
"give me a call. I owe you one, all right?"

Henderson rolled the card around in his hands idly, then
nodded his head. "Thanks."

For a moment, the thought of making an impassioned speech
about reform actually passed through Gunner's mind. Unlike so
many of his homeboys, Henderson had always seemed to be
worth the effort. But in the end, Gunner's pride was too fragile to
take such a risk. If the kid just brushed him off, as he had in the
past, the investigator would feel like an idiot, like a fool who'd
tried to stop an avalanche with a snowplow. Besides, Gunner
reasoned—considering where their conversation had just taken
place—it was probably too late for the kid now, anyway.

"Take care of yourself, Donnell," Gunner said. Then he
turned tail and got the hell out of there.

Mickey had to call him three times, but he finally got Gunner to
stop and turn around before barging through the curtains leading
to his office out back.

"You've got a visitor," his landlord warned him, using a comb
to gesture toward the rear of the shop. The little black boy in the
chair before him waited wordlessly, the torture of his haircut
almost at an end.

"Who is it?" Gunner asked irritably.

"Never seen him before. But he says his name is 'Marvin X
Rush.' Can you dig that? 'Marvin X.' "

He broke out laughing.

Nothing but the name was amusing to Gunner. He was in no
mood for visitors. The curious timing of Noah Ford's death had
added an unwelcome twist to a case he had already decided would
be impossible to solve, and if he needed anything at all right now,
it was time to think. Not talk bean pies with every neighborhood
Muslim who had an armload of the things to sell.

"Mr. Gunner. My name is Marvin X Rush. I hope I haven't
come at a bad time."

He stood up from Gunner's threadbare couch and stuck out
his hand. Gunner's guess was he was in his early twenties, of

medium height and slightly built. He was bespectacled and clean-shaven; handsome, but ordinarily so. And of course, he couldn't have been more wholesome looking if the brothers at his local mosque had just run him through a car wash.

The good news was, he was dressed casually, not in the suit and tie Black Muslims generally conducted Allah's business in.

Gunner shook his hand, eyeing him warily. "Would it do me any good to say you have?"

Rush just smiled, uninsulted. "Of course. I didn't mean to intrude." He started gathering up a stack of papers he had left on the couch behind him, preparing to leave. "I'll come back some other time."

"Forget it. You're here now, and so am I, right? Have a seat, Brother X. Make yourself at home."

Gunner went over to the chair behind his desk and took his own advice. "Can I get you anything? Coffee, tea? A naked white man on a spit?"

Rush smiled again, determined to be civil. Gunner figured he had to be a graduate of the Never-Let-Them-See-You-Sweat school of salesmanship.

"No, thank you" was all he said.

"All right. So to what do I owe the pleasure? You in the market for a private investigator?"

"No. But my business here does relate to your employment in that area."

"Is that right."

"Yes, sir. You see, I am the head of a community services group known as STIFLE, which of course is an acronym for 'Stop The Insanity of Fascist Law Enforcement.' As the name implies, we are a coalition of neighborhood brothers and sisters who have come together to stop the Los Angeles Police Department's abusive and inhumane treatment of the people in this community. Perhaps you've heard of us."

Gunner looked at him blankly. "Can't say that I have."

Rush seemed disappointed. "I see. Well, in the coming months, you won't be able to open a newspaper or turn on the television without hearing our name. That I can promise you. We have a number of fund-raising functions planned that will bring our message to the people, big time."

"Great. I'll be sure to check the newspaper for dates and times."

Rush caught the shallowness in Gunner's voice and stopped, his enthusiasm for the future suddenly dimmed. "You don't mean that, of course," he said. "But that's all right. It doesn't matter. I didn't come here to invite you to one of our rallies, anyway." He stood up and walked over to Gunner's desk, dropping the stack of papers he'd brought along with him in front of the investigator like a lead weight. "I came here to show you this."

Gunner merely glanced at the facing page. It was a statistical printout of some kind, entitled "POLICE MISCONDUCT LAW-YER REFERRAL SERVICE, OVERVIEW."

"Do me a favor," Gunner said, "and pretend I don't know what this is, or what the hell it has to do with me. Because I don't. On both counts."

"That is statistical data outlining the severity of our problem, Mr. Gunner. It's an overview of all the complaints our legal office has received against officers of both the LAPD and the LA County Sheriff's Department in the last six months. Complaints of physical assault, racial and sexual harassment, false imprisonment, illegal search and seizure, and a host of other misconduct charges too numerous to mention. If you'd look at the top line, there, I believe you'd see that the total number of complaints recorded is two thousand four hundred and sixty-five.

"I brought this material to you today because I think you need to see it. If my information about the work you've been doing this past week is correct."

"Information? About me?"

"Yes, sir. About you, and the case you're supposed to be working on behalf of a former police officer named Jack McGovern."

Finally, Gunner understood.

Trying to keep a cool head, he said, "Look. It's none of your business, but I'm going to tell you this, anyway. I'm not working for Jack McGovern. Jack McGovern is dead."

"I know who you're working for, Mr. Gunner. Not by name, of course, but I know roughly who he is, and what he's hired you to do. He's hired you to sabotage the legal suit Harriet Washington's filed against the police on behalf of her son, Lendell."

"I don't do 'sabotage' work for anybody, Brother X. But that's something else that's none of your business."

"The perpetuation of the racist and violent police state presently terrorizing this community is everybody's business, Mr. Gunner. Including yours."

"No shit."

"Jack McGovern murdered Lendell Washington. In cold blood. To suggest otherwise is ludicrous."

"So I'm ludicrous. Is that a crime?"

"We're talking about one of the most sadistic white men to ever wear the uniform, Mr. Gunner. Did you know that?"

"I know all about the man's history," Gunner said.

"Then how do you explain what you're doing?"

"I don't have to explain it. I'm an American. Keeping my reasons for doing the things I do to myself is my God-given birthright."

"Meaning, you don't hold yourself accountable. Is that it?"

"Accountable to who? You?"

"Accountable to your people, Mr. Gunner. To your brothers and sisters out there waging war against the devil in your name."

He had spoken from the heart; his faith in the words lit a fire behind his eyes Gunner had not seen until now.

"I wage my own wars, Brother X," Gunner said, getting to his feet. "But thanks for dropping by anyway, huh?"

"You're selling out, brother."

"Call it whatever you like. Just do it somewhere else. Please."

It was the *please* that did it. Marvin X Rush heard the emphasis his host had placed on the word and immediately understood he was treading on dangerous ground.

He was through the door and out on the street before Gunner could even offer him his literature back.

10

The first thing Monday morning, Gunner made a phone call from home.

"Wiley Legal Services," a diffident female voice said.

"I'd like to speak to Mr. Wiley, please."

"May I ask who's calling?"

"Aaron Gunner."

"Erin Gunnert?"

Gunner repeated his name, spelling it once for her. She put him on hold and gave him some substandard soul music to listen to while she was away.

"I'm sorry, Mr. Gunnert, but Mr. Wiley's in conference right now and cannot be disturbed. Can I take a message for him?"

"Yeah. You can. Tell him I'll be up to see him in fifteen minutes. And if his conference isn't over by then, or he's suddenly gone to lunch, he's going to be needing some new furniture in the receptionist's area. You got all that?"

She said she did, but he doubted it very seriously.

Milton Wiley's law office was on the fourth floor of a hard-luck medical building on Crenshaw Boulevard in Hawthorne, just two blocks north of Rosecrans. The building had one working elevator out of a possible two and a ground-floor pharmacy swarming with wailing children. By the time Gunner reached the door to suite 404, he was ready to wring Wiley's neck.

The heavy-set black woman behind the receptionist's window

rang Wiley's office with comical efficiency as soon as Gunner gave her his name. She was still calling him Mr. "Gunnert."

"He says you can go right in," she said dryly, pointing to a door leading out of the waiting room to Gunner's right.

Gunner had the door open in his hand when a voice behind him said, "Whoa, there, brother! Hold on a minute!"

He turned around to see a broad-chested young black man get up from his chair in the waiting room and move toward him, tossing a dog-eared magazine casually aside with no regard for where it landed. He had an inch or two on Gunner in height, and close to thirty pounds in weight, and he looked like the kind of character who knew how to use it all in a fight.

"My appointment was for eight o'clock. It's nine o'clock now. What time was your appointment for?"

He was smiling pleasantly, but he was doing it from right up in Gunner's face.

"Seven-thirty," Gunner said.

"That would mean they're an hour and a half behind."

Gunner shrugged. "I guess so." He started through the door again, but the big man slid gently to one side, blocking his way.

"I think you missed your chance, man," he said, no longer smiling. "I think if you had a seven-thirty appointment to see Mr. Wiley, you should have been here at seven-thirty. Just like I've been here since eight. Fair is fair, right?"

He looked over at the receptionist behind the window to suggest that she second the motion.

"Mr. Gunnert has an emergency, Mr. Foster," she said, her voice filled with trepidation.

"Shit. Not yet, he doesn't," Foster said, yanking the door out of Gunner's hand.

"Trudy's right, Howie. Mr. Gunner's case is an emergency," Milton Wiley said, suddenly appearing in the doorway. He waited for Foster to release the door, then held it open for Gunner to pass through. "We're running quite a bit behind this morning, and we were unable to get to him earlier. Please forgive the inconvenience, will you?"

Foster didn't look like he wanted to forgive anything, but he let Gunner go without trying to stop him. Gunner could feel the heat of his gaze on his back long after Wiley had closed the door behind them.

The lawyer led the way to his office without speaking. He took a seat behind his desk and waited for Gunner to choose one for himself, neglecting to choose one for him.

"He was right, you know," Wiley said, infuriated. "You had no right to barge in on me like this. It's not fair to my clients."

"I didn't barge in. I called ahead," Gunner said, settling onto a burgundy leather couch against the wall at Wiley's left.

"That's right. With a threat. I didn't appreciate that, either."

"Funny you should say that, Mr. Wiley. Because there are a few things I don't appreciate myself. Such as having my business spread all over the street, like leaflets at a goddamn carnival."

"Excuse me?"

"I'm talking about your boy Marvin X. Mr. STIFLE. He came to see me Saturday to tell me how disappointed he was to hear I've been working the Jack McGovern case. I'm a disgrace to my race, he said."

"I don't understand."

"The hell you don't. You turned him onto me. You're the only one who could have."

Wiley fell silent for a moment, considering his alternatives. "I thought his organization might like to know what you've been doing," he said indifferently.

"I'll tell you what you thought. You thought he'd do exactly what he did. Lay a shitload of crap on me about police brutality, and then infer I'm a Tom for ignoring it."

"And you don't think you are, is that right? Take a look around you, Mr. Gunner. What Marvin had to say about police brutality is very real. People who are your neighbors are being maimed by the police in this city every day."

"I'm well aware of that, counselor."

"Then how can you continue to pursue the case you're presently engaged in? How can you sleep at night knowing that the man you're trying to vindicate was one of the most onerous examples of racist law enforcement this community has ever known?"

"Easy. I just tell myself he was innocent. Not of being a colossal bigot—but of murdering Lendell Washington. That's my only concern in this matter, Mr. Wiley. The rest I don't give a damn about."

"No. Obviously, you don't," Wiley said.

"Look. Let's you and I get something straight, all right? I don't need you, or Brother Rush, or any of your mutual friends at STIFLE, to tell me what kind of law enforcement the black community's been getting around here lately. I've seen more than my share of prone-outs and outright ass-kickings, just like you have. But my turning down the McGovern case isn't going to solve the problem any more than my accepting it will make it any worse. Besides—and I've told you this before—I'm not working for McGovern. My client's interests and McGovern's just appear to coincide in this case, that's all."

"And appearances can be deceiving, I guess."

"That's right. They can. Take you, for example."

"Me?"

"When I met you last Thursday, you appeared to have nothing but contempt for Lendell's cousin, Noah Ford. You said he was a devil. Nobody to trust for the truth."

Wiley was slow to shrug. "So?"

"So he was your client. Wasn't he?"

After another pause: "I represented him, yes. What's wrong with that?"

"Nothing. Except that you did your damndest to keep me from talking to him, and a day after I did, he wound up dead."

Wiley leapt forward in his chair, enraged. "If you're trying to imply I had anything to do with that—"

"Somebody sure as hell did. I'm not that big a believer in coincidence."

"But it *was* a coincidence. Noah's murder was a gang hit, Mr. Gunner. Nothing more, and nothing less."

"Is that what they told you down at Central?"

"Yes. They told me the boy who did Noah was auditioning,

trying to get jumped into a Blood set known as the H-Town Gamblers. Apparently, Noah'd had a run-in once with a Gambler on the outside, and a Gambler on the inside happened to remember it. So when the boy asked them who he could do to prove himself—"

"They picked Noah."

"Yes."

"And you believe that?"

"Of course I believe it. Why shouldn't I?"

Gunner had no answer for that. "Have you talked to the kid yourself?" he asked instead.

"No. Have you?"

"No."

"I see. I guess you could only tell those idiots the bald-faced lie that you were working for me so many times before they'd finally catch on."

"Speaking of bald-faced lies: Why didn't you tell me you were Noah's attorney in the first place, Mr. Wiley? Did you think I might wonder what kind of legal counsel he was getting, retaining the same lawyer as Harriet Washington?"

"I was afraid you might wonder about that, yes. And then jump to all the wrong conclusions afterward."

"Such as how it may have been more profitable to you in the long run to advise Ford with Mrs. Washington's best interests in mind, rather than his own."

Wiley cleared his throat and straightened up in his chair. "Yes. But that wasn't the case, I assure you."

"Of course it wasn't. Never mind that the kid started out blaming the robbery on Lendell, then did an abrupt about-face and took the blame for everything. Everything but holding the gun, that is."

"I would have been insane to suggest he plead any other way," Wiley said. "Thanks to me, the boy only got six months, when he could have very easily gotten three years."

"I think what's more important is that his cousin got a relatively unblemished reputation out of the deal," Gunner said. "One

123

that makes him a much easier sell as a martyr today than he would have been otherwise."

"That's ridiculous!"

"Is it?"

"And if it leaves this room, I'll prove it slanderous. Do you understand?"

"I think so. You're trying to say you'll sue the pants off me."

"That's exactly what I'm saying!"

"You don't think that's a rather predictable threat to make, coming from a shyster such as yourself?"

"I think this discussion is over, Mr. Gunner. That's what I think."

And sure enough, it was.

Gunner pulled one more doughnut from the box in his lap and washed half of it down with the last of a cold cup of coffee.

He was parked across the street from Davey's Market, a nondescript little liquor and grocery store on Avalon Boulevard in Watts, just around the corner from his home on Stanford Avenue. The store got its name from a middle-aged Korean man named David Huong, who along with his wife, Lucy, had been doing business in the predominately black neighborhood for well over twenty years. Back when the Huongs were just starting out, Gunner had been just another basket case of an army vet fresh off the boat from Vietnam, sporadically broke and as lost in his own hometown as any perfect stranger could have been, yet the Korean couple had sustained him on credit when no one else would. Gunner had never quite understood the kindness, but he had been devoted to the Huongs, both as a regular customer and casual friend, ever since.

Twelve months ago, when fire and rage and runaway greed had devoured the streets of South-Central Los Angeles like a tidal wave, the Huongs had watched most of their neighbors on the block lose everything to looters and arsonists, scavengers who had left Davey's Market standing today like a smoke-blackened bunker in the middle of a war-torn battlefield. The Huongs owed their survival of the purge to Gunner and a small army of his friends, men and women who, having realized early on that the Korean-owned market would be a choice target of the mob engulfing the city, had been there to watch over and defend it. It was an act of friendship that had enraged many of Gunner's neighbors, but he had been prepared for that. He was all too familiar with the anti-Korean sentiment that was prevalent among his people, and was no stranger to its causes. He had seen his share of other Korean shopkeepers like David and Lucy Huong conduct business in the black community, and he knew well how openly they held their black customers in contempt. No *thank yous* or *you're welcomes,* no *hellos* or *how are yous.* With these people, it was always just a silent *Give me the money and get the fuck out of my store,* or sentiments to that effect.

But the Huongs were different. Perhaps their English was just as indecipherable at times, and their sense of humor nearly as nonexistent, but they were not of the same school as their less sensitive brethren. They were fair, cordial, and respectful of their customers, and they deserved to be treated as such.

That was why Gunner was here today.

For while getting through the riots of a year ago relatively unscathed was fine, it did not bring an end to all of the Huongs' troubles. Just as there had been before the previous July, there were still members of the black community today who were annoyed by the Korean pair's presence in it, and who liked to demonstrate that annoyance by disfiguring their store's exterior with graffiti, breaking their windows and doors, and just generally stealing them blind. All of this the Huongs had learned to live with, but lately the terrorism they were routinely subjected to had taken on a new dimension, one that, in the last month, had come to their door at least once or twice a week, in the deceptively disarming form of three small boys. They were all about the same age, David Huong had told Gunner—no more than six or seven, maybe eight—and they always came in together, like a tiny swarm of angry bees. Pushing over racks of potato chips, smashing display cases, tossing canned vegetables at the walls—they were only in the action for destruction, pure and simple, and they were as good at disappearing as they were at showing up from out of nowhere. Their timing wasn't bad, either, as the police had yet to catch a minute of their act in progress.

So Gunner had offered to try and catch it, himself, in his spare time.

Sitting in his car eating stale doughnuts and drinking cold coffee as he watched people drift in and out of the market like Chevys on a slow-moving assembly line, Gunner paid homage to the money Mitchell Flowers was paying him to do something else entirely by devoting some serious thought to the murder of Noah Ford, and its place in the McGovern case. The explanation Milton Wiley and Donnell Henderson had given for Ford's death had sounded feasible enough; kids outside the walls of Central Juvenile Hall were killed under similar circumstances every day. But the timing of Ford's murder seemed to suggest that it had been more than just a cruel twist of fate, that perhaps there had been more hands involved in it than just those of an overanxious buster named Pebbles.

Assuming that was true, it followed that Ford had been killed to ensure his silence. But his silence in what regard? What could Ford have known that would have made him such a threat to someone? That he'd given the gun he'd brandished in the liquor store to Lendell Washington before they split up? Or that Washington had been carrying a gun of his own that night? Perhaps. In either case, if he had chosen to admit as much to Gunner or the police, Ford would have been placing the gun in Washington's hand that McGovern had claimed all along he had. Something Milton Wiley, for one, would no doubt have preferred he not do.

On the other hand . . .

Maybe what Ford knew better than anyone else was that Washington had in fact never touched a gun that night—but someone else, besides Ford himself, had. The unknown third accomplice or overreactive drug merchant Gunner had mused about earlier. Either someone Ford had known about from the very beginning, and had been protecting all along, or someone he had only learned about recently, well after the fact. Someone, in any case, who had decided Ford's ability to keep a secret could no longer be relied upon.

Despite the fact that Gunner had just come from a brief canvassing of the homes on either side of the alley where Washington had died, where everyone he had spoken to had claimed that the alley had seemed to be empty before the Washington shooting took place, he was finding the idea of a second party being with Washington just before he died more and more appealing. Because such a theory explained a great deal, starting with how Jack McGovern could have been fired upon out in the street when the only gun Washington ever touched had allegedly been held with a hand he rarely used, and then only to fire two harmless and meaningless rounds into the alley floor at his feet. A second party in the alley also seemed to explain where the missing part of the liquor store money McGovern had been accused of stealing might have actually disappeared to.

Of course, there was one other scenario that answered these questions just as neatly as Gunner's second-party theme, and that was the one that had the LAPD, in the persons of Danny Kubo and Dick Jenner, manipulating the physical evidence at the scene to ensure McGovern's downfall, just as Mitchell Flowers continued to insist they had. Gunner still viewed this theory with some skepticism, yet he knew it was the only one that seemed to fly if Washington—or *someone*—had indeed fired two shots in McGovern's direction while the patrolman was still standing in the middle of Van Ness Avenue. Because somebody should have found at least one of two slugs somewhere outside of the alley if things had really gone down that way—and nobody ever did.

Or, more to the point, nobody ever *reported* having found one.

For over an hour, Gunner vacillated between these two major propositions, police conspiracy or unknown second party, embracing one and then the other, unable to find complete satisfaction in either. And then he faced up to an ugly truth, the very same one he had tried in vain to impress upon Mitchell Flowers two days ago: No matter how Lendell Washington had died, Gunner was going to have to produce a weapon to prove it. And if a) the kid (or some unseen friend) had really had one; b) Gunner's client really wasn't going blind or losing his mind; and c) Gunner hadn't spent the last six days spinning his wheels on a worthless case like a goddamn hamster on a treadmill—then it had to be out there somewhere. In the alley, or in someone's backyard. It sure as hell hadn't just *walked* away.

Or had it?

Gunner suddenly pulled himself erect in the Cobra's driver seat.

He was watching a pair of derelicts rummage through the dumpster behind Davey's Market, looking for scraps of food and clothing. It was a man and a woman—a couple, from the looks of it—and they were finding the pickings pretty thin.

Just as the man they reminded Gunner of had, only three days before.

"Mr. Gunner. This is Deanna Lugo." The station house was a wall of ribald racket behind her. "I just got the message you called."

It was a little after three in the afternoon; Gunner had been waiting since the lunch hour to hear from her.

"Officer Lugo. I have a question for you."

"So soon?"

"It's regarding the guy we saw rooting through the garbage cans last Friday afternoon. The guy in the alley, wearing the tuxedo. Remember?"

"Dancing Fred. Yeah, I remember."

"You know him?"

"Dancing Fred? Sure. Fred's a Southwest landmark, everybody knows him. Why? What's up?"

"I need to know if he was anywhere on the scene the night Lendell Washington was killed. Do you remember seeing him there, at all?"

There was a short silence as Lugo thought about it. "I don't think so. *I* don't recall seeing him there, anyway. Why? You need to find him?"

"Yeah. I think I do."

"No problem. I can think of a couple of places he might be."

She paused. "You want to look for him alone, or would you mind a little company?"

Gunner didn't say anything.

"You want to go alone."

He started to say yes, until he thought about the last phone message he'd received from Claudia Lovejoy, and the Dear John speech she had hit him with before that.

You're free to do whatever you like, she had told him then.

"No. I think I'd enjoy a little company, for a change," Gunner said.

They agreed to meet at the station house in an hour.

Gunner was parked in the loading zone out in front of the building, watching uniformed patrolmen and plainclothes detectives file in and out, like ants in an ant farm. Every now and then, somebody would tell him to move, until he explained he was waiting for Lugo and they let him alone, taking him at his word. He had been there about fifteen minutes when a white man in a brown Christian Dior suit came down the steps and stopped, to smoke a cigarette and stare at him from the sidewalk. He had a ruddy face, a wire-brush mustache, and hair with more oil in it than a small-block V-8, but if, like the others, he wanted Gunner to move, he never said so.

All he did was stare.

When his cigarette was spent, he flipped the butt into the air like a punk in a bad bikers movie and walked away.

Deanna Lugo emerged from the building just in time to see him round the corner and disappear. She was dressed in a heavy blue cardigan sweater, a white, jewel-necked T-shirt, and pleated denim pants, and Gunner couldn't have regretted his decision to bring her along less.

"Who's laughing boy?" Gunner asked her as she stepped into the car, nodding in the direction of the corner.

"You'll never guess," Lugo said, using a smile to disguise her obvious distaste for the man. "That's Maggie's pal from IAD. Dick Jenner."

* * *

Dancing Fred's real name was Harold J. Fenton, Jr., and he had once been a TV repairman.

The way Lugo told the story, his shop used to be on the corner of Jefferson and Third Avenue, as recently as seven years ago. He was a tech school graduate who had built a good little business for himself by being fair to his customers and fast at his work, until the technology of television electronics and the growth of the home video industry started changing faster than he could keep up, and the repeat business he had always counted on for his survival gradually went away. He had had no secondary vocation to fall back on, and no family to turn to for help, so the rest of the house of cards that was his life came down around him in a matter of months. Some people could make the transition between self-reliant businessman and minimum-wage worker rather easily, Lugo said, but some people never could. Harold Fenton was one of the many who could not.

He had been bouncing from city shelter to city shelter, street corner to street corner, ever since, his mind slipping a little further off center with each passing day. At some point, he had picked up the tuxedo he always wore now—no one had ever found out where—and it was then that he became known by all his friends and acquaintances as Dancing Fred, after the late Fred Astaire.

"I've never had to bust him," Lugo said, "but I've had to move him on his way a couple of times. That's the only reason I know him."

She and Gunner had been driving around now for a little less than an hour, trying to track the homeless man down, but they both felt like it had been longer than that. It was a depressing business, touring the haunts and hangouts of the city's dispossessed, especially in the light of a fast-closing day. In alleys and old warehouses, along railroad ties and freeway off-ramps, Dancing Fred's comrades clustered against the cold, trying to eke some dignity out of a beggar's existence. White men in lifeless tweed sport jackets and soleless brown shoes; black women swathed in shawls and blankets three layers deep; children wearing clothing others had given up for rags—all of them made for a slow parade to nowhere that was difficult to take in.

"We'll try just one more place," Lugo said.

Gunner didn't argue with her.

She had him drive to a gas station on Vernon at Normandie, a large, four-island Shell affair with a brightly lit minimarket at its center, and that was where they finally found him. He was standing on one of the islands between two pumps, a spray bottle of watered-down glass cleaner and a roll of paper towels in his hands, asking everyone who passed him if he could pump their gas or clean their windows for whatever loose change they could spare.

It was a common enterprise of the homeless, Gunner knew— and if he were lucky, one that might earn Dancing Fred a dollar and fifty cents before midnight.

Gunner pulled the Cobra into the lot and along the left side of the island where Dancing Fred stood. Neither he nor Lugo had a chance to get out of the car before the bristle-faced man went into his routine.

"Hey, brother. Lemme get those windows for you!"

He was already leaning over the Cobra's windshield, his spray bottle at the ready.

"Later, Fred. We'd like to talk to you, first," Lugo said, smiling. She still didn't get out of the car.

Fred looked at her through the windshield, frowning. "Who . . . ?" He straightened up suddenly, recognizing her. "You're out of uniform! You're out of uniform!"

He was pointing the roll of paper towels at her, making a scene. Several people drifted over from one of the other islands to get a better look at what was going on.

"Take it easy, Fred," Lugo said, stepping out of the Cobra gingerly. Gunner was already moving around the front of the car toward him.

"I have permission to be here!" Dancing Fred cried, stepping backward off the island. "Just ask the manager! Go ask the manager!"

"We don't need to do that. You don't have to leave if you don't want to," Lugo assured him, continuing to close upon him.

"We just want to ask you a few questions, partner. That's all," Gunner said.

"What kind of questions?"

"We're looking for something. And we thought you might be able to help us find it," Lugo said.

The man in the tuxedo seemed to relax a little. "Find what?"

Gunner glanced at Lugo and dipped his head, motioning toward the handful of people who were now standing around them, watching and listening to every word of their conversation.

Lugo nodded slightly and said to Fred, "Let us buy you dinner, and we'll tell you."

Dancing Fred fell silent, mulling the offer over. "What kind of dinner? Can we go to McDonald's? Or Popeye's?"

"We can go anywhere you want," Gunner told him.

After another moment's hesitation, Fred nodded agreeably and said, "Popeye's."

Which was the signal for everyone watching to return to his or her own business, their curiosity unrewarded by bloodshed.

Out in the parking lot of the Popeye's Fried Chicken stand on Western Avenue, just north of Martin Luther King, Jr., Boulevard, under a quarter moon which seemed to have the black night sky all to itself, Dancing Fred cleaned the meat off ten spicy-flavored chicken wings and told them about the gun.

It had all happened eight months ago, but apparently Fred's memory was the one thing he had managed to salvage intact from his past life as a sane man. He knew too many details to be faking it. He said he had indeed found the gun in a garbage can out in the alley where Lendell Washington had been killed, only moments after the kid's shooting and before the area had been secured, but he remembered the can being closer to the Gramercy Place end of the alley than the Van Ness Avenue end, which would have placed it more than fifteen yards away from where Washington's body had been found. It was a revolver, he said, though Gunner had had to describe the difference between a revolver and an automatic for him before he had been able to make that distinction.

And he claimed to still have the gun in his possession.

"A man's gotta have some protection," he said, justifying his decision not to sell the weapon off. " 'Cause it's a cold world out there. A cold world. Just gettin' over, man, that's all a man can do, and you can die tryin' just to do that. Hear what I'm sayin'?" He stared directly into Gunner's face, like a dirty mirror he was trying to see his reflection in. "You can die tryin'."

He nibbled on a chicken bone a while, then said, "So a man, he's gotta have some protection." He was nodding his head at his own wisdom, oblivious to the fact that he was repeating himself. "Somebody said so just the other day, he said, 'Fred, women don't even wanna talk to you no more, you ain't got some kind of protection.' "

The gun was in his cart, Fred said. Over at the camp.

The "camp" turned out to be the open carport of a run-down apartment building over on the fifteen-hundred block of Forty-eighth Street, where a dozen or so homeless people like Fred had gathered for an extended stay. They were huddled in the shadows at the back of the carport, nearly invisible from the street; duffle bags and suitcases, shopping carts and trash bags filled with recyclable bottles and aluminum cans were in evidence all around them.

Gunner didn't see the little man rooting through one of the shopping carts until Dancing Fred—who had been sitting up on the forward edge of the Cobra's trunk lid, above and immediately behind the car's two seats—bounded out of the car and started running.

"What are you doing? *What are you doing?*"

The thief at the cart turned around just as Dancing Fred reached him, a shiny-skinned revolver in his right hand.

"Get away from me, man," the little guy said, annoyed.

Gunner got there in time to make sure Fred followed the order, reaching out with both hands to grab him at the shoulders and pull him back a few steps. Lugo joined them soon after, hovering at Gunner's right elbow.

133

"That's mine, Sulley!" Dancing Fred said, pointing at the gun aimed at him frantically. "That's my protection!"

"You don't want it. You left it here," Sulley argued. The group of people sitting in the oil and grease stains off to his right started inching slowly away from him, mumbling excitedly under their breath.

"Look. I'm a cop," Lugo said, showing Sulley her badge. "Put the gun down and we'll discuss this, all right?"

"He didn't want it," Sulley insisted, still pointing the gun at Fred. He looked to be far beyond the edge of reason.

"That's not true! He's lying! He's lying!" Fred screamed.

"I know how to use it. You don't," Sulley said. "Wanna see?"

He pointed the gun at Gunner's chest and fired.

A white flame lit up the carport as Sulley smiled proudly, his point made.

11

Gunner had always wondered what it would feel like to die.

To have the last booming echo of a gunshot ring in his ears and then slowly fade away; to feel his heart slam to a stop and remain still, never to recover; to see the same mask of horror on all the faces around him, frozen in time like some macabre still photograph.

And now Gunner knew.

The only thing surprising about the experience, as it turned out, was that he was going to live to tell about it.

He had been clutching at a chest wound that wasn't there when the muzzle flash from Dancing Fred's gun completely dissolved into darkness. Lugo beat Fred at snatching the revolver from Sulley's grasp, then moved to see for herself why Gunner was still standing. When they were satisfied he was okay, they looked at each other and silently reached the same conclusion, though they waited for a ballistics man down at Southwest to verify the theory before they accepted it as fact.

"They were blanks, all right," Lugo said. "And the gun was a dummy. Incapable of firing live rounds." She had just returned from using the pay phone at the restaurant where she and Gunner had retreated until the lab tests came back on the gun. Dancing Fred's buddy Sulley was in lockup, awaiting an evidently overdue psychiatric evaluation, and Dancing Fred himself was back at the "camp," where he had promised to sleep every night until further notice, in case Lugo or Gunner needed to find him again.

They had killed just short of an hour here when the police officer's beeper had gone off.

Gunner watched her slip back into her side of the booth and said, "Well, that certainly explains a few things. Doesn't it?"

"Such as why we never found any slugs or trace marks in the alley?"

"Yes."

"We don't know that this gun has anything to do with Washington's shooting yet."

"Technically speaking, no. We don't. But I think we'd both bet our right arm that it does. Wouldn't we?"

Lugo just looked at him over the rim of her coffee cup and said nothing.

"Or don't you want to believe your partner might have been innocent?" Gunner asked.

"I just don't want to get my hopes up. That's all." She was glaring at him. "I mean, let's face it: All this really does is leave us with a whole new set of unanswered questions."

"Like why someone would want to use a dummy gun in a liquor store holdup."

"Yes. Like that."

"Okay. So why would they, Officer Lugo?"

"Actually, that question's easy to answer. Because they probably didn't know that's what they had. They thought the gun and the rounds were the genuine article."

Gunner nodded. "That's one way of looking at it. At least, it would seem to explain why they'd stop to fire the damn thing twice at McGovern when they could have just as easily kept running."

"And the other way of looking at it?"

"Maybe a dummy gun loaded with blanks was the only kind a soft touch like Washington would agree to carry. Maybe he brought it along just for show, and only used it when he had no other choice, hoping it would be enough to hold McGovern off for a while."

Lugo fell silent for a moment, not sure if she wanted to buy that one or not. "Okay."

"Next question: How did the gun get as far away from Washington's body as Fred says it did. Right?"

"Right. Fred said the can he found the gun in was at the far end of the alley, near Gramercy. And that would have put it what—at least four houses away from where Washington went down?" She shook her head. "It doesn't figure. To get it that far, Washington would've had to throw it—and he shouldn't have been in any kind of shape for that. Should he?"

Gunner gave some thought to suggesting that someone other than Washington might have disposed of the weapon—his "Unknown Second Party in the Alley" theory again—but he decided against it, fearful that Lugo was already reluctant enough to follow his convoluted reasoning.

"Maybe Fred was just confused about where the gun really was. In which can, and where," he said.

"I see. He was confused about that, but not any of the rest of it. Is that what you mean?"

"All right. How about this then? The gun was where he said it was because that was where Washington had actually been hit, before stumbling back into the alley and collapsing where his body was found."

"In which case, he'd have left a trail of blood somewhere."

"You're saying he didn't?"

Lugo hesitated before answering. "Actually, I don't remember if he did or not. There was a lot of blood around, all right, but I never looked to see if any of it actually led somewhere. I mean, why would I? Washington was right there, dead; it wasn't like he was missing."

"Sure." Gunner had made every effort not to sound condescending. "Are we through?"

"Not quite. There's still the question of where a kid like Washington would get a dummy gun full of blanks in the first place," Lugo said. "Blank shells and prop guns aren't available over the counter at your local gun shop, you know. They're restricted merchandise, you have to have a special permit to buy them."

"Like all the film companies have."

"Yes. Exactly."

Gunner was sampling his own coffee when he noticed Lugo was staring off into space.

"You just think of something?"

It was a moment before she nodded. "I think I just answered my own question," she said.

Gunner waited for her to explain.

"Last year, back in May or June, I think, they told us about a weapons theft," she said. "Something about some guns being lifted out of a trailer at a locations site, downtown. You know, where they were shooting some scenes for a TV show or a movie, I don't remember which. A few handguns and one semiautomatic, I think they said. All very real, but all very harmless. Incapable of firing live rounds, just like Dancing Fred's."

"And I take it these guns were never recovered."

"Not that I ever heard about, no. They were little more than just toys, after all, so I don't think a whole lot of effort ever went into finding them, you want to know the truth."

"Then they're probably still out there somewhere."

Lugo shrugged. "I guess so. Yeah."

"Then that solves the problem of accessibility, doesn't it? Washington or Ford could have bought one of these guns on the street without ever knowing what it was."

"Yes."

Gunner waited for their waitress to pour him some more coffee, then said, "How long do you think you can keep a lid on news of the gun? Realistically?"

Lugo shook her head. "I don't know. I can keep things quiet about it for a while, I suppose, but if our friend Jenner starts snooping around again. . . ." She shrugged. "It all depends on how lucky I am."

"In that case, I need the rest of those lab tests back. Fast."

"Yes."

"Because if Washington's prints are on it anywhere . . ."

"We can build a good case that he really was armed that night. Exactly." She didn't sound too thrilled with the prospect. "So I guess there's nothing for us to do now but wait, huh?"

Gunner wasn't sure he liked the way she was throwing the words "us" and "we" around—it suggested they had become a team of some kind—but rather than point this out, he just said, "It looks that way. Yes."

"Something bothering you?"

"Me? No." Gunner shook his head.

"Good. Let's get the hell out of here, then."

She was already moving toward the door.

"I think I'd like to go to bed with you," Gunner said.

He had thought she might broach the subject before now, but they were halfway back to Southwest, and she had made nothing more than small talk.

Lugo slowly turned away from the blur of the street to face him. She could have been smiling, but from out of the corner of his eye, it was difficult to tell. "Well. What a coincidence," she said.

"Then you've thought about it, too."

"In my weakest moments. Yeah. But . . ." She let the thought hang in the air.

"But what?"

"But I'm not so sure about the timing of it. For you, I mean."

Gunner stole a glance at her. "For me?"

"Yeah. For you. I get the feeling you're in a weird place at the moment. Romantically speaking, I mean."

Gunner turned around again, eyeing the road.

"Correct me if I'm wrong," Lugo said.

Gunner shrugged. "It depends on what you mean by 'weird.' If you mean unsettled, then you're probably right."

"Ah. Unsettled." Lugo nodded her head knowingly. "I've been there before."

"Have you?"

"Oh, sure. Many times. It's a lot like walking on razor blades, isn't it?"

She grinned, and Gunner followed.

"Do you love the lady in question? Or is that one of the things you're trying to figure out?"

"I don't know. I know that I want to be with her. Beyond that, who knows? She says I'm just looking for a safe haven, that I'm tired of all the bullshit and just see her as a way to retreat from it for a while. I think there's more to it than that, but . . ." He shrugged again. "I'm not always the best judge of these things."

"But she is, I guess," Lugo said.

"Actually, no. She isn't. She seems to be just as confused about her feelings for me as she is about my feelings for her."

"So she told you to go away for a while. Is that it?"

Gunner just nodded his head.

"I see. So what are the ground rules?"

"Well, that part *is* weird. We don't seem to have any."

He slowed to catch a red light ahead, then stopped the car and turned to look at her, waiting to see what she would say.

"Sounds like you're both free agents," Lugo said simply.

"It does, doesn't it?"

"So what do you want to do about it? Wait around to see what develops, or . . .'"

"Fool around with you?"

She laughed. "I like that. 'Fool around.' It has just the right amount of commitment to it."

"You have a problem with commitment, do you?"

"Not a problem, no. I just don't have any interest in it anymore. Some people would say that makes me promiscuous; I say all it does is make me as open to suggestion as you are." She smiled again, a childlike sparkle in her eye. "And you *are* open to suggestion, aren't you?"

Gunner smiled back at her and said, "Completely."

He didn't miss another signal the rest of the way to Southwest.

She had opened the blinds at her bedroom window to let the moonlight in.

Her body was firm and taut, and utterly without blemish. She was the same rich hue of golden brown from the top of her head to the tip of her toes, except for the bands around her breasts and hips where a bathing suit had shielded her flesh from the sun. She had large-buttoned nipples that grew hard as glass, and chiseled legs she could lock like a vise around him. He could literally see the bands of muscle in her buttocks relax and contract as she moved all about him.

She was as generous and exciting as any woman he had ever been with, and she gave him every chance to be likewise. But Gunner was not up to reciprocating. He was not up to much of anything.

The most that could be said for him was that he was functional.

The worst was that he was lousy.

"That was pretty bad, wasn't it?" Lugo asked.

"You noticed," Gunner said.

Lugo rolled over to his side of the bed, laughing. She didn't bother to pull the sheet up over herself. "Well, I guess you have your answer. Don't you?"

Gunner looked at her, smiling gamely. "Is that what that was? My answer?"

"I think so. You aren't usually—"

"No! Hell, no!"

They both laughed.

When the moment had passed, and they were both riding the gentle waves of Lugo's water bed in silence, Gunner said, "You were supposed to have scars."

"Scars?" Lugo looked over at him blankly, not following his meaning.

"You said anybody who'd ever ridden with McGovern had the scars to prove it, whether they knew it or not. Remember?"

"Oh."

"And I don't recall seeing yours. Unless . . ."

"Unless they're the kind that don't show."

"Yes."

Lugo fell silent for a moment, then said, "Most of the time, that's true. They *don't* show. But sometimes . . ." She let the thought float on the air. "Sometimes they show just fine. Catch me on a bad day out on the street, for instance. You'd see."

"What kind of a bad day?"

She tried to smile, but it wouldn't work. "The kind that makes you want to say, fuck it all," she said. "This miserable existence they call being a cop, I mean. The kind of day where the hate rolls in off the street through the open windows of the car, it's so intense. When it seems like every radio in the world is playing that song the kids love so much: 'Fuck Tha Police.' You know the one?"

Gunner nodded. It was a rap song by the group N.W.A., and you couldn't take five steps in any South-Central neighborhood without hearing somebody singing it, or blasting it on their boom box, or even just mouthing the words.

Fuck the police.

"There are times when the faces all around you make you feel less than human," Lugo went on. "When the wisecracks and the taunts cut down to the bone and then slice right through even that. When all you're doing is trying to keep a crowd back behind a strip of yellow tape, and they treat you like you've just put a bullet through the eye of a ten-year-old kid.

"You want to see my scars? Find me on a day like that." She eyed him evenly. "But don't let me catch you fucking up if you do."

Gunner knew she wasn't finished. "Because?"

"Because then I might forget that you're a human being, too, and not just an animal too stupid to know better. Or I might remember some piece of racist trash I heard somebody say down at the station once, and suddenly think I can see the truth in it. Do you understand? Those are the scars I've been talking about— my doubts about *you*. About what your life is worth to society, in general—and what it's worth to *me,* specifically."

She blinked her eyes to see him past a veil of tears, more angry than she was hurt. "Cops like Maggie, they have no doubts. They make their minds up early on that white is right, and blue is better. Everyone else be damned."

She fell silent, kneading the corner of a pillow aimlessly. Gunner didn't say a word.

"Where will I be able to reach you when the lab work comes in tomorrow? Your office?"

Gunner looked at her. "That should work, sure. I may have one or two errands to run, so I'll be in and out. But you can always leave a message with Mickey if you miss me."

"Mickey?"

"My landlord."

"Your landlord?"

"And my barber. Yes."

Rather than ask him to explain that, Lugo said, "These errands you're talking about. They have anything to do with Maggie? Or the gun?"

"Possibly." He had said it so his resentment for the question would show through. "Why do you ask?"

"I don't know. I just wondered."

"Well, don't. You're into this thing with me deep enough already."

"So?"

"So the less apparent that is to your fellow officers, the better. All right?"

"I can take care of myself," Lugo said.

"Yeah, I know. You're a cop."

He waited for her to roll over and turn her back on him before closing his own eyes and trying for sleep.

12

The minute Lilly Tennell caught sight of Little Pete Thorogood, Gunner knew he was going to hear about it.

"Look. Why you always have to conduct your business with this man in *my* place?" she demanded, talking about the neighborhood hot weapons dealer like he wasn't even there. "Haven't you got somewhere else you two fools can go?"

She was a businesswoman above all else, Lilly, and she was only thinking about the reputation of her establishment. As if the Acey Deuce weren't known throughout the free world as one of the raunchiest and most unspectacular bars in existence.

"You're very lucky I'm not a sensitive man, Lilly," Little Pete said. But of course, looking as he did—like a thirteen-year-old beggar boy with a peach-fuzz beard growing on his face—that was precisely what he *did* resemble: a sensitive man.

Lilly wiped the counter in front of him with relish, just to show him how thick and massive her right arm—her fighting arm—still was. "I suppose you're gonna want a drink," the giant bartender said.

"Please." Little Pete smiled at her, climbing up onto his stool the way a toddler would climb up and into a high chair.

Lilly edged off to the other end of the bar and got busy with his drink.

It was only a little after ten on a Tuesday morning, so they pretty much had the place to themselves. The only other patron in the building was an old homeless man named Mr. Cecil, who was over in a corner booth drinking coffee and working a crossword puzzle. Lilly's coffee and the morning paper was Mr. Cecil's daily reward for sweeping the Deuce's floor at closing time the previous night, whenever he could find the time in his busy schedule to show up.

Gunner let Pete throw down a few swallows of his drink before he explained what he needed. The little man's face didn't betray much recognition as the story was being told, but when it was over he seemed to know more about it than Gunner did.

"I recall the product you're talking about. Sure," he said, nodding his head. "It was one semiauto rifle and four pistols. The semi was a big AR-seventy, I believe, and the pistols were all forty-fives. No. Scratch that. It was three forty-fives and a thirty-eight. Yeah." He nodded his head again.

"It's the thirty-eight I'm interested in," Gunner said.

"Okay. I have to warn you right now, though—I didn't handle any of the merchandise myself. And I'm not going to say who did. But anything I can tell you about the rest of it, I will. Fair enough?"

"Fair enough."

"Okay, then. Shoot."

"Well, I think maybe we should make sure we're talking about the right gun before we do anything else. What do you think?"

"I think, yeah. That makes sense to me. The piece I'm talking about was supposed to be a Ruger or a Rossi—something like that. Definitely not an S-and-W. Maybe an SP-one-oh-one, or an Eighty-fifty-one. Four-inch barrel, stainless steel. That sound like the one you had in mind?"

Gunner nodded. "Yeah. That's it." Dancing Fred's revolver had been a modified Ruger SP-101. "But you can't tell me who moved it. Is that right?"

"No."

"But you do know who it was."

"Yeah. I know. The individuals who actually lifted the product brought it around to me first, of course, but you know, I had to tell 'em to take it down the street. Because these fools tried to tell me the shit was genuine. Like I wouldn't know a cap pistol when

I saw one, right? So it got a little ugly, and they made some noise before leaving. You know, tellin' me where they were gonna take the stuff, and how much they were gonna get for it. I just laughed."

"And that's where the stuff ended up? With this other buyer they mentioned?"

"That's my information. Yeah."

"Can you tell me what kind of business this individual runs? I mean, like who his customers are, what neighborhood he works out of—that sort of thing?"

"I can tell you he doesn't cater to the kiddies. Man doesn't believe in it."

"No kids?"

"That's right. No kids. He's like me, in that respect: he's scrupled. Both of us work to a strictly adult crowd. No minors allowed."

"He couldn't have made an exception in this case?"

"He could have. Yeah. But I don't think so." Little Pete shook his head.

"Then my boy must have gotten it secondhand," Gunner said, more for his own benefit than Pete's. *Yet another complication,* he thought to himself. To Pete, he said, "Listen. Any chance this guy would remember who the buyer was, you think? Is he that sharp? Or that conscientious?"

Little Pete shrugged. "Man, that's hard to say. Only way I could know that would be to ask him."

Gunner pulled a hundred-dollar bill out of his wallet and pinned it beneath the little man's glass.

"Then go ask him," he said. "Please."

Little Pete lifted his glass just one more time before leaving.

An hour later, Lugo called Gunner at Mickey's.

"The news isn't good," she said. He could hear heavy traffic roaring past the phone booth she was using.

Gunner grimaced, saying a silent prayer. "Washington's prints aren't on the gun," he said.

"No. They aren't. They found a few latents on it, all right—

Dancing Fred's and that maniac Sulley's, of course, plus a few others they couldn't identify—but that was about it. How did you know?"

"Just a lucky guess." He sighed. "It would've been too much like getting a break, having the kid's prints turn up on the gun."

"Yeah. I guess it would have, huh?"

Gunner didn't answer her.

"Helluva coincidence, though. Having somebody dump that gun in the same alley where Maggie shot Washington."

"Coincidence?"

"Yeah. Coincidence. What else would you call it? I mean, we've proven it wasn't his, right?"

"So it wasn't his. That doesn't mean somebody else didn't use it that night."

"Somebody else? What somebody else?"

"I don't know. Another kid, maybe. Or one of those crack dealers you talked about the other day, the ones you say are always hanging around over there. How should I know who it was?"

"But there *was* no other kid. All Maggie and I ever saw were Washington and Ford. And a dealer—" She left the sentence incomplete.

"What?"

"Well, if there'd been a dealer there, somebody would have seen him. Either Dancing Fred, or one of the other witnesses. Right?"

"Dancing Fred? Dancing Fred wouldn't have seen shit. He didn't arrive on the scene until just before you did, well after the fact of Washington's shooting. Remember? He told us that. And as for the other witnesses . . ."

"Yeah?"

"I'm going to clue you in on a little secret: I don't think any of *them* saw shit, either. All their colorful testimony to the contrary."

"You're saying they were all lying?"

"Not exactly. I'm just saying I wouldn't bet a dime that any of them were telling the truth."

"I don't know. It sounds like you're reaching, to me."

"Okay. So I'm reaching."

"I mean, hey, nobody wants to believe your client's story more than me, but if Washington didn't touch the gun, he didn't touch the gun. Why start making wild assumptions about someone else being there to use the gun that night just because you can't place it in Washington's hands?"

"Because I don't believe in coincidences that big. That's why. There's no way somebody living on that block just happened to toss a piece filled with blanks into the garbage the same week Washington was shot. No way."

"Why not? Stranger things have happened. I mean, I admit the timing's a little weird, but so what? Could be the person who owned the piece had just that week found out what it was—a theatrical prop gun just a little more dangerous than a toy—and decided to chuck it out with their regular trash. People do that sort of thing all the time, we find broken and dysfunctional weapons in people's garbage every day."

Gunner didn't say anything.

"But, hey, it's your case, right? You pursue it the way you want to pursue it," Lugo said.

"Thanks. I will."

"So. Where do you go from here, you don't mind my asking?"

"I don't know. I'm going to have to get back to you on that." He wanted to get off the phone.

"I'd appreciate it if you would," Lugo said. "Because none of this is any of my business, I know, but now that I've sort of been drawn into it . . . Well, I'd just kind of like to stay informed of your progress, that's all."

"Sure. No problem."

Lugo fell silent for a moment. "You talk to your lady friend, yet?"

The sudden change of subject threw Gunner off balance a little. "No. Why would I? To confess I bored another woman to tears last night?"

"No. I just thought . . . you might have wanted to check in with her. So to speak."

"I suppose you'd like to stay informed about that, too."

It was a lousy thing to say, but Lugo didn't bother to tell him so.

She just said a quick "fuck you" and hung up in his face.

Gunner caught up to Charlene Woodberry at the laundromat. He'd found her Dalton Avenue address in the phone book and paid the manager of her apartment building five dollars to suggest a few places where she might be when no one came to her door. He really couldn't blame her for not wanting to be home; her apartment building was a smoke- and roach-filled firetrap and her landlord was a tipsy old snoop with sour breath.

As luck would have it, though, the old snoop had given Gunner his money's worth; the laundromat had been the first place she'd told Gunner to look. It was over on Normandie and Forty-fifth Street, and like all the inner-city laundromats he had ever known, was as warm as a brick oven and as crowded as a rush-hour bus. The sound of heavy dryers and overloaded washing machines at work was overpowering.

Most of the people in attendance here were Hispanics, but among them were three middle-aged black women who seemed to fit the vague description of Woodberry Gunner's fiver had also purchased from her landlord. For a brief moment, he thought about standing on a chair and shouting out her name, just to see if such a shortcut would work, but the din ringing in his ears quickly ruled that out. So he did things the hard way instead, and approached each woman one at a time, bracing himself for attack should any one of them misunderstand his intentions.

The first woman he tried the name on shook it off with a smile, but the second one nodded her head in recognition, with all the reluctance of an embezzler admitting her crime to the boss. She was a tiny, oddly constructed woman, full in the hips but thin as baling wire everywhere else, and she looked like she'd withstood all the bad news her heart could take.

Gunner noticed this last right away, and so made his introductions as light and easy going as possible, handing her his ID to inspect up close, rather than just flashing it from a distance, and endeavoring to smile at the end of every sentence.

"You're the one called me," Woodberry said, handing the investigator his wallet back.

"Yes. You remember."

Woodberry nodded and went back to the business of folding a basketful of clothes, keeping her eyes on him all the while. "You was out there at the prison talkin' to Noah the day he died."

"Actually, no. That's not quite true. I never did get to see Noah that day."

"Harriet's lawyer says I shouldn't talk to you."

"That's because Mr. Wiley is confused about who I represent in this matter, and why. He thinks I'm working for the police, but I'm not. Believe me."

She turned her eyes away from his in order to reach for some more clothes, and to give herself a moment to decide how much she *wanted* to believe him. "So what you want with me?"

Gunner grabbed a handful of bath towels from her basket and surprised her by starting to fold them. "I want to know if anyone else was with Noah the night he and Lendell robbed that liquor store last September. Were they alone that night, or did they have someone else along for the ride?"

Woodberry shook her head at the question rapidly, as if to say he'd been crazy to think she could help him with it. "I don't know that," she said. "I don't know nothin' about what those boys did that night."

"You don't know who else they might have been with?"

"No."

"Noah didn't have any other friends who might have gone in for such a thing? Or Lendell, maybe?"

"No. I didn't *know* none of Noah's 'friends.' I didn't *like* none of Noah's friends. Lendell was the only child I ever wanted Noah runnin' with, an' I didn't know none of his friends, neither. You wanna know about Lendell's friends, you gonna have to ask Harriet about that, not me."

Gunner shook his head. "I tried that. I called her at home just before I came over here, but her lawyer friend Wiley's convinced her not to talk to me."

"Well, look. That ain't my problem, is it?"

"Mrs. Woodberry—"

"Look, I'm tellin' you: I don't know nothin' about what you're askin' me. I didn't know none of Noah's friends, 'cause I didn't *wanna* know none of 'em. I didn't wanna know their names, their faces . . . nothin'. 'Cause all them little fools he liked to hang with, couldn't none of 'em do a damn thing right but die. Or lie, or steal, or kill innocent—"

She stopped, suddenly aware that she was furious. Looking away from Gunner once more, she pretended to watch as her trembling hands smoothed out the wrinkles on a freshly folded bed sheet sitting atop a pile of warm clothes beside her.

"I'm sorry, Mr. Gunner," she said. "But I can't help you. My son was a stranger to me, see, and I was a stranger to him. I was his mother, I know, but I made up my mind a long time ago to mind my own business where Noah was concerned. You understand?"

"I think so. Yes."

"Good."

"And I can't say that I blame you for feeling that way. I'm sure it must have been very hard for you, trying to raise a boy the right way, only to see others come along and lead him down a wayward path."

"Yes. It *was* very hard."

"And now he's dead. They talked him into all the trouble they could, and then they killed him."

"Who?"

"His friends. His homies. All the kids you say you know nothing about."

"Noah wasn't killed by one of his 'homies.' Noah didn't even know that boy!"

"Maybe not him, no. But I'll bet he knew whoever it was that put that kid up to killing him."

"What?"

"I'm talking about murder for hire, Mrs. Woodberry. A contract hit. I don't think that kid killed your son just to get in good with his friends. I think he was told to do it. I think Noah was murdered because somebody he knew didn't like the idea of him talking to me about the night his cousin Lendell died."

Woodberry was just staring at him, trying to understand what all this was leading up to.

"Lendell didn't shoot at that cop from that alley that night," Gunner said. "But somebody else did. I've found the gun they used; I know. What I don't know is who this person was. That's why I'm here, talking to you."

"But I *told* you—"

"I know what you told me. You didn't know any of Noah's friends."

"That's right."

"But you must have seen a few of them around from time to time. And heard their names mentioned on occasion."

Woodberry didn't say anything.

"All I'm asking you to do is give the subject a little more thought, Mrs. Woodberry. That's all. You're the only one I can talk to about this, like I said. If you don't want to do it for my sake, fine. But at least do it for Noah's. Please."

Woodberry stared at him a brief moment longer, then nodded her head, her eyes telling him that, even as she did so, she fully expected to be betrayed.

"All right. Think," Gunner told her. "On the day of the robbery itself. Who was Noah hanging around with, and what were they talking about? It was a long time ago, I know, but try to remember."

Noah Ford's mother looked off into space, her gaze directed at one of the impotent ceiling fans moving cigarette smoke and hot air around above their heads, and started folding clothes again, trying to see details in her mind's eye that were obscured by ten months' worth of random memory and minutiae.

"Noah came home from school late that day," she said in time. "And he didn't have nobody with him. 'Least, he didn't bring nobody inside."

It took Gunner a moment to figure out she was finished. "And then?"

She was staring at him again.

"After he came home from school. What did he do then? Did he stay in most of the night, or go out and come back again? What?"

"Oh. He stayed home. He was home all night, with me, 'til Lendell called him. Then he went out."

"Lendell called him?"

"Yes."

"What time was this?"

"I don't know. 'Bout ten or eleven, I guess."

"You know for certain it was Lendell?"

"Yes." She nodded her head. "It was him."

"How do you know? Did you speak to him?"

"Yes. I was the one answered the phone. And I heard Noah use his name a couple times, while they was talkin'."

"Then you heard their conversation."

"I heard some of it. Yeah. I wasn't tryin' to listen to 'em, or nothin', but Noah was on the phone in the kitchen, 'cause the phone in the bedroom was broke 'round that time, and I could hear 'im from the livin' room where I was sittin'. A little bit, anyways."

"And they were talking about the robbery?"

"I didn't know what they was talkin' about. All I could tell was, Noah was tryin' to talk Lendell into doin' somethin' he didn't wanna do. That's all."

"Did he mention any other names besides Lendell's that you can recall?" Gunner asked.

Woodberry thought about it for a minute, then shrugged. "I don't remember."

"Try, Mrs. Woodberry. Please. This could be the kid I'm looking for."

The black woman nodded and entered her contemplative state again, letting her eyes wander about the laundromat as she folded clothes unconsciously, yet flawlessly.

"Ben," she said eventually.

"Ben?"

"Yes. That was it. Ben. Don't ask me what he said 'bout this Ben, though, 'cause all I caught was the name. Ben."

Gunner quickly scratched the name down in his notebook. "Did Noah know a kid named Ben? Or you?"

Woodberry shook her head again. "I don't. And if he did, that was the first I ever heard of it."

"Could it be a nickname for somebody you *do* know? Is that possible?"

"I don't know. It could be, I guess. People be havin' all kinds of nicknames these days, especially kids. But 'Ben'? What kind of nickname would that be, 'Ben'? Ben's just short for Benjamin, right?"

"Generally speaking, yeah."

Woodberry shook her head again. "I don't know no Benjamin," she said.

"Maybe it was somebody Noah'd just met. You know, a friend of a friend, or something."

Woodberry shrugged once more. "Maybe."

"How could I find out about that, do you think? Who could I ask?"

He was trying to be clever, asking her in a roundabout way for the names of Noah's other friends when she'd already told him she didn't know any. But he got away with it.

"There's an older boy, used to come 'round the house," Woodberry said, the flatness of her tone informing Gunner that she was playing along with his game, rather than succumbing to it. "Noah called him Duck. Maybe he could help you."

Again, Gunner recorded the name in his notebook, nodding. "Duck," he said out loud. "You wouldn't happen to know—"

"No," Woodberry snapped. "I wouldn't."

Gunner looked up at her, and immediately became aware that he had pushed her as far as she was ready and willing to go. He put his pen and notebook away and said, "That's okay. I'll ask around the neighborhood for him. Maybe even go down to the schools."

Woodberry didn't even pretend to care.

Gunner offered her a hurried thank you and stayed around just long enough to help carry her laundry out to her car.

He never did find Duck.

He spent all of what was left of the day trying, dropping the kid's name from one end of town to the next, but no one big or small ever offered him a hint of recognition for his trouble. The closest he came to a "Duck" was an overweight nine-year-old named "Quack," who'd earned his unenviable nickname more for the way he walked than the way he talked. When his feet got going beneath him, the poor kid waddled from side to side like a toy tugboat lilting on a choppy sea.

It was around seven in the evening when Gunner finally gave it up and went home, to shower, take the load off his feet, and eat dinner, in no particular order.

He ended up eating dinner last, a fast-food pseudo-Mexican affair that he wolfed down lukewarm as he watched one of those tabloid news shows on television. The program gave him all the suggestive sex and violence he could have asked for to hold his attention, but all he really did was aim his gaze in the screen's direction and watch the images projected upon it move and change shape as he thought about the case he was working, instead.

It had taken him longer than it should have to embrace the idea, he knew, but he was finally convinced that someone other than Lendell Washington had fired the shots at Jack McGovern his client claimed to have seen the night of Washington's death. It was the one theory that seemed to pull all the little odds and ends of the case together. Like the evasive answer Noah Ford had given him when he'd asked the kid whose idea the liquor store holdup had been: *"I don't know whose idea it was. . . . 'Cause, like, it wasn't his idea, an' it wasn't my idea. Right? We just did it."*

And it also seemed to put a different spin on what Washington could have meant when, upon seeing his cousin Ford take off from the liquor store in a direction opposite the alley behind Forty-second Street, he had allegedly screamed, "You're goin' the wrong way!" Deanna Lugo had assumed the kid had had his and

Ford's homes in mind at the time, but if he'd been thinking about the alley, instead—where a shy or frightened third party to the pair's little late night holdup was patiently awaiting their return in the dark. . . .

More and more, it seemed obvious that that was how it had all gone down. It explained everything—even the missing portion of the liquor store cash McGovern had been accused of lifting from Washington's body.

So now Gunner felt he knew the likely *how* of it; he just didn't know the *who*. He had a probable name to work with—*Ben*—and a possible acquaintance in somebody named *Duck*—but that was all. No sex, no age, no height or weight. Finding this kid armed with a profile like that was going to be like searching for a marshmallow in a snowstorm. At least, that was the way things looked to Gunner before the phone rang a little after ten o'clock.

And Little Pete Thorogood said hello.

It only took ten hours of surveillance the next day, Wednesday, for Gunner to know he was following the right man.

"My man tells me the person you're lookin' for is a young, junior executive–type brother," Little Pete had said the night before. "You know, a Buppie. Nice hair, nice shoes; wearing a C-and-R suit that fits like a second skin. You know the kind I mean."

Gunner did.

"This Buppie, he told my man he wanted something just for show. Something he could flash if he got in a tight pinch, to discourage anybody who might mistake him for an easy mark. He said he wasn't looking to hurt anybody with it, and my man says he knew that was for real, because the Buppie didn't look like he could've pulled the trigger on you if you had one hand on his balls and the other on his throat. He was harmless.

"So what my man does is, he tells the guy, 'I have just the piece for you.' Right? And he sells him the thirty-eight, the cap gun, without ever tellin' him it's not for real. You know, as a gag. Tryin' to be funny. He says he even opened the chamber and rolled the cylinder around so the guy could see the shells, to make him think he was getting a full load, on the house. And the guy bought it. Can you believe that shit?"

Gunner could.

He had only once seen the man he was now following, and then very briefly, but his quarry couldn't have fit the description Little Pete had given him for the original owner of Dancing Fred's revolver better if Pete had been standing right beside him with a magnifying glass. Still, Gunner might not have made the connection had he not already known the name Noah Ford had apparently pinned on this individual, no doubt because the irreverent little bastard thought it was funny and disrespectful both at the same time: Ben.

As in *Uncle* Ben, the instant-rice king.

Or Uncle Pervis, as his better behaved nephew Lendell Washington had probably referred to him.

Gunner had traded his Cobra for his cousin Del's inconspicuous Hyundai early Wednesday morning, then driven directly to Harriet Washington's place. Pervis Hilton had emerged from the house about an hour later, just a few minutes past nine, and Gunner had been with him ever since. Driving an old Chevrolet Corvette, its orange fiberglass body lined with cracks and bad patches, Hilton had gone immediately to the Fox Hills Mall in Ladera Heights, where he disappeared through a rear door marked Employees Only. Gunner had had to wait until the mall opened up for customers at ten to pick him up again, but he found him easily enough, selling suits and slacks and overpriced silk handkerchiefs at Zeidler & Zeidler, the men's clothing store. Gunner had caught a quick glimpse of Hilton within, then taken the escalator up to the mall's second level, out of Hilton's frame of view, to watch the store's entrance from there.

There wasn't anything to see until Hilton broke for lunch three hours later.

He had come out of the store and gone directly out to the parking lot and his car, stopping only at a women's shoe store along the way to exchange double entendres with a gorgeous black salesgirl working within. Hollywood Park in Inglewood had just opened its gates an hour or so earlier, and Hilton and Gunner both made it there in time for the second race. Gunner followed Hilton's lead in paying for general admission and then watched him go directly to a pari-mutuel window to lay down several bets, barely eyeing the track itself as he walked by. The investigator couldn't see the denomination of the bills Hilton was handing the clerk from where he was standing, but he could tell Hilton wasn't just wagering his lunch money, because he was keeping a close eye on the players in line behind him, as if he were worried somebody might see more of his transaction than it would be safe to allow them to see.

Afterward, Hilton had bought himself a hot dog and pushed his way up to the rail to watch the third race, making notes in his racing form as he eyed every movement on the track like a hawk. A three-year-old filly named Simplicity Itself rode the inside to victory less than a half-length ahead of a mare named Same Way Twice, paying off handsomely at $14.60, but if Hilton had expected this result, he had an odd way of showing it: He shredded one of his paramutuel tickets into confetti and called it a day, leading Gunner out to the parking lot and their respective cars.

From there he drove back to work, having never given Gunner any reason to believe he didn't do this sort of thing every day.

Hilton and Gunner then spent the final four hours of the former's work day much like they had the first three, with the exception that Gunner slipped away from his post on the mall's second floor for a few minutes to call an old friend down in Vegas from a pay phone. By the time Hilton left work a few minutes later to have dinner in Hollywood with a fat Samoan Gunner knew to be a bookie named Papa Ho, Gunner felt as if he had Hilton pretty much figured out.

Hilton was getting in the Corvette, out in the dark parking lot of the restaurant in Hollywood, when Gunner finally made his presence felt.

"Hello, Pervis," he said.

Hilton turned, the color draining from his face even before he could complete the motion. Gunner was just standing there, waiting.

"What the hell do *you* want?" the clothes salesman managed

to ask, almost with genuine backbone. The relief in his eyes seemed to imply he had expected to be ambushed by someone else.

Someone he had reason to fear.

"You remember me, then," Gunner said.

"Yeah. I remember you. You're that rent-a-cop my idiot sister invited into the house the other day. The one the cops hired to try and fuck up her case against them."

"Actually, you're only half right. Despite the common assumption, I'm not working for the cops. I'm working for a neighbor of yours. Somebody who saw something last September I think you might be interested in."

Hilton's sneer lost just a fraction of its arrogance. "Last September? Like what?"

"Like the two shots you fired at the cop who killed your nephew Lendell. The ones that drew the cop's fire to Lendell in the first place."

This time, Hilton's face took the whole fall, like an old theater curtain dropped from the rafters. With his last ounce of false courage, he said, "I don't know what you're talking about."

"Oh, I think you do. Lendell didn't get shot that night because Jack McGovern was a racist pig looking for a little target practice. He got shot because you tried to kill McGovern first, when you saw it was a cop Lendell had brought back with him into that alley instead of Noah Ford. What you did was, you panicked. And then you ran away."

"That's a lie! You're crazy!" Hilton said.

"I'm not crazy. Just tired. And maybe a little hungry. I've been following you around all day today, and it seems like all I've seen you do is eat. First at the track, during your lunch hour. And then just now, breaking bread with Papa Ho. What was that you had in there, by the way? Veal? It looked pretty good."

"Look, fuck you. I don't have to listen to any more of this shit." Hilton sat down in the car and started to close the door behind him.

"I have your gun, Pervis," Gunner said.

Hilton froze, the car door still hanging open in his hand.

"The one you tossed in the garbage can at the end of the alley, before you ran away."

Hilton came alive and tried to slam the door shut, but Gunner stepped forward to stop him. He looked down into the low-slung car at him and said, "I could have taken it straight to the police, and watched them yank you out of your sister's house without calling first to say they were coming. But I thought maybe Harriet had seen enough policemen around for a while, and deserved to hear the news from you, in whatever way you'd care to present it. But if that's not important to you . . ." He backed away from the car. "I'll just see you downtown. Sooner or later."

Gunner put his hands in his pockets and waited for Hilton to make up his mind.

Hilton killed some time scanning the parking lot beyond the Corvette's windshield, just to give him something to do with his eyes, then slowly pulled the keys out of the car's ignition and stood up. He slammed the door closed, locked it, and turned around, looking not unlike a second-grader about to be marched down to the principal's office.

"Smart man," Gunner said.

He didn't realize there was someone moving up behind him until the expression on Hilton's face abruptly changed, and he heard gravel popping beneath someone's feet, just at his back.

Gunner only got halfway turned around, and one hand out of his pockets, before his skull slammed into something hard, and the world shut down for the night.

13

When the fog finally rolled out, big-time pain rolled in.

It started at the back of Gunner's head, just behind his right ear, and then radiated outward, sending signals of discontent throughout his entire body. It felt like somebody had slung a manhole cover like a Frisbee and planted the damn thing in his skull. He thought about opening his eyes, but discovered to his dismay that the thought alone was enough to drive the manhole cover an inch farther into his brain. So he resigned himself to keeping perfectly still. For the rest of his life, if necessary.

So as not to make himself completely useless, he took a little inventory. What he found was that he was laying on his back, unbound, on what felt like the soft leather flesh of a divan. And that whoever his hosts were, they were not happy with each other at the moment.

"Why in God's name would you bring him here?" he heard Milton Wiley say.

"I told you. Because I thought I was doin' you a favor."

This voice was vaguely familiar, but not yet identifiable.

"A favor? What kind of favor?"

"He was talkin' about takin' homeboy here to the police. It sounded like he knew the whole deal. So I thought, you know, maybe you'd wanna talk to him."

"Talk to him? For what? He was only a nuisance to me. He couldn't prove anything. But by bringing him here like this, you've tied my hands. Do you realize that? You've put me—you've put all of us—in a completely untenable position."

"What the hell does *untenable* mean?"

This time, Gunner recognized the voice. It was his impatient friend from Wiley's waiting room. Howie Foster.

"It means we have no choice now but to kill him. Unless he can somehow see his way around to being reasonable."

"Kill him? What do you mean, kill him?"

This was Pervis Hilton.

"Shit. I'm in enough trouble as it is. I'm not getting involved in any goddamn murder!" Hilton said.

Gunner opened his eyes. The jolt of discomfort he had been expecting followed the act, all right, but it was mercifully short-lived. His vision cleared after a moment and he could see the three men positioned around Wiley's office distinctly. To his right, Wiley was sitting on the front edge of his desk, facing a standing Foster, while Hilton was sitting in a chair between them, looking as distressed as ever.

It was Foster who saw him first.

"Hey. Looks like he's wakin' up," the big man said. He sounded slightly amused.

Gunner grabbed the back of the leather divan with his right hand and pulled himself up into a sitting position, doing what he could to ignore his body's violent protestations. Afterward, he had to wait a while before the room and its occupants drifted back into focus.

"How's the head, homeboy?" Foster asked, grinning.

Gunner looked at him, rubbing the back of his neck with his right hand, and said, "I think you can guess the answer to that. 'Howie.' "

"You can call me 'Mr. Foster,' asshole."

"And you can call me 'in your ass,' you ever come near me again. All right?"

Foster just laughed.

Wiley stood away from his desk to get a closer look at Gunner and said, "For what it's worth, Mr. Gunner, I had nothing to do with your being brought here this evening. This meeting was entirely Mr. Foster's idea, I'm afraid."

"So I heard," Gunner said.

"You heard? You mean, you were awake when we—"

"Were discussing the probability of having to kill me? I heard that. Yeah. As I recall, the vote was one for, and one against, with your boy Howie here abstaining. Though, I'd imagine if you asked him to vote again—"

"You'd be dead. Damn straight," Foster said.

He was standing directly in Gunner's path to the office door. Deliberately.

"Nevertheless. We were talking about something that never has to happen," Wiley said. "For all your insipid disruptions of my business, Mr. Gunner, you still strike me as an intelligent man. One who can be bargained with, given death as his only other alternative."

Gunner shrugged, and winced when it cost him. "You're asking me to forget an awful lot, counselor. Don't you think?"

"On the contrary. I think I'm asking you to forget very little. Mr. Hilton's connection to the gun you say you've found, number one. And the details of this meeting—and the kidnapping that preceded it—number two. Is that too much to ask in exchange for one's life?" He shook his head. "I don't think so."

"That's because you're oversimplifying things a bit. You're not just asking me to forget the gun was Hilton's—you're asking me to forget the part he played in the robbery that got his nephew killed. Or hasn't he told you yet that the robbery was his idea?"

"Shut the fuck up, man!" Hilton said, actually threatening to rise from his chair. "You don't know what you're talking about!"

"The young man has a serious gambling problem," Gunner said to Wiley, as if Hilton hadn't even spoken. "He spends his lunch hours betting on the sixth-place horse in every race out at Hollywood Park, and a little birdie I know down in Las Vegas says he's as regular a loser there as he is at the track. He's in the red everywhere he goes, and people who stay in the red sometimes do desperate things. Especially if they've fallen too far behind the eight ball with a bookie like Papa Ho. Papa Ho isn't a patient man, from what I understand."

"The fat bastard was going to kill me," Hilton said to Gunner, his jaw set so tight the words just barely passed through his teeth. "For thirty-five dollars. Thirty-five dollars!"

"Shut up, Pervis," Wiley said.

"Why? He already knows, right? He's so goddamn anxious to hear the details, right? Well, let him hear them, then. Fuck him!"

"We don't know *what* he knows. But if you blurt out the whole damn episode . . ." Wiley paused, to make sure Hilton caught his meaning. "You're going to have to accept some responsibility for the consequences."

Hilton surveyed the three faces in the room, trying to read them. Foster was clearly pulling for him to speak his mind, but neither Gunner nor Wiley appeared to give a damn what he decided to do.

In the end, he looked at Gunner and said, "I was into Papa Ho for almost a thousand. Nine hundred and seventy-two dollars, man, that's what I owed him. And I had it, too. Everything but thirty-five dollars of it. Nine-hundred and thirty-seven dollars was all the green I could scrape up. I'd had a bad run and . . ." He shrugged. "I was busted. Didn't have anything more to sell, didn't have anything left to hock. I asked around for a week, trying to borrow the money, but . . . I'd borrowed money before, and I guess I'd made a mess of it.

"Anyway, come my last day to get the money, I was still lookin' for it. Papa Ho said, he understood it was only thirty-five dollars, but he'd already cut me some slack once before, the year before that, and this time he wasn't going to let it ride. It was the principle of the thing, the fat motherfucker said. So . . ."

He couldn't get the rest of the sentence out.

"So you put your two nephews up to knocking off a liquor store for you," Gunner said.

Hilton nodded. "I tried to lift some of my sister's jewelry at first, just to hock it for a while, and then put it back, but I'd already hit her up like that once, so she put the shit away. Hid it somewhere in the house where I couldn't find it. I was tearing up the place lookin' for it when Noah came in lookin' for Lendell, and saw me. That's when I got the idea to have him get the money for me."

He shook his head, thinking about it. "But the little fucker wouldn't do it alone. He said Lendell had to come with him."

"And you didn't have time to argue with him."

"No. I didn't." He fell silent for a moment, melancholy setting in. "When I look back on it, I can see that's where it all got fucked up. Him insistin' that Lendell go along." He shook his head again. "I should've never let that little fucker talk me into that."

"You should've never done a lot of things," Gunner said. "Including go into that alley with a gun that couldn't have stopped that cop if you'd stuck the barrel in his ear and emptied it."

Hilton just looked at him, dumbfounded.

He really didn't know.

"What the hell are you talking about?" Wiley asked, agitated.

Gunner looked up at the attorney and said, "I'm talking about blanks. The kind they use in the movies." He turned to Hilton again. "The next time you buy a gun on the street, Rambo, read the fine print. That piece you bought to protect yourself was a fake; you couldn't have punched a hole in a paper bag with the shells it was loaded with."

"What?" Hilton's voice had been little more than a whisper.

Foster fell out laughing again. "Rambo!" he said, holding his sides to keep from bursting.

"Fuck you," Hilton told him, with unexpected authority.

"You better watch your mouth, boy," Foster said, still chuckling.

"I see no need to hear any more of this, Mr. Gunner," Wiley said. "I think it's safe to say you know more about Pervis's and my situation than we would prefer. What do you say we just leave it at that?"

" 'Leaving it at that' is not what people in my profession do best, Wiley," Gunner said. "But then, respecting the law isn't always what people in your profession do best. Is it?"

"That all depends on whose law you're talking about."

"I thought there was only one."

Wiley laughed derisively and went back around his desk to sit down. "There has never been only one law in this country, Mr. Gunner. You know that. From the moment your ancestors and mine were first brought here, there has always been two separate codes of behavior in effect: the white man's and the black man's. That I spent seven years of my life learning to practice the former does not mean I am ignorant of the latter."

"I see. This is a black pride thing. Not a matter of simple greed."

"There is money to be made for me in all of this, certainly," Wiley said matter-of-factly. "Even if we should settle out of court—which I don't expect we will, by the way—Pervis's sister and I stand to make in excess of three-quarters of a million dollars in our suit against the LAPD. If I were to sit here and tell you that financial reward isn't one of my incentives in this matter, I'd obviously be lying to you.

"However, I'm not just in this for the money. The money is only secondary to me, at best. My primary purpose in this endeavor is to effect change. To force a conscience upon a system of law enforcement that has basically functioned without one for decades."

"A conscience," Gunner said.

"That's right. A conscience. A heretofore absent sensitivity that would make the system work for everyone, equally, without regard for race or social status. My associates and I want to drive the bigots and sadists who have historically shaped and populated the police force in this city out into the street, Mr. Gunner. Forever. Chief Bowden will merely reshape the machine, at best. We intend to rebuild it."

"By suing the department for a million dollars over an officer-involved shooting you know was justifiable homicide."

Wiley snapped forward in his chair and said, "No. By publicly crucifying an icon. By exposing and then vilifying a man who represents, even in death, everything evil about the system of law enforcement we are subject to today. Shame and public humiliation—that's what we're after here. Not the money. The LAPD costs the taxpayers in this city thousands upon thousands of dollars in court cases similar to ours every year, and the losses have yet to make any measurable impact on the way the department serves the black community."

"But you think raking Jack McGovern over the coals on the six o'clock news every night for a month will," Gunner said.

"Yes. We do. At least, we believe it's a start."

"You keep referring to yourself as 'we.' What 'we' is this? You and these two losers?"

Wiley smiled. "I'm afraid the odds you're presently facing are substantially larger—and broader—than that, Mr. Gunner. Suffice it to say that I speak for a group of people who are committed to attacking the same problem from a number of diverse angles, all in order to achieve one common goal: to change the way the LAPD does business. To expose its senseless cruelty and bigotry to every living American with a television set, until its professional pride will no longer allow it to tolerate the status quo."

"Even if a few innocent heads have to roll in the process."

"If that's yet another insinuation that I had something to do with Noah Ford's death at Central, I can only tell you what I told you before: that I don't know anything more about Noah's death than what I was told by the authorities there."

"Then it was just pure luck on your part."

"What's that?"

"That the only other person besides Hilton and yourself who knew Mrs. Washington's suit was groundless got himself killed in prison before he could talk to me."

Wiley grinned and said, "You underestimate Noah, Mr. Gunner. We had an arrangement, that young man and I. In exchange for his keeping his uncle's participation in the liquor store heist our little secret, he was to receive a nominal percentage of his aunt's eventual compensation award. His desire to earn that money had kept him quiet to this point, and I was confident it would continue to do so, no matter how you or anyone else chose to grill him."

Gunner turned to Hilton, who had been curiously silent to this point. "Maybe not everyone's confidence in Noah was as unshakable as yours, Mr. Wiley," he said.

Hilton tried to ignore that, but Gunner's gaze was insistent. In time, even Foster was staring at him, demanding an answer. "I don't know anything about Noah's death," he said. "Except that it couldn't have happened to a more deserving little mother-fucker."

He smiled.

Gunner was starting to feel like himself again; it still hurt to blink, but the room wasn't swimming in a dingy haze anymore. Of course, he wasn't on his feet yet. If he tried to get to the door now, he'd have to put Foster on his back to do it, and he didn't know if he had that kind of stamina. Besides . . .

Foster was looking right at him.

"Come on. Do it," the big man said, grinning from ear to ear. "Make my fuckin' day."

"Time is running short, Mr. Gunner," Wiley said, reacting to Foster's obvious impatience. "If there'd be any point to us discussing a deal similar to the one we had with Noah, now is the time to say so. Otherwise . . ." He shook his head sadly. "I'm afraid we'll have to resort to measures we had hoped to avoid altogether."

He glanced in Foster's direction.

"All I have to do is look the other way," Gunner said.

"Yes—and no."

"No? What's the no?"

"We'll also need to know where we can find your client. So that we might offer him the same chance to cooperate with us we've offered you, of course."

"Of course."

"You may be under the impression that he would be adverse to taking money for his silence, but we happen to know for a fact he is more than open to that possibility."

"And how would you know that?"

"Because he told us as much. How else?"

"When was this?"

"Oh, quite some time ago. Months before you were hired, anyway. But of course, he wouldn't mention that to you, would he? You might not turn the screws as tightly if you knew it was all for show."

Gunner didn't know how to answer that. He was too busy feeling like a jackass. What Wiley was inferring was that Mitchell Flowers had tried to blackmail him a while back—and failing that, had hired Gunner to either make the lawyer pay for dismissing him, or merely encourage him to be a little more open-minded about paying Flowers off. All that business about receiving threatening notes and phone calls from some anonymous blackmailer of his own must have just been something Flowers fabricated to get Gunner to go along.

P. T. Barnum had been right. There was a Gunner born every minute.

"It's unfortunate we couldn't come to some agreement when he first approached us," Wiley was saying, forging right ahead. "But I'm afraid his idea of a fair price for his silence was highly inflated, at least at that time. Perhaps we'll find him more realistic this go round.

"In any case, as I've said, time is running short. So I'll need your answer, now. Can you meet our terms for a truce as I've described them, or not?"

"I can't give you my client's name," Gunner said.

"Nobody asked for his name. I asked where we could find him."

"Wait a minute. You don't want his *name*?"

"We already *know* his name. What we don't know is how to contact him. Quit stalling, Mr. Gunner. It's very late, and I'm tired."

Now Gunner was really lost. They knew Flowers's name, but they didn't know where to find him? It didn't make sense. Unless Flowers wasn't listed in the telephone directory. An unlisted phone number *would* make him more difficult to track down than most people—but what the hell would a man like Flowers want with an unlisted phone number?

"Hurry up, Mr. Gunner. I'm waiting," Wiley said impatiently.

"Okay. Let's say I tell you what you want to know," Gunner said, trying to buy himself a little time. "You're still screwed,

Wiley. Any way you look at it. Nothing's going to change that now."

"Is that right? Do tell how."

"The police have Hilton's gun. That's how. They're probably peeling his prints off the grips as we speak."

The news hit Wiley about as hard as a feather riding a light breeze. "Let me worry about the gun," he said simply.

Gunner found his calm more than a little disturbing.

"You can't trust him, Wiley," Hilton said. "No matter what he says."

"My feelings, exactly," Foster agreed.

"If we let him go now, it'll be over for all of us," Hilton added.

"I thought you said you wanted no part of murder?" Wiley asked him angrily.

"I don't. But . . ."

He turned to Foster for help.

"Looks like the deal you've been offering's just been taken off the table, Wiley," Gunner said. "But then, it was never really meant to be taken seriously, was it?"

Wiley just glared at him.

To Hilton, Gunner said, "I suppose all of your bitching just now could have been part of the act, Pervis, but I'm betting it wasn't. You really were afraid Milton here was going to let me go, once I'd told him what he needs to know. Weren't you?"

When Hilton wouldn't answer him, Gunner grinned and facing Wiley again, said, "The boy just doesn't understand, does he, counselor? How far you'll go to get your way in all this, I mean."

"I've been negotiating with you in good faith, Mr. Gunner."

"Sure you have. And you keep a big ape like your pal Howie here around just in case you need some walnuts opened. You need me to point you in my client's direction, and then you need me *dead,* Wiley. That's the only play you've got, let's face it."

It was small consolation to Gunner, but Wiley really did look shaken up. He glanced over at Foster and said, "I don't want him found for at least a week. Do you understand?"

Foster nodded his head and said, "No problem." For a change, he wasn't smiling. He stepped over to where Gunner was sitting and said, "Let's go. Very slowly, and very easy. All right?"

Gunner didn't move.

Foster grinned, feeling playful, and reached down to get a handful of Gunner's collar.

Gunner caught him coming forward with a right hand that had all he had to offer behind it. He felt a knuckle crack in his right hand as the blow broke the big man's nose and sent him backpedaling, his arms flailing about like the wings on a bird filled with buckshot.

But Foster didn't go down.

He caught his balance and threw his weight into Gunner's path as the investigator made a dash for the door, connecting on a solid body block that sent Gunner flying head over heels halfway across the room. Gunner hit the wall at an awkward angle and discovered to his horror afterward that he couldn't move to get up.

Foster's bloody face was leaning over his own momentarily.

"Sheeeeit," the giant said, laughing heartily.

Gunner watched him cock his fist back over his head, and just closed his eyes.

He awoke in the trunk of a car.

A big car, from the feel of it. And the feel of it was all he had, because the trunk was as dark and stale as a tomb. He was taking flight with each bump in the road, lying on his right side in a stretched-out, halfhearted fetal position. His feet were bound together and his hands were joined similarly behind his back, probably with the same duct tape Foster had slapped across his mouth. As the car continued to bounce along, its springs squealed like mice in his ears and his head kept hitting what felt like a spare tire behind him. His left eye seemed to be swollen shut, and he had the taste of his own blood in his mouth.

His first instinct was to start kicking at the walls of the trunk for all he was worth, to try to attract someone's attention, but he put that idea out of his head quickly, because it wasn't likely to get him anywhere, and he had a hunch he was going to need that kind of energy later.

If he was lucky.

When his eyes had adjusted to the darkness somewhat, he began to notice two pinholes of light that kept appearing and disappearing on the face of the trunk lid before him. He tucked his body into a tighter ball and shimmied forward, toward the rear end of the car, until he was able to identify what it was he was looking at: two bullet holes in the sheet metal, one right above the other.

He brought his good eye up close to the top one and peered out. His field of vision was naturally poor, and the lighting out on the street kept vacillating, but he could nevertheless see the three lanes of traffic Foster was leaving in his wake. It took him a while, with the scene jouncing in and out of his view, but eventually he became convinced that he was looking at La Brea Avenue, as seen from a car moving north along it, in the middle lane. He saw a big blue street sign reading "3rd Street" go by, then one for Beverly Boulevard, and realized they were cruising past the Miracle Mile district into Hollywood.

They stopped at a light, and all Gunner could see was the grille of the car behind him. It almost seemed close enough to touch. When Foster pulled off again, the grille fell back and Gunner saw that it belonged to a full-sized Oldsmobile station wagon with a manic-looking white teenager behind the wheel. The kid had a New York Giants football cap on his head, and was slapping his right hand on the car's dash to the beat of a song Gunner couldn't hear, his lips moving to the occasional lyric he could remember.

Gunner knew there was nothing he could do behind his little bullet hole that would catch this character's attention.

He lay back and tried to think, resting his one good eye for a moment. Where could Foster be taking him? The Hollywood Hills were less than fifteen minutes away, and Wiley had specifically requested that Gunner's body not be found for a while. If Foster was looking for the kind of scrub and brush that could camouflage a grown man's corpse for days and sometimes weeks at a time, he could do a lot worse than the dense ragweed that covered the hillside for miles up along Outpost Drive. Or Beach-wood Drive. Or Nichols Canyon Road. Or . . .

Gunner tried to pry his hands loose, but it was no good; it felt like Foster had used half his roll of tape just on his wrists alone. To complicate matters further, Gunner was finding it harder and harder to breathe. Lack of oxygen was not a problem yet, but he knew it would be soon.

He waited a few more seconds, then leaned forward to squint through the bullet hole again.

The kid in the Oldsmobile was gone, replaced by a featureless figure driving a red, late-model Chrysler Le Baron with a wind-shield too filthy to see through. A tan pickup truck of a make and model Gunner couldn't make out lagged several car lengths be-hind, in the fast lane to Gunner's right, while nothing at all showed itself in the slow lane to his left. Both the Chrysler and the pickup were a good distance back; if he tried to bow the rear fender of Foster's car out with his feet, he doubted either driver would notice. And even if they did, he could guess what they would do about it. Go home and greet the wife with a story that would start with *I just saw the funniest damn thing . . .* That's what. The situation seemed hopeless . . .

. . . until Gunner saw the black-and-white police cruiser move up to pass the Chrysler on its right-hand side.

He recognized immediately that the cops inside were on their way somewhere; the car was moving too fast. Foster was driving leisurely, no doubt looking as innocuous inside the car as a man as physically imposing as he possibly could, and he didn't even have the radio on, let alone cranked up to any conspicuous level. Unless he did something reckless or stupid inside the next fifteen seconds, there was little chance of his drawing the preoccupied cops' attention. Gunner was going to have to do that on his own, or the opportunity to save himself—very likely his last—would be gone.

Still, his earlier problem remained: What could he do from behind two little puncture wounds in the car's trunk lid to create the kind of diversion he required?

He glanced about the trunk he was trapped in frantically, and for the first time he noticed how much light from outside was visible around the edges of the taillight assembly near his feet. He kicked at it gingerly and felt it give; the damn thing was loose. Foster had apparently taken a hit back there, and much of what the taillight had been anchored to no longer existed.

Gunner flipped himself over on his other side, quickly, turning his back on the assembly in order to use his heels on it at the best possible angle. He felt around for the target, found it, and then kicked down and out on it with everything he had.

He heard the taillight shell explode and the sound of glass and metal hitting the street. Somebody—probably the faceless driver of the Chrysler—stood on their brakes and locked them up, causing several other drivers, either alongside or behind, to do likewise.

Gunner rolled over onto his other side again as Foster's driving became erratic for a moment, no doubt a result of his being distracted by the chaos occurring behind him. When Foster had recovered, once more manipulating the car like a man with nothing to hide, Gunner looked down to see that his kick had broken the taillight assembly in half, ejecting the far half into the street and completely dislodging the other. He could see the pavement in the big car's wake roll by through the gaping hole that remained.

By the time Gunner got into position to peer through his tiny porthole again, the black-and-white was already riding Foster's tail, the lightbar on its roof spraying the night red, its siren calling for Foster's attention in short, angry bursts. Gunner figured the game was over.

Then Foster stepped on the gas.

The big car leaped forward, and Gunner was tossed toward the front of the trunk like a rag doll. He hit the back wall face first and cut his cheek open just below his left eye on a jagged ridge of sheet metal. As Foster started dodging in and out of traffic, bouncing his car off those that couldn't or wouldn't get out of his way, Gunner slammed off the surfaces of the trunk unmercifully, the full cry of the squad car's siren now screaming in his ears. More than once, he almost lost consciousness, and before long he was certain that this was how he was going to die: trussed up and helpless, like a kitten some twisted child had thrown into a clothes dryer.

A second siren joined the first, initially faint, then gaining fast, and Foster's driving grew even more frantic. The big car wasn't built for speed, and he was clearly having a tough time holding it on the road.

When he finally couldn't manage it anymore, the car went into a long skid of some sort, jumped over what felt like the curb, and slammed to a stop with a deafening, gut-wrenching crash.

Gunner could not move. He was pinned toward the back of the trunk, his legs caught awkwardly beneath him, the car's spare tire pressed up against his chest. If he gave his pain too much thought, he knew he would pass out.

The first thing he noticed was that the car's engine was still running, though the car itself remained still.

Then he heard other things.

Car doors slam. Feet racing across pavement. The hammers on revolvers and pumps on shotguns being slid back noisily. And finally, orders. Lots of orders. The kind that were not to be confused with polite suggestions or casual requests.

These were the kind a man followed to the letter, without delay, if he wanted to see the next second of whatever it was he thought of as his life.

"You! In the car! Stick your right hand out the window!"

A pause.

"Now your left! Come on!

"Open the door with your left hand! Your *left* hand! That's right! Let's go!

"Now . . . Keep your hands out where we can see 'em and exit the car! *Hands in front,* I said!"

Behind him, Gunner heard Foster force the big car's driver's side door open, its apparently twisted and misshapen form moaning and popping in complaint.

"Do not face me, sir! Turn around! *Turn around!*"

"You heard what the man said, goddamnit!" a second voice shouted.

"Now lock your hands behind your head! That's right! Take three steps back and get down on your knees! Keep your hands behind your head! All right, get down on your knees!"

There was another pause, and then a flurry of moving feet.

"What the fuck'd I do?" Gunner heard Foster demand belligerently.

But nobody answered him. Inside the trunk of the big man's car, Gunner heard the familiar rattle of handcuffs, followed by what sounded like Foster grunting as he was forced to the ground, perhaps leading with his face.

"He wants to know what he did," one of the officers outside said, sarcastically.

Foster started making strange noises, as if he were trying to talk while his mouth was being pressed to the pavement.

"Get the fuck off 'im, Red," somebody said.

After that, a host of voices joined in on the conversation, making it impossible for Gunner to keep track of who was saying what.

"For what? Homeboy could've killed somebody back there."

"I think you busted one of his teeth."

"Jesus."

"What, that? He did that in the car."

"Yeah. In the crash. On a CD case, or something."

"That's right. It was a CD case. I saw it."

"You guys . . ."

"A Public Enemy CD it was, I think."

"No. You mean Public *Enema.*"

"Yeah, yeah. That was it. 'Fear of a *Coonskin* Planet.' "

They all cracked up.

Gunner waited for the party to end before he made any effort to let them know he was there.

14

"We have a problem," Detective Denny Loiacano of the Los Angeles Police Department, Hollywood Division, said.

He was a short, compact Italian with a face too kind for police work, and it had fallen to him to check out Gunner's story. It seemed an unfair thing to do to so nice a guy. Soft-spoken, courteous, and neat, wearing his tie loose around his unbuttoned collar seemed to be as disheveled and unprofessional as Loiacano knew how to get.

Twenty minutes ago, he and his partner—a bean-pole redhead named Conlan—had left Gunner alone in this spotless interrogation room with Ira "Ziggy" Zeigler, Gunner's fifty-three-year-old lawyer, after having heard the investigator's explanation for his kidnapping four times. Now the two detectives were back, bearing fresh cups of coffee for all. Loiacano had even thought to bring extra cream and sugar.

"What kind of problem?" Gunner asked him. He had an ugly patch over his left eye, a bandage on his cut cheek just beneath that, and a still-drying plaster cast on his right hand, the last to protect the middle knuckle he'd broken like a china dish on Howie Foster's face. When he breathed too deep, he could literally feel the point of impact of every punch the big man had pummeled him with.

Loiacano cleared his throat and said, "Officer Lugo says she doesn't know anything about this gun you're talking about. She says she spoke to you once, out at the scene of the Washington shooting last Friday, and that was it. She hasn't seen nor heard from you since."

"What?"

"She says she told you you were wasting your time then, but that you refused to listen. Is that true?"

"Shit. I don't believe it!"

"Answer the man's question, Mr. Gunner," Conlan said, holding up the wall behind his partner's chair. Apparently, that was his role on this team: the Designated Mouth.

"Of course she told me I was wasting my time. I haven't talked to anybody yet who hasn't. But that doesn't mean she didn't change her mind later."

"You're saying she's lying, then," Loiacano said carefully.

"That's exactly what I'm—"

Seated at Gunner's immediate left, Ziggy kicked the leg of the investigator's chair and said, "What my client is saying is that the officer's memory appears to be a little short. Perhaps if you were to question her in person . . ."

Loiacano shook his head. "I don't think that would be a very good idea at this time, counselor," he said.

"Why not?" Gunner asked, jumping in.

"Because I happen to believe her. This is a police officer we're talking about here—not some bimbo off the street. And I'm not going to drag her halfway across town for questioning until I have just cause."

"I need the gun, Loiacano. You know that."

"I don't know what I know, except that your story's pretty wild and farfetched. Don't you think?"

"It's the truth."

Conlan mumbled something unintelligible as Loiacano shrugged. "Okay. It's the truth. But right now, you've got nothing in the way of evidence to prove it. And neither do we."

"What about Foster? You've got him, don't you?"

"Yeah, we've got him. But if you think he's talking to us, you're nuts. According to him, sticking a strange man in the trunk of his car had to be somebody's idea of a joke. He had no idea you were in there until we told him, he says."

"Bullshit. He put me in there himself, after beating the crap out of me at Wiley's office. Or do you think I did this to myself?" Gunner waved a hand over the patch covering his eye.

"Look, Mr. Gunner. Nobody's saying we don't intend to investigate your story thoroughly. We do. I'm just warning you not to expect too much, that's all. Because it shouldn't take a genius to know how your friends Wiley and Hilton are going to play it when we get them down here to talk. They're going to act just as dumb and stupid as Foster. And if they do . . ."

He shrugged again.

"Then you'll talk to Lugo again," Gunner suggested forcefully.

Loiacano smiled. "We'll see. Let's take this thing one step at a time, all right?"

Gunner and Ziggy shared a glance, then wasted no time finding the door.

Ziggy drove Gunner back to the restaurant parking lot in Hollywood where the investigator had last seen his cousin's car. Ziggy owned an old '67 Ford Thunderbird that was in better shape than most cars half its age, and he liked to keep a cooler full of ice-packed fruit behind the passenger seat, where he could reach it easily while driving. He was big on vitamin C, Ziggy, and like his car, he was in the kind of condition that put most men his age to shame.

Tonight, he was methodically working his way down to the core of a Washington apple.

"I think we're in a world of hurt on this one, son," he said.

Gunner stared at the road ahead and nodded. "Yeah. That's what I was thinking."

"You figure somebody got to Lugo? Or did she just get cold feet?"

"I don't know. But I intend to find out."

Ziggy glanced at him, alarmed. "How's that?"

"By asking the lady," Gunner said. "What else?"

"You think that's advisable?"

"You're the lawyer. You tell me. Do I have a prayer of proving any part of what I just said back there if I can't convince Lugo to produce Hilton's gun?"

Ziggy thought his answer through, though he knew that wouldn't change it. "No. My guess is you don't," he said. "Because the man was right, of course. All your friends Wiley, Hilton, and Foster are going to do is play stupid, in order to put the onus on you to provide them with a motive for your kidnapping. And since Hilton's gun is that motive, and you don't have it . . ."

"We're in a world of hurt," Gunner repeated for him.

Ziggy nodded his head.

"I still say you should have let me file a complaint against those assholes who handled Foster's arrest," Gunner said, changing the subject.

"No. That would have been a mistake. I can't think of anything else that could have made Loiacano more reluctant to take your story seriously than he already is than that."

"They made a goddamn laugh-in out of busting him, Ziggy," Gunner said angrily.

"I know, kid. I know."

"And he didn't lose those three teeth on a fucking CD case, either. He was talking just fine until after they cuffed him."

"Yeah. It's a shame. Really."

Gunner turned to watch him take another bite of his apple. "You think I'm overreacting," he said.

"I didn't say that. I just think you'd be better off looking at the bright side of things, that's all. Why sit here worrying about how Foster lost his teeth, when you should be thanking God he didn't put a bullet in the back of your head and dump your body in a ravine somewhere?"

"Because a man shouldn't have to hear every watermelon joke a cop knows every time he gets taken downtown," Gunner said. "That shit gets old after a while, all right?"

Ziggy turned to look at him, but Gunner quickly glanced away. It wasn't Ziggy's fault. It wasn't anybody's fault.

It was just the way things were.

* * *

Early Thursday morning, when Deanna Lugo tried to pull her car out of her Los Feliz apartment building's underground garage, Gunner was standing there waiting for her in the driveway, barring her path to the street. He had been waiting here for nearly three hours to surprise her, never once picking up the security phone out front to try to talk his way into her apartment, and from the look on her face now, a surprise was exactly what he had given her. She looked like someone who had just caught a glimpse of the Grim Reaper himself.

She rolled her window down as he approached the car and said, "What do you want?"

"I want the gun," Gunner said, showing remarkable restraint. "What do you think I want?"

"I don't know what you're talking about."

"Look—in case you haven't noticed, somebody tried to kill me last night, and you're the only one who can stop them from trying again. So quit fucking around and give me the goddamn gun!" He dented the door on her side with the heel of his left hand.

"Get away from the car," Lugo said.

Gunner started pulling on her door handle, ignoring her.

"I said get away! Now!"

She had her service weapon out, aimed at Gunner's chest.

The black man stopped pulling on the door, but did not retreat. "That's not going to stop me," he said, shaking his head.

"I don't *have* the gun anymore, all right? IAD has it."

"IAD?"

"That's right. IAD."

"You mean Dick Jenner?"

She lowered her eyes to avoid his. "He came to see me down at the station house yesterday. He said they were opening up Maggie's case again, and they knew I had the gun someone had used against him the night he shot that kid. He told me if I turned it over without asking any questions, and promised to keep my mouth shut about it afterward, they'd forget about my having had it run through the labs without going through the proper channels. What could I do? I had to give it to him."

Gunner didn't say anything.

Lugo looked back up at him and said, "It was an official request, for God's sake. I had no choice."

A car horn honked behind her. They both turned to find a rough-idling blue Isuzu pulled up to her rear bumper, an impatient black woman sitting behind the wheel, waiting to exit the garage.

"I have to go," Lugo said. "I'm sorry."

Gunner put his hand on the car to stop her and said, "I don't get it. I told you two days ago you didn't want to get too involved in this, and you just shook me off. 'I can take care of myself,' you said."

"That's right. I can." She put the car in gear. "What the hell do you think I'm doing now?"

She almost knocked him on his ass pulling away.

"Man. What the fuck happened to you?" Sonny Flowers asked, grinning.

"It's a long story," Gunner said. He was standing out on Mitchell Flowers's front porch, waiting for Flowers's baby brother to open the screen door and invite him in.

The investigator was in a sour mood, for a variety of reasons, and he didn't really care if Sonny Flowers knew it or not. He had made one stop before this one after leaving Deanna Lugo's apartment building a little over two hours ago, and the scene that stop had led to hadn't played out the way he had thought it would at all. In fact, it had thrown him off stride considerably, and he had a strong sense it was going to put a damper on his whole day.

"My brother ain't here," Sonny Flowers told him. "He's at work."

"I didn't come here to see your brother. I came here to see you."

"Me?"

"Yeah. Do we have to sit out here on the porch swing to talk, or can I come inside?"

Sonny Flowers grinned wide, then unlocked the screen door and just limped away from it, to find a seat for himself in the living room. He had pajamas on again, both the top and the bottoms this time. He watched Gunner step into the house and join him, sipping from a cup of coffee without bothering to offer Gunner one of his own.

"What's your name again?" he asked curiously, as Gunner sat down in front of him.

"Gunner."

"That's right. Gunner." He drank some more of his coffee, then said, "Man, we look like a matchin' set. With our eyes an' all, I mean." He laughed. "So you was going to tell me what happened to you. That shit sure as hell didn't happen down at no bowlin' alley."

"No. It didn't."

"Somebody kicked your ass."

"As a matter of fact, yeah. Somebody did. And I think you probably know the guy. He's a big young brother named Foster. Six-four, maybe six-five, and an easy two hundred and forty pounds. Very well spoken, very polite. His friends all call him 'Howie.' "

For an amateur, Sonny did a good job of keeping the look of recognition off his face.

"I don't know nobody like that," he said, trying to smile. "I know some big brothers, but—"

"This one made a one-eyed cripple out of you. Does that help you at all?"

This time, Sonny's face completely collapsed, then coalesced into an angry, hate-filled mask. He put his coffee cup down and said, "All right. So I know the man. So what?"

"So you and your brother have been playing me for an idiot. That's what. Your brother wasn't out by that alley the night Lendell Washington got shot—*you* were. *You* saw McGovern get shot at before he killed that kid, not him."

"What kid? McGovern who? Man, you're crazy."

"I'm not crazy. Just stupid. Milton Wiley had to practically spell it out for me last night before I finally figured it out. He acted like he knew who my client was—yet he didn't know how to find him. That seemed damned odd to me, considering your brother's in the book. I know; I checked. He also said something to the effect that my client had tried to blackmail him before, but had gone away empty-handed because he and Wiley couldn't agree on price. What that suggested to me was that whoever Wiley's blackmailer was, he'd tried to pinch Wiley for more than he wanted to pay, and blackmailers who do that usually end up one of two ways: either dead—or all broken up. That's when I remembered you.

"You're the one Wiley's looking for, Sonny. Not your brother. You've been hiding out in this house, not recuperating in it."

"You're full of shit."

"You put the squeeze on Wiley and Wiley had Foster put the squeeze on you. Full force."

"I don't know what you're talkin' about, 'blackmail' an' 'squeezin',' " Sonny said, climbing to his feet. "We didn't blackmail or squeeze nobody! All we did was offer to help the man win his case. That's all." He started hobbling around the room, like a steer in the slaughterhouse waiting for its turn under the hammer. "I called him up an' told him what Mitch told me to tell him, that it wouldn't be right for me not to go to the cops, to tell 'em what I saw the night that kid was shot, now that they were gonna get sued for somethin' they didn't really do. But if—"

"Wiley wanted to make it worth your while, you might consider keeping quiet about it anyway," Gunner said.

Sonny nodded his head. "Yeah. That's it. That's all I said. I told him I was just thinking 'bout the kid's mother. I didn't wanna see her lose a son and a chance for all that money, too. I mean, so what if it wasn't really murder, the way the cops killed that boy? They've murdered plenty others, right? Hundreds of 'em! So I told the man, if he was interested, I wanted to help. That's all I said to 'im."

"And you don't call that blackmail."

"Hey, did I threaten anybody? No. All I did was make the man a business proposition. Take it or leave it."

"And obviously, he left it."

"What?"

"He didn't pay you."

Sonny shrugged, treating the subject like something he had hoped wouldn't come up. "Yeah, he paid me. Five fuckin' grand. Mitch said, have him put the money in a kid's lunchbox and leave it on a bench at the park, late at night. And that's what he did."

"Only what? He had Foster waiting for you when you tried to make the pick up?"

Sonny shook his head. "Not the first time. He played it straight, the first time."

"The 'first' time? What do you mean, the first time?"

Sonny wouldn't answer him.

"You mean, you tried to hit Wiley up *twice*?"

"Man, what do you think? Five thousand dollars wasn't no kind of money for what I was sellin'! He an' that kid's mother were gonna make *millions* suin' the police, and all he wanted to give me outta the deal was five grand! Mitch, he said we was lucky to get that, but I knew that was bullshit."

"So you called Wiley again. Is that it?"

Sonny nodded again. "All I asked him for was another ten. Fifteen thousand, that was all I was ever gonna ask him for. And the motherfucker sets his boy on me. In the park, just like you said." He shook his head, fighting back tears even as he choked down his anger. "He didn't have to do that, man." He flipped the patch over his right eye out of the way and pointed to the black, fleshy socket beneath. "He didn't have to take my goddamn eye over no motherfuckin' ten thousand dollars!"

Gunner watched him fall back into his chair, his single eye rimmed with red, his chest heaving. It was hard to tell if he even knew Gunner was still in the room.

"Whose idea was it to hire me?" Gunner asked him after a while.

Again, Sonny wouldn't answer him.

"I'll take that to mean it was Mitchell's," Gunner said.

"He's my brother, man. He loves me. You think he was gonna just sit by and do nothin' after those motherfuckers nearly killed me? Shit." He laughed. "Don't let my man's looks fool you. Mitch don't fuck around. He said, you wanna get even with assholes like that, you don't go to the cops. You just fuck with their money. Mess their action up so bad, it don't work no more."

"And that's where I came in? To mess their action up?"

"That was the idea. Yeah." He grinned, looking Gunner over. " 'Cept it looks like you got your action messed up instead."

Though he wasn't entitled to it, Gunner let him have his little joke. He had too many questions left to ask, and he didn't want to bring their meeting to a premature end by adding a mouth full of broken teeth to Sonny's already formidable list of physical injuries.

"The money your brother used to hire me—that was his share of the five thousand you got from Wiley?"

Sonny nodded, still smiling. "Yeah. He said that would make it all the sweeter. Usin' their own money to fuck their shit up with."

"Did you know Lendell Washington didn't fire the shots you saw the night Washington was killed? That someone else in the alley did?"

"Someone else? Like who?"

"Then you didn't know."

"Man, what the hell are you talkin' about?"

"Never mind. It isn't important. What is important is that we stop Wiley's little game while there's still time. Before one of us—or all three of us—ends up dead."

"Dead?"

"You heard me. Dead. I gave Wiley and Foster up to the cops last night, Sonny. Because I thought I had enough to put them away. Unfortunately, I was wrong; at least about Wiley. My one piece of evidence against him took a walk on me, and I think it was a cop who made that happen. Are you smart enough to understand what that means?"

Sonny didn't say anything.

"It means our asses are swinging in the wind, brother, that's what it means. It means Wiley and someone with the LAPD are only going to let us run our mouths off about their business so long before they decide to shut us all up permanently. Evidence or no evidence." He stood up and walked over to where the one-eyed man was sitting. "We have to stop them before they stop us. It's that simple."

"Stop 'em how? And what is this 'we' shit?"

"We have to go see a man. You and me. Right now."

"What man?"

"I'll explain that to you on the way. Let's go."

It wasn't an invitation; looking up into Gunner's face, Sonny understood that immediately. Still, he said, "Hey. Fuck you. I'm not goin' anywhere, all right?"

Gunner was reaching for his client's brother's throat when someone behind them said, "Yes, you are, Sonny."

Mitchell Flowers's wife was standing at the threshold of the dining room, eyeing her brother-in-law with the cold, unflinching determination of an angry kindergarten teacher. How long she had been there, neither man could say; she had appeared from the rear of the house without making a sound.

"You're going to do whatever this man tells you to do," she said firmly. "Or I'll go to the police myself this instant. Do you understand?"

"Sissy, this ain't none of your business," Sonny said.

"This is my business. Anything that involves my husband is my business."

"Shit. You don't know what you're talkin' about."

"It's one thing for the two of you to get yourselves killed trying to blackmail somebody. But when you pay someone else to do your dying for you, under false pretenses . . ." She glanced at Gunner and shook her head. "Someone has to bring you to your senses."

"Woman, you the one needs to be brought to her senses!" Sonny argued, struggling to his feet. "You want Mitch to go to jail? Is that what you want?"

"No. But I don't want to see him dead, either!" Flowers's wife left the dining room at last to square off with her brother-in-law at close range. "Look at yourself!" She gestured at Gunner. "Look at him! Look what these monsters you've been messing with have done to you!" She shook her head. "This isn't going to happen to Mitch, Sonny. I'm not going to allow it. And neither should you."

"Sissy . . ."

"He's always looked out for you. Always. You know as well as I do, he only did this foolish thing because he thought he was helping you. Well, it's time for you to do something for him for a change. Before it's too late." She turned to Gunner again. "I hope you'll forgive me for not having said something sooner, Mr. Gunner. But I was so afraid for Mitch . . ." She let her eyes drift down to the floor for a brief moment, then raised them again. "I don't know if there's anything you can do for him. But if there is . . ."

Gunner shrugged, knowing he was about to say something he might regret later. "I can't promise you anything, Mrs. Flowers. Partly because I'm in no position, and partly because I'm in no mood."

"I understand."

"But whatever I can do to minimize your husband's involvement in all this, I'll do. For your sake—not his."

Sonny's sister-in-law smiled and reached out to shake Gunner's hand. "Thank you. You're very kind." Facing Sonny again, she said, "I'll be going back to my room now, Sonny. If you and Mr. Gunner are still here when I come back, I'm going to call Mitch at work and tell him to meet me down at the police station. You can join us there, if you like."

She was all through talking. Without another word, she turned and walked away, into a hallway past the dining room and out of sight.

"Shit," Sonny Flowers said.

The screen door slammed as Gunner just left him standing there.

After a moment, Mitchell Flowers's little brother threw on some clothes and limped out to the investigator's car.

15

Gunner didn't waste his time looking for Milton Wiley.

He knew Wiley wasn't going to be around. The attorney was too smart for that. The man he had ordered killed the night before was still alive and on the loose, and his favorite henchman was cooling his heels in jail, waiting to be brought up on kidnapping and attempted murder charges. Wiley would see Gunner coming a mile away, and make himself scarce. Just as Pervis Hilton would.

Unfortunately for Hilton, only Wiley had the resources to do the job right.

While Wiley might have already put oceans and continents between himself and Gunner, the best Hilton could do toward the same end was take a day off from work and hide in the far reaches of his sister's home. At least, that was where Gunner and Sonny Flowers found him a few minutes before noon, after one of his Zeidler & Zeidler co-workers at the Fox Hills Mall had told them Hilton had failed to report for work that morning.

Hilton's Corvette had been nowhere in sight upon their arrival, but Gunner had instructed Sonny to ring Harriet Washington's doorbell anyway, while he went around to the back of the house to watch the back door. Standing inside Washington's backyard gate, peering around a rear corner of the house, Gunner had heard Sonny use the doorbell twice, then knock once, before he spotted Hilton easing his way out of a rear bedroom window.

He was standing there to greet him before Hilton's feet even hit the ground.

"Yo, Ben. Nice to see you again," he said.

Hilton spun around and froze, reacting first to the terrible shape Gunner was in, then to the gun that was staring at him from the investigator's right hand. Gunner had retired his nine-millimeter Ruger automatic to his hall closet ever since agreeing to take the McGovern case, not wanting to risk the volatile mix of concealed firearms and officers of the law, but now he felt an overwhelming need for its company. It seemed unlikely that the gun could land him in any more trouble than he was already in.

"Do me a favor and don't ask me what I'm doing here," Gunner said. "You used that line last night. Remember?" He patted Hilton down, finding only a set of keys in one pocket. "Your sister home, by any chance? Or do you expect her home soon?"

Hilton shook his head.

"Mind if we go back inside, then?"

Gunner used the Ruger to indicate the back door.

Maintaining his silence, Hilton took back his keys, opened the door, and led the way inside, taking occasional peeks at Gunner over his shoulder all the while. They passed slowly through the kitchen and ended up in Harriet Washington's living room, where true to Hilton's word, they heard nothing to indicate the woman of the house was home.

"Open the front door and tell the man waiting outside to come in," Gunner said.

Hilton was already as paper white as a black man could become, but the discovery that Gunner wasn't alone here seemed to edge him even closer to the shade of a bloodless corpse. Gunner had to pull the slide back on the Ruger for emphasis before Hilton found the nerve to do as he had been told.

His nerve was quickly lost again, however, when Sonny Flowers stepped into the house to join them, an expression of sheer boredom on his face. He still wasn't sure why he was here, doing Gunner's bidding, but of course, Hilton didn't know that. To Hilton, the limping, one-eyed black man probably looked like the Angel of Death incarnate—and that was exactly the reaction Gunner had made this trip to elicit from him. He could have waited to see if Hilton would crack under Denny Loiacano's questioning, it was true, but this seemed to be an approach to loosening Hilton's tongue that showed infinitely more promise.

"Pervis, I'd like you to meet my client. This is the man who saw you shoot at Jack McGovern the night you inadvertently got your nephew Lendell killed."

"Look," Hilton started to say, finding his voice at last, "I didn't have nothin' to do—"

"He has your friend Foster to thank for the way he looks," Gunner said, cutting him off. "Just like I do. But whereas I'll be relatively whole when I heal up, he never will be. Not quite, anyway."

Gunner nodded at Sonny, and the one-eyed man lifted his eye patch to give Hilton the same good look at his black, hollow eye socket he'd given Gunner earlier.

"I'm tellin' you, man! I didn't have nothin' to do with that!" Hilton cried as he turned his eyes away, disgusted. "Howie works for Milton, not me!"

"The three of you are in this together, Pervis," Gunner said. "You're as much to blame as they are. And since we can't get our hands on Foster or Wiley . . ." He shrugged. "I guess you're going to have to pay for this man's losses all by yourself."

"What?"

"You heard me. This is payback time, homeboy. For him, and me."

"Hey, man. I *told* you—"

"*Fuck* what you told me. Your denials don't mean shit to me, and they mean even less to him." He turned to Sonny. "Look around the house, see if you can find something we can tie him up with."

Sonny nodded his head and started to hobble off, toward the back of the house.

"Waitaminute! Waitaminute!" Hilton said, blinking back tears. "Don't do that, man! Come on!"

"Come on, what?"

"Let's talk about this a minute! All right? Let's just talk!"

Gunner studied Hilton's face in silence for a long moment, as if he might actually turn the younger man's offer down. Finally, he said, "Okay. You want to talk, we'll talk. For a minute." He looked at Sonny again. "Go back out to the car and wait for me there. I'll call you if I need you."

The sullen, one-eyed man just stared at him, doing his best to feign disappointment, then turned away wordlessly and left, slamming the front door closed behind him. He was no Danny Glover, Sonny, but he'd put on a pretty good show.

When he was gone, Gunner said, "That man wants to dig you a grave, Pervis, and I'm going to let him. Do you understand? Because that's the deal I made with him: If I can't get the goods on you and the others, I let him have you, to do with what he pleases. Today or tomorrow—whenever he feels like coming to get you."

"You wouldn't do that," Hilton said.

Gunner laughed. "Shit. You better take another look at my face, brother. After what you and your pals have done to me, I could eat popcorn in the stands while you got what's coming to you."

"But Milton—"

"Milton's not here. You are. And let's face it: Wiley might've masterminded this whole thing, but it really all started with you. Didn't it?"

Hilton knew better than to answer that.

"You're getting deeper into the shit every minute. This could be your last chance to put some distance between yourself and Wiley before it's too late."

Hilton knew it was true immediately, but he didn't nod his head to admit it until several seconds had passed. Lowering his eyes to the floor, he sighed and asked, "What do I have to do?"

"You have to come clean. About everything. Both for me, and for the police."

"The police?"

"Of course. They've got to hear your story from you, not me."

Hilton fell silent.

"What's it going to be, Pervis?"

It was a long time coming, but a shrug finally made it up to Hilton's shoulders.

Gunner grinned. "Good man," he said. "You're doing the right thing, believe me." He glanced around the house until he found the phone, then waved the Ruger at Harriet Washington's plastic-covered couch and said, "Take a seat and relax for a minute while I make a call, all right?"

He watched as the listless Hilton sat down, then went to the wall phone in the kitchen and did what most people in big trouble always did first: He called a cop.

He had to make two separate phone calls before someone finally showed up. The first was to Denny Loiacano in Hollywood, the second to Danny Kubo downtown.

In both cases, the officers he was trying to reach were unavailable, so he'd left an identical message for each, consisting of little more than his name, Harriet Washington's address and phone number, and an urgent plea for help. It was Loiacano he really wanted to see, but Kubo was the one who responded to his call roughly an hour later, acting as put upon and disgruntled as when they had last met.

Predictably, Kubo wouldn't listen to anything until Gunner had explained the patch over his eye and the cast on his right hand with a brief overview of his run-in with Wiley and friends the night before. Kubo thought he was getting the straight scoop, but Gunner flat out lied and told him he had made up a story for Loiacano during questioning, rather than try to sell the Hollywood detective on the truth. Gunner knew Kubo wouldn't appreciate his drawing another cop into a case Kubo had implored him to drop almost a week ago, and he couldn't spare the time right now to listen to the IAD man complain about it.

Only Gunner and Pervis Hilton were there when Kubo arrived, as Gunner had sent Sonny Flowers home, hoping to avoid involving either of the Flowers brothers in the McGovern affair unless Hilton's confession made it absolutely necessary. He had feared an hour would be more than enough time for Hilton to change his mind about turning himself in, but he needn't have worried. Hilton started talking the minute Kubo sat down and made himself comfortable, clearly anxious to explain to someone, anyone, how little a role he had played in Wiley's scheme to turn Lendell Washington's death into the goose that laid the golden eggs.

As Gunner and Kubo took turns asking him an occasional question or two, Hilton took them through the whole sordid affair step by step, from his ill-fated purchase of the gun he had fired at Jack McGovern the previous fall, right up to his reacquaintance with Gunner in his sister's backyard only hours earlier. He had confessed all to his sister's attorney within days of his nephew's killing, Hilton said, because he expected that either Wiley or the authorities would learn of his part in it eventually, and he was looking ahead to the possibility of having Wiley represent him when the time came. In retrospect, Hilton admitted, he should have been able to foresee that Wiley would choose to just sit on the information, considering everything that was at stake, but he hadn't, and once that mistake had been made, there had seemed to be nothing for Hilton to do but stand back and watch Wiley go to work. Which was just what he did.

"He told me not to worry, that no one would ever find out I was even there when Lendell got shot," Hilton said. "And he was right. No one did. He talked Noah into keeping quiet about my putting them up to the robbery, and that was it. The show was on. The only way something could go wrong was if the cops found my gun, he said, but they never did. We figured it got picked up with the trash where I dumped it and was gone for good. But then you said you found it."

"I did," Gunner said. "But I didn't have it for long. I think Wiley has somebody inside the police department who made sure it got lost again."

"Somebody inside the department? Like who?" Kubo demanded.

Gunner nodded in Hilton's direction and said, "Ask him."

"What? Man, I don't know who Milton's cop is." Hilton shook his head.

"But he does have one."

"Hey. I don't know one way or the other. I've heard him say he's got a man on the inside, yeah, but I always thought he was just talking. 'Cause what kinda cop would want to help *him*, right? He's jackin' up the police for a million bucks!"

Gunner and Kubo just looked at each other, leaving the name Gunner had in mind unspoken.

"We still haven't heard what happened to Ford, yet," Gunner said to Hilton, moving on to a new item on his agenda before a debate he knew he couldn't win broke out between himself and Kubo. "Or are you going to try and tell me his getting killed down at Central last Saturday was just an odd coincidence, too?"

"I don't think it was a coincidence. Hell no."

"How about telling us what you *do* think it was, then," Kubo said.

"I think it was a hit. Sure. I just don't think Milton had anything to do with it. I mean, he could've done it, I guess, yeah. But why would he?" To Gunner specifically, he said, "Noah wasn't going to tell you anything, man. You could've spent the next fifty years of your life tryin' to get that little motherfucker to talk to you, and it wouldn't have done you a damn bit of good. Milton told you that last night, remember?"

"He told me a lot of things last night," Gunner said.

Hilton just shrugged, having already rested his case.

Gunner looked at Kubo and asked him if he'd heard enough.

"I guess so," Kubo said. He nodded toward the kitchen, suggesting they confer there in private.

Gunner stood up and followed him out of the room. Hilton watched the two men step just inside the kitchen doorway and stop, too far away to be heard, yet close enough to keep an eye on him.

"Well? Do you believe me now?" Gunner asked.

Kubo shrugged. "I don't know if I do or not," he said. "This guy isn't exactly star witness material, if you know what I mean."

"What?"

"I mean, some of what he says makes sense, I suppose. But a lot of it doesn't. All this talk about Wiley having a man on the inside, for instance—that's a load of crap, Aaron, and you know it."

"Do I?"

"You do if you've got half a brain in your head."

"Half a brain is a fourth more than you've got if you still can't see what's going on here, Danny."

"All right, all right. Take it easy. I didn't say his story isn't worth looking into. I just said it's got a few holes in it, that's all."

"Then you are going to look into it."

Kubo nodded his head after a long pause. "Yeah. Somebody has to, I guess." He moved to the phone on the wall and picked up the receiver. "By the way. Anybody else know about this besides me?"

Gunner shook his head. "Who would I tell?" He was lying through his teeth again, of course, but there was no way for Kubo to know that. Though Sonny Flowers had been here earlier, Gunner had made a point of steering Hilton off the subject just as it was about to come up.

"Are you sure about that?" Kubo asked, skeptical to the last. He was punching a number in on the phone.

"Yeah, I'm sure." Gunner's eyes were on Hilton, who was wiggling around on the couch like a man trying to ignore a full bladder.

"Good," he heard Kubo say behind him.

Somehow, Gunner knew there was a gun in the policeman's hand before he turned around to actually see it: a Smith & Wesson nine-millimeter automatic, blue-skinned and angry looking.

"What's the gag, Danny?" Gunner asked Kubo solemnly.

Kubo's head inched from side to side. "It's no gag, partner. Sorry." He was all business now, just a cop doing his dirty work with cold, deliberate efficiency. He hung up the phone with his free hand, then took a side step deeper into the kitchen, removing himself from Hilton's field of vision. He moved in closer to Gunner and gingerly lifted the Ruger out of the holster under the black man's left arm, holding his own Smith & Wesson up under Gunner's chin all the while.

"I thought you said Wiley having a man inside the department was a load of crap," Gunner said.

Kubo stepped back again, shoving the Ruger inside the waistband of his trousers, and said, "Wiley doesn't own me. He doesn't even know me. We're just two people who happen to share a common goal, that's all. We cooperate with each other."

"Ah. I get it. Sharing and cooperating. Just like on 'Sesame Street.'"

"Look. This is going to be hard enough. Do me a favor and can the wisecracks, all right?" He used the Smith & Wesson to direct Gunner back into Harriet Washington's living room.

Hilton came up off the couch when he saw them coming, sizing the situation up immediately, but Kubo said, "Stay where you are, Hilton," and he sank right back down again, his eyes glowing white with fear. Kubo told Gunner to take the seat next to him but stayed on his feet himself, preferring to look down upon both men from a safe distance.

"There's something I haven't told you yet, Danny," Gunner said. "Something I think you should know before you do anything stupid."

"If you're going to tell me about your girlfriend Lugo, forget it. I know all about her."

"Yeah?"

"Yeah. She's a nice kid. Too bad you had to drag her into this."

"I needed her help, Danny."

"You dumb ass. The lady's going to lose her badge for trying to help you. Or worse."

"Or worse?"

"That's right. Or worse. The stakes in this thing are that high, Aaron. When the hell are you going to figure that out?"

Gunner didn't answer that.

"What are you going to do to us?" Hilton asked Kubo, taking advantage of the lull in the pair's conversation to speak for the first time. He wasn't looking too healthy.

"I haven't made up my mind, yet," Kubo told him, unconvincingly.

"Shit. Don't bullshit the man, Danny. You made your mind up about that on your way over here," Gunner said.

"Okay. Maybe I did. But that doesn't mean things have to go down the way I planned. You want to change the script, Aaron, be my guest. What I told you last week about us being even, we both know that was bullshit. The way I see it, I still owe you one more favor, at least. A big one. So consider this one it.

"Get the hell out of here and forget you ever heard of Jack McGovern. He was a sorry fuck who didn't deserve your time, or your worry. What happened to him eight months ago was for the best, believe me, and to undo it all now—that would be a mistake."

"I don't think your friends downtown would see it that way. Do you?"

"To tell you the truth, I don't have that many friends downtown. So I don't really give a shit how they would see it. Most of those idiots actually thought highly of McGovern; I'd hardly expect them to see the value in ensuring he remains a disgrace to the department."

"I assume you mean excluding Chief Bowden, of course."

"Bowden? Bowden's reasons for dumping on McGovern were strictly political. He wasn't as much interested in how right it was as how good it would look to the people he's counting on to make him mayor someday. The long-term benefits to the department of the move totally escaped him."

"You want to know something? They seem to escape me, too."

"Maybe that's because you're not a cop. A *real* cop. Badge-heavy jackasses like McGovern, they aren't police officers; they wear the uniform, all right, but that's it. They don't give a damn how much damage they do to the public trust, because the public trust isn't a priority with them.

"But *real* cops—all the ones busting their asses trying to make the words 'To Protect and Serve' actually *mean* something in this city again—they *do* give a damn. And they're the ones who pay the price every time the system gives a bad egg like McGovern the keys to the asylum so that he can re-clone himself, over and over again."

"Re-clone himself?"

"That's right. You trying to tell me you haven't figured out yet that McGovern was a goddamn *training officer,* for Christ's sake? The man was out there on the street, creating new officers in his fucked-up image every day."

"And that's what this was all about? Stopping McGovern from corrupting future recruits?"

"The sonofabitch *had* to be stopped. They all do. Cops like that are poison, and they've been rubbing off on the rest of us long enough. The time has come to weed the fuckers out of the ranks. Any way we can."

"And you think this is a good way to start. By fitting every last one of them for a frame."

"I didn't frame anybody. I just didn't go out of my way to spare McGovern the dishonor he'd had coming to him for a long time. There's a difference, Aaron."

"Sure there is. Just like there's a difference between vigilantism and murder."

"Murder?"

"You were the one who had Noah Ford killed, Danny. Not Hilton here, or Wiley. They both knew Ford too well to think he'd talk to me, but you didn't. You couldn't be sure about him, one way or the other."

Kubo was obviously uncomfortable making the disclosure, but he shrugged and said, "The way I figure it, he should have died back in that alley last September anyway. Not his cousin Washington. Kids like Ford don't make this world a better place to live any more than cops like McGovern do."

"I want to know how you did it," Gunner said.

"How I did it? What the hell difference does that make now?"

"You want me to throw in with you, it makes a difference. They said Ford had been killed by a gangbanger in the H-Town Gamblers set. Is that right?"

His answer came at the end of a long pause. "Yes."

"So what's your connection to the H-Town Gamblers?"

"I don't have one."

"Then how the hell—"

"All I did was get a rumor started about him. I had somebody spread the word around that he'd dissed a Gambler on the outside once."

"And their homeboys did the rest."

"Yeah."

"So who spread the word for you? A guard on the inside?"

"Maybe. Look. We're digressing, and time is running short." He glanced at his watch and frowned. "I'm afraid I need your answer, partner. Right now. You want to be reasonable here, or not?"

"Look, man—" Hilton started to say, again breaking a lengthy silence.

"Shut up," Kubo told him. He didn't even make the effort to turn the clothes salesman's way.

Stunned, Hilton did as he was told and looked over at Gunner, like Kubo anxious to hear what choice the investigator was going to make. He was still unwilling to accept the fact that Kubo was going to kill *him,* no matter what the man seated beside him decided to do.

Only when Gunner shook his head at Kubo did Hilton surrender all hope for himself.

"Not that I don't admire your motives, Danny," Gunner said. "But I'm sorry. I just can't hang with you on this one. Your methods are a little too drastic for my tastes."

"I'm only doing what's going to be necessary to get the community back on our side again," Kubo said coldly.

"Even if I thought that were true, I still couldn't help you. But you knew that before you asked me, didn't you?"

Kubo shrugged again, a veil of disappointment changing the shadows on his face. "We used to be pretty tight once, you and me. I figured I at least owed it to you to ask."

He pulled Gunner's Ruger from the waistband of his trousers with his free hand.

"Oh, shit," Hilton moaned.

"As long as we're paying off old debts," Gunner said, "I told you there was something I thought you should know before you did anything stupid. Remember?"

Kubo waited for him to elaborate.

"I went to see your friend Dick Jenner today. It was a dumb thing to do, I know, but at the time I was thinking he was the one working with Wiley, not you, and I wasn't sure I'd be able to convince Hilton to talk. So I decided to see if maybe he would.

"Naturally, he told me he didn't know what the fuck I was talking about. And I believed him. I didn't want to, but I did."

"Make your point," Kubo said. He was furious.

"Well, I was just thinking," Gunner said. "My going to him like that might have started him wondering about you. That would only be natural, right? And if he were wondering about you, he might want to . . . keep an eye on you for a while."

Kubo was already moving toward the window at the front of the house, backpedaling as he shoved the Ruger back into his pants. He kept his body turned in Gunner and Hilton's direction as he parted the drapes and peeked out at the street, looking for a sign, any sign, of his partner's presence there. He had his eyes off Harriet Washington's living room for all of five seconds.

But that was long enough.

"Put the gun down, Danny," Dick Jenner said.

He was standing at the threshold of the kitchen, training his own nine-millimeter automatic on Kubo's chest. He had entered the house through the back door without making a sound.

Kubo turned around slowly and smiled, holding the Smith & Wesson up high in his right hand, aimed at the ceiling. "Man, am I glad to see you," he said. "These two assholes—"

"I said toss the piece, Danny," Jenner ordered again, taking a step closer to him. "Do it, partner. Please."

"Look, Dick. You don't understand . . ."

Gunner wasn't sure, but the Smith & Wesson in Kubo's hand seemed to be descending.

"I understand plenty. I've talked to Lugo, Danny. She gave me the gun," Jenner said. "But we can straighten this thing out, man. Believe me. Just *don't get crazy on me,* all right?"

Kubo still refused to obey. "I'm not crazy," he said.

201

"Jesus Christ. I'm begging you. Don't make me do this, god-damnit!"

Kubo's right hand released the Smith & Wesson as if to surrender it, just as his left went for the Ruger at his waist. Jenner hit him once over the heart, and the blast propelled Kubo backward like a doll on a string, into the wall behind him. He knocked over a table and the lamp atop it fell to the floor, smearing Harriet Washington's floral wallpaper with blood as the Ruger tumbled out of his grasp. He was still breathing when Jenner got to him, but everyone in the room knew he was a dead man.

Hilton started to get up, but Gunner put an arm out and forced him into his seat again, where Gunner himself intended to remain. A cop had just killed his own partner, and in a minute, Gunner knew, he was going to start looking around for someone to blame. Leaving the couch before being given permission to do so might not be enough to win the honors, but you never knew.

When Jenner finally turned around to face them, they knew that Kubo was dead. He came over to where they were sitting and stood over them, just as Kubo had done only minutes earlier, and gave them a good, hard look at the gun in his hand.

"I've got you to thank for that, you son of a bitch," he said to Gunner.

If he was looking for an argument, he wasn't going to get one.

"He was a good cop. I don't give a shit what you say. And I don't want to see his reputation go down the toilet." He paused. "But that's exactly what's going to happen, I bring you two in. Isn't it?"

Gunner still wouldn't say anything.

Jenner put the nose of his automatic up against the black man's forehead and smiled.

"Decisions, decisions," he said.

16

Sometimes, luck was enough.

And Gunner held no delusions about his living to see another day being anything else but. He had told Danny Kubo what he thought was a lie, only to discover he had told him the truth, instead. While he had indeed gone to see Dick Jenner Thursday morning, before his confrontation with Sonny Flowers at Mitchell Flowers's home, he hadn't believed for a moment that Jenner might have actually followed Kubo to Harriet Washington's residence. That had just been something to say in order to draw Kubo's attention to the window. The idea was to wait for Kubo's eyes to turn away, then make a break for the kitchen and the back door beyond. No one had been more surprised—and relieved—than Gunner when Jenner's appearance in the kitchen doorway had rendered such a desperate gambit unnecessary.

Another cop in Jenner's shoes, facing the choice between besmirching his dead partner's memory and killing a pair of black nobodies who were at least indirectly responsible for his partner's death, might have put the bullet in Gunner's head that Jenner had ultimately refused to. It wouldn't have been that difficult to make up a story that would explain two more bodies in the room, if Jenner had wanted to do that; as an IAD man, he almost certainly would have known what to say, and what not to. A lie, and the small measure of revenge that would have come with it, was the most attractive option Jenner had available to him—and yet he had refused to tell it. Despite the cost to Kubo's name, he had opted for the truth instead. Turning Gunner and Hilton over to Denny Loiacano, he had stood back while they buried Kubo under a mountain of dishonorable allegations, then supplied Loiacano with the gun he had talked Deanna Lugo into giving him, just for good measure. In short, he had played the good cop, because that, ironically, was what Jenner was: a good cop.

Hell yes, Gunner had been lucky.

And in the days that followed, his good fortune held. Pervis Hilton's sudden willingness to talk to the police might have persuaded Milton Wiley to do little more than turn himself into the authorities, but it had moved Wiley's friend Howie Foster to start talking like somebody who was getting paid by the syllable. Gunner kept waiting for someone to mention his client's attempts to extort hush money from Wiley, but no one ever did, and the omission made Gunner's life just that much easier. Neither Mitchell Flowers, nor his brother Sonny, really deserved the break, but Gunner felt as though *he* did, and he was glad to get it. So much so that he refused to worry that Wiley might choose to blow that particular whistle later, whenever—and *if* ever—he finally decided to come clean.

All in all, Harriet Washington and Dick Jenner represented the only real down side to the end of Gunner's work for Mitchell Flowers. Washington, because she had had to learn the truth about both her lawyer and her baby brother in the same fashion as most of the general public: by watching the evening news on TV Thursday night; and Jenner, because he never spoke to Gunner again. He knew how much his making peace with the investigator would help to assuage Gunner's guilt over Danny Kubo's death, and he had no interest in doing Gunner that particular favor. The half-dozen or so calls Gunner made to him downtown once the police had sent the investigator home for good never received an answer.

What Jenner didn't know was that Gunner's reasons for wanting to talk with the IAD man went beyond mere forgiveness. He was also looking for answers. He was comfortable with the knowledge that his old friend Kubo had died an insane man, but it bothered him that he could not say where Kubo's insanity had begun, and his wisdom had left off. For Kubo had made it sound as if no other measures but his own would stand a chance of ridding the LAPD of the racism it was becoming more and more infamous for. And if a *cop* felt that way . . .

Gunner didn't want to believe the system was really that far gone.

So he tried to get Dick Jenner to consent to a little reassuring heart-to-heart, only to have his invitations go unacknowledged. It took some time, but eventually he convinced himself that it didn't matter; whatever the ingrained state of the department's prejudices, it was none of his business, and not his worry.

And then one day, the flowers came.

Long-stemmed red roses; an even dozen. The strange looks he had gotten from Mickey, Weldon Foley, and Foley's homie, Joe Worthy upon his entrance into Mickey's shop that morning had been confusing until he had seen the bouquet, resting in a familiar gold lamé box atop his desk, a gift card attached.

Mickey followed him like a puppy dog into the back of the shop and, watching him read the card, said, "Lady left those for you early this mornin'. You know her?"

Gunner felt a grin slide over his face. "I think so. Yeah."

"Not well, I hope," Mickey said. " 'Cause I got news for you—"

Gunner waved him off and read the card:

> My Darling Aaron,
> I was wrong about you. You were wonderful. Please give me a chance to apologize? Tonight? I'll be sitting at the bar at McQueen's. You know the place. Eight o'clock. Don't be late!
> Love,
> H.K.

"So tell me somethin'," Harry Kupchak said, doing a sloppy job of refilling Gunner's empty beer mug. "How'd the boys down at the office like Peaches?"

He was already laughing.

"Exactly as you might expect. They think I've taken a walk on the wild side," Gunner said.

"No shit."

"No shit. I think my landlord's drawing up eviction papers as we speak."

Gunner smiled as Kupchak fell out again, then went to work on his beer and took a good look around. McQueen's was a boisterous little bistro on Figueroa and Flower streets that was apparently where every self-respecting cop working out of the Southwest station house spent his or her after-hours. Laughter and vulgarity spilled across the room from all directions, and smoke lingered in the air like levitating ghosts at nearly every table. The lighting was as subdued as the oldies music emanating from the jukebox.

Had it not been for one plainclothes officer in a corduroy jacket shooting pool over near the door, Gunner would have been the only black person in attendance tonight.

"How the hell'd you find her, anyway?" Gunner asked Kupchak, picking up their conversation right where it had left off.

"Just because I'm an asshole, Gunner, that doesn't mean I don't have friends. The guy who was at the desk the day you dropped her off at the station, I had him and an art department guy put together a composite for me. All I had to do after that was show it around, 'til I found somebody who knew her, and where I could find her."

"You have to do much talking to get her to do it?"

"Are you kidding? I think she's startin' to enjoy the work. It's a lot easier than what she's used to, right?"

They both laughed.

"Anyway, this makes us even," Kupchak said.

"I guess it does."

"Except, you need another favor. Don't you?"

"Did I say I need another favor?"

"You didn't say it. It's just a feeling I get, watching you. Maybe I'm wrong."

Gunner let him stare for nearly a full minute, then said, "I've got a few questions I wanted to ask you. That's all."

"What kind of questions?"

Gunner shrugged, trying to downplay the significance of the subject. "Questions about cops like McGovern. Bigots who wouldn't recognize a decent black man if one fell out of the sky on top of them. You know the kind I mean."

"Yeah?"

"Yeah. I want to know where they come from, Kupchak. I want to know what happens to them out there that they forget what it's like to give a damn about anybody but themselves."

Kupchak tightened his jaw to keep the cordial smile on his face in place, then raised his beer mug to his mouth and said, "Forget it. You wouldn't understand."

"Try me. I might surprise you."

Kupchak kept him waiting. He didn't speak until the last of his beer was gone, and only then after he had refilled his own glass. "War, Gunner," the policeman said. "That's what happens to 'em. Only nobody wants to admit it.

"People wanna believe it's just a job, police work. Like driving a cab, or selling insurance. But you tell me what cabbie has to clean up the mess a drunk leaves behind after he's bounced his baby girl off the walls of his apartment like a goddamn basketball. Or what insurance man has to wrestle with an old woman wielding a butcher knife on her front lawn while all her neighbors stand around shouting obscenities at him. 'White motherfucker' this, and 'asshole' that. Shit. You call that a job?"

"So being a cop's a dirty business. Everybody knows that going in."

"Nobody knows jack shit going in. That's the trouble. Rookies always think they're prepared for what's coming, but they never are. Nobody could be. Crack houses on every other corner; nine-year-old kids committing execution-style murders; women being cut up or beaten senseless by jealous boyfriends or dusted pimps. Some cops, they learn to live with it after a while, sure. But others . . ." He went back to his beer to fill a short silence. "They get a little crazy. Out of control. But that's what happens in a war, right? Not everybody comes out whole."

"Except you people aren't grunts, Kupchak. And this isn't some jungle in Cambodia. The people you're talking about being at war with are US citizens, man, not the goddamn Vietcong."

"So what the hell's the difference? We were the enemy over there, and we're the enemy right here. The people of this community hate our guts just as much as the gooks ever did."

"I think you're wrong. I think you're confusing hatred with fear."

"Fear?"

"That's right. Fear. These people are too busy being afraid of you to hate you, Kupchak. You've got them scared shitless."

"Yeah? Well, what a coincidence. They've got us scared shitless, too. Because we're the only ones tryin' to fight this fight by any rules, Gunner. All the fuckin' crazies we have to go up against—all the kids with their Uzis, and whacked-out car thieves with their tire irons and baseball bats—they don't give a fuck about the rules, all right? They don't *have* any rules. We're the ones who have to try and be civilized about this shit, not them."

"You're talking about the lowlifes. I'm talking about everybody else. You can't keep lumping us all in with the scumbags just becuase we all happen to look alike to you."

"Shit. All we *see* are lowlifes," Kupchak said. "What do you think? This isn't Malibu we're talking about here, Gunner, it's the fuckin' *ghetto*. And by and large, the people we run into aren't CPAs or Boy Scout troop leaders. They're drunks and crack heads, ex-cons and cons-to-be. Drug pushers and wife-beaters, professional crybabies who don't do a fuckin' thing all day but hang out, while the rest of the world is busting its ass trying to pay for their food stamps. I hate to say that, but it's true."

"Bullshit," Gunner said.

The room had suddenly grown quiet. Somewhere over the last several minutes, Kupchak and his black civilian friend had become the center of everyone's attention.

"Hey, Harry! You need some help over there?" a voice called out from a far corner of the room.

208

"Bullshit? What's bullshit?" Kupchak asked Gunner, ignoring his friend across the way.

"Everything you just said. All that crap about your seeing nothing but lowlifes. If that's really how you feel, Kupchak, you boys need to have your eyes examined. Because you're only seeing part of the picture."

"And the part of the picture we're missing is what? As if I couldn't guess," Kupchak said.

"Only the vast majority of people you're supposed to be serving down here. That's all," Gunner said.

"So I exaggerated a little. There are good, law-abiding citizens in this community, sure. We see 'em all the time. But we see the other kind more. And mistaking one kind for the other can get a cop killed faster than anything else I know. I've seen it happen too many times."

"Goddamn straight," somebody at the next table agreed.

"So you assume the worst about everybody, just to be on the safe side," Gunner said. "Is that it?"

"You'd better believe it. I told you, Gunner: This is war. And the enemy in this war wears a million disguises and comes at you from a thousand different directions. You can't make it down here giving people the benefit of the doubt, all right? You *can't.* You can get yourself blown away trying that Mr. Nice Guy shit down here."

"How about just being human? Is that a safe proposition, or are you asking for trouble there, too?"

"Anything we do out here is asking for trouble. That's my whole point. You want to be a human being first, and a cop second? Fine. That's your privilege. But they'll be pinning all your medals to a dead man's chest later, friend. Believe it."

A rumble of assent rolled throughout the room, and at last Gunner understood the futility of the argument he was engaged in. Kupchak's view of the world had been set in stone years ago, and there wasn't a power on earth strong enough to change it now. Basically, Gunner thought, the policeman's lament wasn't much different from Dancing Fred's, as the homeless black man had expressed it that night at the Popeye's Fried Chicken stand:

The world was cold; life was dangerous; and all you had to do to meet a sudden end was have the audacity to attempt to survive it all.

"You can die tryin'," Fred had said sadly.

Abruptly, Gunner tossed back the last of his drink and stood up. "It was nice talking to you, Kupchak. It's been enlightening, to say the least."

"What happened, Gunner? I hurt your feelings?" Kupchak asked him, remaining seated.

Gunner simply grinned at him and walked away.

"Hey! Don't be a stranger, now!" Kupchak called after him, watching the black man wind his way through the muttering crowd to the door. "Drop in again any time, huh?"

Tickled by his own sarcasm, Kupchak started laughing, causing several people in the house to erupt right along with him.

By the time Gunner reached his car outside, there wasn't a single cop in McQueen's who wasn't having the time of their life at his expense.

The next day, Gunner found himself parked out in front of Davey's Market again.

As usual, he was supposed to be watching out for the three pint-sized holy terrors who had been vandalizing David Huong's establishment, but today his eyes were all over the place, his mind wandering.

He should have never had that talk with Harry Kupchak.

The things he had learned at that table in McQueen's he would have preferred not to know. It was the kind of harsh reality that made a man wonder why the world was still turning, when the immeasurable weight of mankind's love for self-destruction should have stopped it in its tracks eons ago. Kupchak was only one cop, it was true, but Gunner had little doubt the policeman's views were shared not only by his friends at McQueen's, but by many of his fellow Southwest officers, as well. All you had to do was watch the latter in action to know that.

And Danny Kubo had died trying to warn Gunner that more of the same were on the way.

It wasn't a heartwarming thought, if you were one of the "good" black people cops like Kupchak had such a difficult time acknowledging. It meant that you had to prove more than your mere innocence when you were unfortunate enough to come up against them; you had to prove your worth as a human being first, before anything else. Because the system in which they operated had taught them to question not only your good intentions but your right to be considered their equal, as well. Along with all the amusing names they liked to use for you came any number of misconceptions, and all you had to do to get along with them was dispel those misconceptions one by one, time and time again.

While the hell that was their daily bread out on the street kept reinforcing all their fears and prejudices against you.

The description "no-win" seemed to fit this situation to a T, Gunner thought.

Someday, he tried to reassure himself, the LAPD and the black community would find a way to break the vicious cycle that was pulling them further and further apart with every passing day. All the finger pointing would stop and the healing process would begin. It was not inconceivable. But in the meantime, there would only be a continuation of what Harry Kupchak had accurately described as a war, and everyone involved would lose. Some would lose a son, some a daughter; others, a partner or a friend. Almost no one would be spared.

It was insane.

"I thought that was you," Claudia Lovejoy suddenly said.

Gunner looked up, startled, to see that she was standing on the sidewalk beside his car, staring at him. Her late-model Honda Accord had somehow snuck up behind him and parked, a few car lengths down on the same side of the street.

"I was driving by, and I saw the car. And I thought, if you'd seen me, and I didn't stop . . ." She shrugged, as if she thought that would make her explanation seem more plausible. "I just didn't want to seem rude, that's all."

"I see," Gunner said.

"Maybe I should have just kept going."

She'd caught the pained expression on his face before he could turn it away from her.

"No. Not at all."

"But you look like you're working."

He showed her a shrug of his own, careful not to put too much annoyance in it. "Some kids have been giving Davey over there a hard time lately, so I told him I'd keep an eye out for them when I could. It's just something to do, really." He looked back across the street at the market again, afraid to keep giving her his undivided attention. She looked as beautiful as ever.

She stared at the back of his head for a moment, then said, "You look good."

"Thanks. So do you." He'd turned his eyes toward her, but that was all.

"I haven't been very kind to you lately, have I?"

"Claudia . . ."

"No. No. It's true. That message I left with Mickey the other day . . ."

"Forget about it. I was being hardheaded, and you were just tired of dealing with it. You did what you had to do. It's okay."

"No. It isn't." She waited patiently for Gunner to finally turn around again. "Okay, I mean. In fact, it's been far from that, you want to know the truth."

She showed him a thin smile and a shrug.

"So welcome to the club," Gunner said.

"Yeah. Thanks."

"Look. This is your party, remember? Any time you want to call it off, you can."

"I know. And I want to. But . . ." She shook her head. "Not just yet. I still need a little more time."

Trying his best not to sound bitter, Gunner said, "We *all* need a little more time, Claudia."

She was behind the Honda's wheel by the time regret fully set in. He watched the car pull off in his rearview mirror and then followed its course with his eyes as it vanished down the street ahead of him, making every light. Without thinking, he fired the Cobra up and started to go after her, to demand some explanation for the scene she'd just cast him in, but the sound of his own name being shouted in the street brought him quickly back to his senses.

He killed the car's ignition and looked off to his left just in time to see a trio of young boys in laceless sneakers and bright-colored clothes cross 108th Street on the dead run, leaving a furious and frantic David Huong in their wake. Huong was standing out in the street in front of his market, screaming and gesturing at Gunner to give chase, forcing southbound traffic on Avalon to bob and weave its way around him.

Gunner grabbed his keys and took off running, flying after Huong's little tormentors like a dog yapping after a mailman. The kids were almost two full blocks ahead of him at the start, but his stride was much greater than theirs and he made up ground on them easily. They fled east on 107th Street, trying to lose him, but it didn't do them any good. He was on his own turf now, only houses from his home, and there was no way he was going to lose any race being run in his own backyard.

By the time the three boys reached McKinley Avenue, imploring each other on through the labored breathing of foot soldiers at boot camp, all Gunner had to do was decide which one he wanted to scare the shit out of. The one taking up the rear would have been easy pickings, of course, but the investigator went for the smaller kid in the middle of the pack, instead. He clamped a hand around the boy's bony neck and just reeled him in, leaving the remaining pair to make good their escape. They waited until they were far out of reach to stop and look back at him, then showed him the middle finger of their right hands and laughed, daring him to do something about it.

The oldest of the two couldn't have been more than eight years old, and already they knew how to tell a man to go fuck himself without even saying a word.

Meanwhile, the friend they'd left behind was giving Gunner all he could handle, screaming at the top of his lungs and clawing at the black man's hands with both of his own, trying to break Gunner's grip on his neck. He kept shouting the same thing over and over again, like a talking doll stuck on a single recorded phrase: "I didn't do nothin'! I didn't do nothin'!"

"I'm going to kill you," Gunner told him, shaking him out like a wet rag doll just to wear him down a little. "I'm going to walk you over to the freeway and throw your ass down over the side. Come on."

He started dragging the kid back toward Avalon Boulevard and the Harbor Freeway far beyond.

The boy struggled against him frantically, making one last, great effort to save himself, but Gunner remained unfazed. As Avalon loomed closer and closer, the little man finally broke into tears and went limp in Gunner's hands, certain that his life was over.

"I'm going to drop you on a blue car," Gunner said casually, watching for the kid's reaction. "That okay with you? Blue?"

The boy just kept crying. He had a smooth brown complexion and a handsome, unmarked face, and tears were cutting a swath through the thin film of grime on his cheeks. He was just a baby, six, maybe seven years old, but he was already making plans for his own funeral, like his buddies were down the street. They just didn't know it, yet.

"But I didn't do nothin'," the little man sobbed, forcing the words out between sniffles.

"Yes you did, goddamnit!"

Gunner stopped walking and snatched him around, ending the game. "You fucked up! You went in that store and jacked it up, just like you did the last time! Don't lie about it!"

"But it was Pee Cee—" He started to point a finger at one of his accomplices hovering in the distance.

"Fuck Pee Cee! You went in there with him, didn't you? That makes you just as guilty as he is. You let him talk you into doing something stupid, sweet pea, that's *your* problem, not his."

"But—"

"What's your name?"

The kid was rubbing his eyes now, trying to pretend he didn't hear the question. "Huh?"

"You heard me. Your name."

The kid kept on rubbing his eyes, his head down, and said, "Gaylon." He had done everything possible to make the name unintelligible.

"Gaylon what?"

"Gaylon Brown."

"How old are you, Gaylon Brown?"

"Six."

"Six, huh? Well, let me tell you something. A six-year-old man has no business letting anybody tell them what to do. You understand? You're too old to be somebody else's punk."

"Punk?"

"That's right. Punk. You know what a punk is? A punk is somebody who does shit he knows he shouldn't do just because he sees one of his homeboys doing it. Like this Pee Cee, for instance. You do everything Pee Cee tells you to do?"

Gaylon Brown shook his head emphatically.

"Bullshit. Yes you do. Don't lie. You're his punk."

"I ain't nobody's punk!"

"Did he come back here to help you? Did he run to your mother or father to get help? Hell no. He didn't do shit. He's standing over there right now, just waiting to see what I'm going to do to you. You think he's your friend? Shit. . . ."

Gunner shook his head and laughed.

"It's like this, Gaylon Brown. I'm going to let you go—this time," Gunner said. "But I'm going to be watching you. You understand what I'm saying? I'm going to be *watching you*. And if I ever see you messing up again—jacking up somebody's market, or snatching somebody's purse—*whatever*—I'm going to take you over to the freeway. And I'm going to throw your sorry little ass down onto the fast lane, in front of a big blue Oldsmobile. So help me God. You believe that, Gaylon Brown?"

The kid nodded his head, trying to keep from crying again.

"All right, then. Raise." Gunner released his grip on the little boy's neck.

Gaylon Brown started running and didn't look back until he was safely among his friends again, too far away to be concerned about Gunner ever reclaiming him. When the trio of boys broke out laughing and raised their middle fingers skyward in salute to him, like miniature musketeers proudly crossing swords in defiance of the king, Gunner wasn't much surprised.

But neither was he amused.

Walking slowly back to his car, he considered Gaylon Brown's mistake. The poor kid had thought he was bluffing, because the freeway threat was so outrageous. He'd assumed because that part of Gunner's act was hollow, all the rest of it had to be, as well. What he didn't know was how much of Lendell Washington Gunner had just seen in him, or how much his relationship to his friend Pee Cee reminded the investigator of the bond Washington had allegedly had with his cousin, Noah Ford.

And Gaylon Brown certainly didn't know what a pain in the ass Gunner could be, once he decided to make a perfect stranger's business his own.

Had he only understood that, the boy might have kept his bony little finger in his pocket where it belonged, and never seen or heard from Gunner again.